SPECTER

SPECTER

KATIE JANE GALLAGHER

HIDDEN
BOWER

HIDDEN
BOWER

ISBN: 978-0-578-50818-4

First Edition First Printing
Cover Illustration Copyright © 2019 by LianaM.
Wilderness font by Centric Studios.
Rise of Kingdom font by Vladimir Nikolic, licensed under the 1001Fonts Free For Commercial Use License (FFC).
Eau de Rose font by Qkila.

www.katiejgallagher.com

For my family, who taught me to love stories.

And for John, who helped me tell another one at last.

Chapter 1

IT TURNED OUT all the books and movies had gotten ghosts dead wrong. Still, I knew what I was dealing with from that very first glimpse. Just like you can tell a cat from a dog, some instinct thrummed through me, real deep and low in my gut, and I *knew*. The dead aren't the living, and it was the dead I saw that day.

Day, not night—see? Granted it was October, but the way early bit of October, too early for even me to be getting excited about America's best holiday. Plus it was sunny, *plus* it was a Tuesday. If the days of the week were people, Tuesday would be bumbling, adorable, and absolutely average—perhaps the younger cousin of trendy and aloof Thursday. Nothing notable is supposed to happen on Tuesdays, let alone anything supernatural.

I was in bed, wrapped up burrito-style in my blankets, shivering from a fever and halfway to miserable—only halfway because it was just about the time Mrs. Morrie would be handing out the math test I was supposed to be taking. It's funny how things work out; the night before I'd considered faking sick to dodge the test, and now here I was, sick for real.

I was just sinking into a nap when the door creaked open, followed by the light pad of footsteps. I snaked an arm out from under the warmth of my comforter, my hand meeting soft fur.

"Hey, Mustard," I croaked. The virus hadn't spared my throat. I patted the bed, and my golden retriever jumped up and began snuffling my face, all whiskers and dog breath.

"Gross!" And as I pushed him away, I saw a flash of blue-tinged skin in the corner of the room.

That was the next thing that wasn't right. It—she—had none of the silvery translucence from the stories. In fact, she wasn't see-through at all, her figure cast in slow-moving blue shadows, like the sun making mottled patterns on the seafloor.

There was a ghost in my room—a ghost my age, her hair a big mess of feathery curls straight out of an eighties movie, her clinging black leotard and jeans vintage to match. And she was looking right at me.

I jerked back, yelping as my head collided with the headboard. The ghost's eyes widened. In my peripheral vision, Mustard was making circles at the end of the bed, preparing for his thrice-daily nap. Didn't he notice? Weren't dogs supposed to have a sixth sense for the paranormal? They could predict earthquakes and sniff out cancer, after all. In the movies, dogs always gave early warnings about evil spirits…

And that's why all the smarter ghosts in those same

movies always found some sinister way to get rid of the dog. I scrambled forward and gathered Mustard up into an unhappy, squirming ball, then tried to leap out of bed, only to get caught in the blanket. I tumbled to the ground, and Mustard wriggled free from my arms. Shooting me a wounded look, he trotted from the room.

The bed skirt was blocking my view of the ghost. I sucked in a steadying breath and willed myself to get up. Surely she'd be gone when I stood up again, going for the jump-scare-then-leave kind of haunting. What a great story this would make, narrated by upturned flashlight around a clichéd campfire. *I was lying sick in bed, then…*

I pushed up from the floor with a groan.

"Fuck!" There she was, blue and muted, though she stood directly in the sunlight beaming through the window. A vague, familiar feeling quivered at the back of my mind…

The ghost was tracking me with her eyes. After a long, silent moment, her lips twitched up into some horrid semblance of a smile. She took a step forward.

"M-Mom?!" But my call was useless reflex only; she'd deemed my fever just low enough to go into work for a few hours, rather than shuttling me to the doctor. I was alone in the house—well, no one else alive was in the house.

You're hallucinating. Call Mom so she can take you to the hospital. For that must be it—my fever had climbed too high. Yet the ghost looked so *real*, and I couldn't help but scan my room for something, *anything*, to use to fight back. I didn't keep my room stocked with weaponry, so I settled for the bedside table lamp, yanking the cord from the wall and clutching it baseball bat-style.

Time for the first and likely final showdown between Lanie Adams and Ghost Girl.

But she took another step forward — her sneakers were also some retro style, I noticed — and icy fear rooted me in place. Just a hallucination — a hallucination of a ghost who shops at Goodwill. I drew together my fleeing scraps of courage and poked the lamp toward Ghost Girl's stomach.

It passed straight through, without even a ripple at the edges. I lurched back, gripping the lamp to my chest like a safety blanket. "Not real," I whispered, and the ghost frowned at me, as if to say, *I beg to differ.*

"What do you want?" I managed. My voice was a trembling wreck. Didn't ghosts usually have some sort of purpose, some wrong to be righted or atrocity to be avenged? She opened her mouth to answer…

The words erupted as a garbled stream of syllables.

Fine, she could have the room; I was willing to vacate. I threw down the lamp and vaulted over the bed, hurtling towards the door —

— Where I leaped straight through another bluish ghost, this one a teenage boy standing right on the threshold.

That was when my hopes that this was all just a hallucination evaporated away. Have you ever taken a bath in a ghost? Suffice it to say that the experience is not pleasant — an aching kind of cold that seeps to the bone in the space of a heartbeat, banishing all memories of warmth.

But I didn't have to endure it for long. White sparks clouded my vision, then the world wavered and contracted to a pinhole.

Chapter 2

"LANIE? OH MY God, hon, what are you doing down there?"

Down where? I opened my eyes, and my mom's worried face swam into view. There was a crick in my neck from sleeping without a pillow...

It all came back in a horror-soaked rush: Mustard, ghost, lamp, sneakers. And then a second ghost. I shot upwards, and my mom gasped.

"Are you all right? Why—?"

"I was, uh, feeling better, so I started playing with Mustard on the ground. But then I felt sleepy so..." The lie fell neatly into place, out of my mouth before I could reconsider. Something long dormant, more feeling than memory, brushed softly against the edges of my mind once more. What was it? My brain felt sluggish from being passed out on the floor for God knows how long...

My mom was squinting at me. "Right. Well, I'm glad you're feeling better, but let's just take your temperature."

"Okay..." I rubbed at my eyes, trying to get rid of the brain fog. "You're home early? How was the meeting?"

Her lips twisted. "The artist wasn't a good fit, so we wrapped it up quick. Figured I'd come home and keep you company. Dad'll be home at the regular time."

I got slowly to my feet as she went to grab the thermometer. My muscles were stiff, but the cold-hot fever tingles were gone. Maybe the stress had burned the sickness away, my body deciding there were more important things to worry about than some 24-hour virus.

My shoulders tensed as I peeked into the bedroom—empty, as far as I could tell. But that really didn't mean much; the ghosts could be in hiding.

That was, after all, what made ghosts so deliciously terrifying: the rules were that there *were* no rules. They could hang around, bat-like, in a high corner of the room, or fold up into the dark pocket between your hair and the nape of your neck. They could flutter around behind you, whispering in your ear, then dance away the instant you turned to look. I'd never counted on developing a fear of monsters under the bed at sixteen, but here I was.

My mom came back with the thermometer in hand. I popped it in my mouth, and she gave a satisfied nod when it beeped a moment later. *98.6.* "That's good. You feeling hungry? Soup, maybe?"

I nodded, my eyes flicking once more towards my bedroom. A nervous energy pulsed just beneath my skin. How was I supposed to sleep in there tonight?

"I'll just take a shower first," I told her. A shadow of that penetrating cold remained, like my blood had turned to ice water.

In the shower, I left the curtain half open, just in case my new blue friends decided to invade the bathroom. Not that I'd be able to do anything about it if they did; I just didn't want to be surprised by one of them popping through the curtain. Call me a bit of a horror snob—I've always held that jump scares are a cheating way to scare people, and I wasn't prepared to suffer them in my real life.

Even with the open curtain, it had never felt so good to get clean. A grimy, dried layer of sweat coated my body from the fever—plus I'd charged headlong through the second ghost, and that *had* to dirty you up in some way, right? I squirted more body wash onto my loofah, then attacked my skin until it was lobster-red.

I only shut the shower off when the hot water started flagging. Chest tight, I wrapped myself in a towel. My feet felt rooted to the bath mat, unwilling to make the journey down the hall to my bedroom—the scene of the crime.

But I could hear my mom downstairs in the kitchen; I couldn't stay in here forever. Giving myself a silent countdown, I went on three, darting back into my bedroom and tugging on the first clothes I could lay hands on—dark jeans, amethyst Overlook Hotel T-shirt. Then I was out the door as quickly as I'd come and down the stairs, heart hammering, every inch of me screaming *away away away*.

"Must be feeling better," my mom said, oblivious, as I entered the kitchen. She brought two steaming bowls of tomato soup over to the table. "Sounded like a stampeding elephant coming down those stairs."

"Mmm," I said vaguely. Sitting down, I curled my hands around the bowl, letting the warmth radiate through my palms, trying to banish the feeling of jumping through the boy ghost. I hadn't gotten a good look at him—just a blurry, blue male figure.

Beside me, my mom kept her eyes glued to her tablet as she ate her soup, scrolling through prospective artist portfolios for our family's gallery. *Flick*—a set of stormy seascapes rendered in oils, the waters roiling and foamy. *Flick*—a series of whale photographs, the framing zoomed-in tight. Through the photographer's lens, the whales were gargantuan, grotesque—almost Cthulhu-ish. My kind of art.

"Those ones are nice," I said.

She nodded. "We actually have a meeting set up with the photographer in a couple weeks. But he's becoming a bigger deal lately, so I'm not sure if he'll want to sign with a little gallery in Connecticut."

She scrolled on to the next artist's portfolio, and I swirled my spoon through the soup. How best to poke at the topic without letting on that I was seeing things?

"So," I started, "we have this project in history. We, um, have to research someone who used to live in Enville. Like an old mayor or someone."

My mom shut her tablet off, suddenly all ears. "A group project?" I pressed my lips together, suppressing a sigh.

"No, it's individual. Anyway, I was thinking about doing someone who used to live in our house. Do you know anything about the people who owned it before us?"

She sipped her soup, thinking. "I'm afraid not. We bought it in '89, but I couldn't even tell you the name of the previous owners. They were a middle-aged couple, that I do remember. Moved down south somewhere, I think."

"Did they have kids?"

"They may have mentioned a daughter…? I don't think we met her, though." She paused. "You know, the deed would have their names. But we'd have to go to the bank and get it out of the safe deposit box, and the schedule's tight with all these prospective meetings. But if you really need…"

I waved my hands. "Don't worry about it, I'll find it online." Surely some magical website could spit out the information I needed. Now to the real question. "I guess what I was really wondering was… did anyone ever die in this house?"

She set her spoon down with a clink, her eyebrows meeting in a frown. "You know, maybe you should give those horror movies a rest. What kind of question is that?"

"Well, think about it. Say you're living in England—chances are somebody passed away in your house, since everything's so old there."

She fixed me with a dry look. "Yes, but we're not *in* England."

"Enville's pretty old, though, as far as U.S. towns go—right? Wasn't the house built in the twenties? So all I'm saying is that maybe someone actually died here. Don't realtors have to tell you that? I thought I read that somewhere."

She shook her head at me slowly, looking at me like another piece of art—one that was a little too experimental and definitely too morbid for her tastes. My mom was kind, caring, compassionate, really all the Mother's Day adjectives, but her tastes ran pretty vanilla. "Not sure about the realtor thing," she said, "but I never heard anything like that about our house. You can always ask Dad about it, I guess. You're really set on this?"

"I just have a hunch it's exactly what Mr. DeBraav's looking for."

"Well, he's the history teacher, not me," she said, her eyes still a bit disapproving. "How about if you ask him if there's a way to find that out?"

"Yeah, all right." Damn it. I'd been looking for easy answers, not an extracurricular history project.

In school the next day, I took a few extra moments at the end of history class to straighten my books and papers. When the last student finally slipped out the door, I cleared my throat, and Mr. DeBraav looked up from his class notes and smiled.

"What's up, Lanie? Question?"

"Yeah, not on class, though. I was just hoping for a little advice." He motioned for me to go ahead, and I dove in with my questions, leaving aside the ghost stuff, of course. *How do I figure out who used to live in my house? Is there a way to tell if someone died in the house?* I wasn't worried about his reaction, since Mr. DeBraav never glossed over history's vilest moments. The classes detailing the Rape of Nanking or the Nazi medical experiments had made more than a few of the class's wimpier students get up and take a break, their faces pale and queasy, but not me.

As I spoke, I could already see that I'd struck gold; his eyes had lit up behind his glasses. "So I wondered if you had any suggestions," I ended.

"Well, sure," he said. "Have you tried a séance?"

I blanched, and he chuckled. "Kidding. Anyway, in terms of whether anyone died in the house, I've never heard of a reliable service to check that. But interviews with the previous homeowner would likely turn up some answers. You've probably already searched your address online?"

I nodded. "I didn't find much." My house was number 3 at the very end of Ferngrove Lane, a winding road that dove straight into the heart of Enville's sprawling forest. But a whole slew of Ferngrove Lanes peppered the United States, and most of the search results were just housing price estimates. So I'd tried a few more imaginative searches, all some hopeful combination of "3 *Ferngrove Lane Enville Connecticut murder teenage girl boy eighties serial killer death suicide homicide.*" An hour of searching had yielded nothing, save for a worrying browser history. Hopefully the FBI wouldn't put me on some list—possible future psychos of New England, perhaps.

Mr. DeBraav was tapping a finger to his chin, thinking. "I'd start with the house deed or tax assessment records. Those would list the previous homeowner."

"How do I find those documents?"

"The county keeps some tax records online, actually."

I pulled out my math notebook—mostly blank, due to

my long-standing feud with algebra—and jotted down some notes. "And what if I wanted to find the names of the family members of the homeowner? They wouldn't be listed, right?" The ghosts had looked my age, definitely no older than seventeen or eighteen—far too young to be buying houses.

"Right. Lanie, it sounds like you're interested in someone specific?"

He was too smart for his own good—time to lay on the bullshit. "I also thought of making it a multi-generational, family history thing. How did these people end up in Enville, and where are they and their children now? Like *The Joy Luck Club*, sort of." We were reading it in English.

He rocked back on his heels. "Ambitious! Well, your first order of business should be to find the name of the previous homeowner. Then I'd try to contact them on social media and go from there."

This was something I could work with. I might not actually *know* my so-called friends on social, but I could use Facebook as well as anyone else. "Thanks, I'll do that."

"Of course. Let me know if you need any more help. And by the way, try getting some more sleep. Bit too much yawning in class today."

If only he knew. I'd woken up every half hour last night and fumbled for my phone flashlight, shining the light into the corners of the room, up at the ceiling, down toward the sides of my bed, searching for blue…

Next period was study hall, which I begged out of to go to the library to work on my invented history project. It felt comforting to be surrounded by books as I began a deep dive into online tax records. Surely I wasn't alone; one of these thousands of authors had to have experienced an honest-to-God haunting.

Mr. DeBraav's advice was spot on. It took a bit of poking around on the county's website, but soon I was scrawling down more notes: my house's parcel ID, the date and reference number of the 1989 sale, the full zip-code. There was even a blueprint of the house, which disappointingly lacked any indication of hidden passageways or boarded-up rooms. It would have been too easy, of course, for my house's spirits to be emanating from desiccated corpses squirreled away in the walls.

My real triumph was discovering that the so-called "grantor" meant "seller" in non-legalese. I had my name: *Holt, Edgar F.*

My imagination spiraled in a thousand directions as I scoured the Internet for Edgar Holt. Why had he and his wife moved away—something innocuous like a job offer or an early retirement to Florida? Or maybe some more sinister reason—a house that wouldn't stop haunting them? Or perhaps something yet more fantastical… I sank into fantasies of Mr. and Mrs. Holt teaming up as joint serial killers, a grizzly police detective just close enough to discovering the truth to necessitate a speedy departure.

Yet I could already tell I'd have a tough time finding the

answer. I was running into the same issue I'd had Googling my street: there were pages and pages of Edgar Holts. In the end I rattled off a quick message to the top contenders. Hopefully the Edgar Holt I was seeking checked his Facebook.

That done, I took a field trip to the library's paranormal and occult section. It was decidedly lacking. Most of the books were as hokey as you'd expect: crimson title fonts leaking blood droplets, cover illustrations akin to B-grade eighties horror flicks. The spooky aficionado in me reveled in this stuff, but I needed something more serious.

Then I caught sight of a gray-green canvas volume at the end of the shelf. I wrinkled my nose as I pulled it out; the spine had a light coating of dust.

Ghosts and Monsters from Around the World: A Compendium. A quick flip through revealed detailed descriptions of such creatures as the *jiangshi*, some sort of Chinese zombie-vampire mash-up, and the *cihuateteo*, Aztec mythology's ghosts of women who died in childbirth.

Well, maybe the author had seen fit to include my blue-skinned ghosts, or at least some distant cousin. I walked back to my table and started skimming.

The real question bugging me was, *why now?* I'd lived at my house my whole life—ample time for the ghosts to reveal themselves. It didn't make any sense...

"Hey!" The whisper-shout came from a guy with a mop of mouse-brown curls seated at the next table over. He was lanky, legs sprawling so that he seemed to take up the whole table, even though there were three empty seats. His

T-shirt featured a cartoon ruby-encrusted sword; the gold text underneath read *Proud Warrior of Viningal.*

I eyed him coolly over *Ghosts and Monsters.* I had nothing against gamers, but "Viningal" sounded like a venereal disease. "What's up?"

"Just wondering—is that for some elective?" He jerked his chin at my book. "Looks way better than this shit." He held up a copy of *Dracula.* From the corner of my eye, I saw the grandmotherly librarian on the other side of the room shoot us both a dirty look, though I couldn't tell if it was for the whispering or the swearing or the dissing of Bram Stoker's seminal work.

"What's wrong with *Dracula*?" I whispered back.

"I mean, the first bit was decent, but the second half's killing me. The only scary thing about it is I might die of boredom."

"You're reading *that* in English?"

"Yeah, the Intro to Horror elective with Mrs. Naples. I'm more a math guy, so I wanted to get away from Shakespeare and Fitzgerald—thought we'd talk about modern stuff like *Resident Evil* or whatever. But everything we're studying is super old…"

Wow. How had I never heard of this class? I always just went with whatever humdrum English offering my guidance counselor recommended for college.

"Well, it's not for a class," I said with a nod at *Ghosts and Monsters.* "I'm just doing some, ah, personal research."

"'Personal research?'" he repeated, but didn't press me when I stayed quiet. "Anyway, I'm Ryan."

"Lanie."

"Huh, interesting name."

"Short for Melanie."

"Cool, cool. Well, I'd better get back to this. I have a paper due next week." He scowled at the snarling face of the eponymous villain on the cover, fangs in full, pointy glory, before flipping open to a dog-eared page in the middle.

I spent the rest of the period speed-reading through the first half of *Ghosts and Monsters*. None of the creatures so far matched my blue ghosts, though I held out hope for the latter part of the book. All I needed was some scrap of a detail to point me in the right direction.

I stared down at the blank sheet of paper on the desk. Last class of the day, and my English teacher was out sick, but it didn't mean she hadn't mustered the strength to assign us two in-class pages to write about a formative event in our lives, à la *The Joy Luck Club*. Normally this kind of thing might be sort of fun, but I was so tired from my sleepless night that all creativity had fled my body.

I eyed the clock—forty-eight minutes to go—then fiddled with my pencil, smacking the eraser on the paper with a satisfying thump.

What. To. Write.

And then, as my brain floated away towards meditative boredom, I felt that tug of memory once more.

A waiting room. Seated next to my mom, I'm watching a TV

playing a Disney movie when an older woman emerges from somewhere to usher me away—just me. My mom stays behind, watching me go, and I feel our growing distance like a physical ache.

The woman brings me to a different room—soft music in the background, pastel colors. She motions me to sit in a chair, and I do so, squirming under her gaze. The room's a bit too warm, and I'm wearing shorts, the backs of my thighs sticking to the seat...

Some sort of doctor's office—and a hazy feeling intertwined with the memory, like an aftertaste concealed by other flavors.

Blue. Revulsion. Fear.

Chapter 3

"YOU ALL RIGHT?" I'd let out a gasp, and the girl at the desk next to me—Emma? Emily?—was eyeing me warily. I shook my head at her, my tongue dry, then rose from my seat and walked over to the sub on shaky legs.

"C-can I go to the nurse?"

I was in luck: the head nurse, crotchety from decades of calling malingering teenagers' bluffs, had left early, leaving her younger, kinder cohort in charge. I rattled off a few symptoms—nausea, headache—and she pointed me into a dark, quiet room adjacent to the main room with a few empty beds.

I kept my eyes screwed shut as I tried to make sense of the memory. How old had I been? Why had I been in that doctor's office? But the memory was too hazy, too mashed-up to give me any answers.

I jumped when my phone vibrated. The screen shone bright as a spotlight in the darkness.

Message from Edgar Holt: Not me, sorry. Good luck with that.

Well, it had been naive to think I would find the right one straightaway.

In fact, it took almost a full twenty-four hours before the right Edgar Holt finally replied. I was in the library again, buried in *Ghosts and Monsters*, when my phone buzzed, earning a glare from the librarian. She had good hearing, this woman—probably more curse than blessing in her line of work.

That's me, the message read. What do you want to know?

In his profile picture, this Edgar Holt was a balding man smiling at the camera. His cheeks were a bit pink from what looked like a touch of sunburn.

I frowned down at my phone. What exactly *did* I want to ask him? Opening with ghosts seemed like a sure-fire way to shut down the conversation.

In the end I settled for the same story I'd fed my mom and Mr. DeBraav. I'm doing a project about all the different people who have lived in my house—what brought them to Enville, what their lives were like when they were here, etc. My family's owned the house ever since you sold it in 1989. It would be really helpful if you could tell me how long you lived in it, who lived there with you, stuff like that. Thank you!!! I wasn't normally the three exclamation points type, but I needed all the help I could get.

Half a minute passed, then an ellipsis bounced in a new bubble underneath my message. I drummed my fingers on the desk, waiting for his response.

How about talking on the phone about the details? I don't mind sharing, it's just that the later years in the house were a complicated time for my family.

A thrill coursed through me. *A complicated time*—what could that mean? I was close; I could feel it.

And then, once I knew *why* my house was haunted, I could figure out my next step—hopefully nothing that involved digging up unmarked graves in the backyard.

We exchanged phone numbers and arranged to talk at seven. My stomach was fluttery as I set my phone down and reached for *Ghosts and Monsters*.

"Lanie!" Ryan waved to me from the next table over. I hadn't even noticed him sit down.

"Oh, sorry," I whispered back. "Didn't see you."

He shook his head at me in feigned disappointment, hazel eyes twinkling. "How's it going? All that texting for your 'personal research?'"

I laughed quietly. "Yeah, actually it is. Got myself a hot phone date tonight with this old guy. I'm interviewing him for a history project."

He made a face. "Have fun with that."

"Thanks. How's *Dracula*?"

"Oh, you know… Terrible." He had his finger in the book to mark his spot. It looked like he hadn't read more than ten pages since yesterday.

"Hey, you know…" I could hardly believe I was saying this. "Umm… If you ever need help with that class, horror's sort of my thing. I-I've read *Dracula* like three times."

He raised an eyebrow as his eyes slid from me to the book. "*This* book? *Three* times?"

"Don't hold it against me!" The librarian gave me a

furious shush, and I flushed, then lowered my voice. "I promise I'm not a vampire. I'm just saying I could look over your paper if you want."

"You'd do that?"

"Yeah, why not? But you said you're good at math, right?"

"Yes…?"

I picked at a piece of lint on my jeans. *Just ask him—no turning back now.* "Math's sort of kicking my ass right now. Turns out doing homework matters. So maybe you could look over my math homework, and I can check your paper?"

Ryan leaned back in his chair and grinned. He was definitely cute, in an infrequently-combs-his-hair kind of way. "Okay, why the hell not? It's a deal." He sighed when the bell rang, then looked back to me. "See you back here tomorrow?"

"Sure. See you then."

I gathered my things and left the library, slightly dazed. The interview with Holt, the study date with Ryan—it was an unprecedented amount of social commitment for Lanie Adams, loner extraordinaire.

But maybe it was time to try some new things. A brush with death can give you funny ideas, I guess.

"Did I get sick a lot as a little kid?" We had all just sat down to dinner. My dad gave me an amused look as he spooned a heaping portion of lasagna onto his plate.

"Sick? No, not as far as I recall. Wait, there was the time that girl was being mean to you in second grade, and you kept saying you had a stomachache because you didn't want to see her in school. Was it Julia...?" He squinted in thought. "Or Jennifer...?"

"Jessica Acker," my mom replied, spearing a green bean a tad too forcefully. "I'd forgotten all about that. Can't say I was mad when her family moved."

I sighed lightly. "I mean, were there any times I was *actually* sick, not just faking?"

"Well, sure," my mom said. "I mean, every kid gets sick. You got the chicken pox in first grade, of course. Oh, and then you got a few plantar warts on your feet—from the showers at the YMCA pool was always my guess."

Gross. "But never anything serious besides that?" I said, eager to leave the topic of my warts behind. "Where I had to see a specialist?"

My dad stabbed a finger in the air. "Oh! What about that one visit to the psychologist?"

My breath caught. The memory—this had to be it. "I think I sort of remember that... But why did I have to go?"

"You were having nightmares," my mom said, and I felt something shift within me. Like shining a flashlight into a long-abandoned room. Like dusting off a once-beloved book, the details now just wisps of memory.

"Nightmares?"

"That's right," my dad said, looking to my mom. "How old was she?"

"Third or fourth grade," she answered. "You don't remember that?"

"N-no!" I sputtered. Cold dread slithered from the back of my neck down my spine, pooling in my gut as a hard, solid weight.

My dad smiled. "You started waking us up in the middle of the night yelling, 'Go away! Go away!' And you told us that some people were messing with you in your dreams, making them scary. We tried a bunch of different things, but nothing really worked. Truth be told, we were a bit concerned." He chuckled. "Not least because your daughter developing the habit of screaming you awake at three in the morning isn't exactly ideal. All three of us were zombies after a couple days, and that kept on for… oh, a week, at least." He took a bite of lasagna, then looked up at me, the corners of his eyes crinkling. "I sure hope you're not thinking about starting that up again."

"Not really." Inside I was reeling. "And you took me to go see a psychologist about it?"

He nodded. "That's right. Your mom here was quite worried about what was going on in that sleepy little head of yours!"

She scowled at him. "Don't you think that's downplaying it a bit? Lanie, you were telling us all *sorts* of things about the people in your dreams. You said they were *real*. It felt like…" She shook her head, frowning. "It felt like you were starting to believe in Santa Claus again. You were a young kid, but you weren't in kindergarten. You had a good sense of what was and wasn't real. And I got worried how you were telling us all about these people in your head, how they were talking to you, bothering you. I thought maybe…

Well, I don't know *what* I thought, but it wasn't good."

My jaw dropped. What must she have suspected? That her daughter was beginning to suffer from schizophrenic episodes?

"In any case," my dad continued, "the psychologist wasn't concerned. The appointment was just a one-time thing, really to reassure us nothing serious was going on. She gave us a few ideas to try, and I guess they worked, since the bad dreams stopped for good a day or two later." He took a sip of water. "Anything else you were wondering about?"

I steeled myself to ask my next question. "Did I say anything about the people? Who they were? What they were doing?"

He scratched his head. "Hmm. Well, this was a while ago, but I think you said they were a funny color. Green or blue or something."

I felt near-catatonic for the rest of dinner, picking listlessly at my lasagna. The ghosts had visited me in my dreams when I was a little girl—which meant they could just as easily storm my dreams tonight. Waking or sleeping, I wasn't safe anywhere.

Perhaps I really was going crazy. Or maybe I was slowly realizing the ability to commune with spirits. Well, at least if it were the latter, I had a back-up plan if I didn't get into college: holding séances.

"Didn't like it?" my mom asked as I set my half-finished plate on the ground. Mustard wouldn't complain.

"No, it was good," I said. "Just wasn't feeling very

hungr— Oh, that's my phone." I could hear it ringing up-stairs; I'd put it on max blast, not wanting to miss Edgar Holt's call.

I took the stairs two at a time, closed the door, and snatched up my phone from my bed.

North Carolina number.

"Hello?"

"Hello, this is Edgar Holt calling for Lanie Adams?" His voice was deep and even-toned.

"Uh, yes, that's me. Thanks for agreeing to talk to me." I opened up my laptop to type some notes.

"Well, I think it's a fantastic sort of project that you're do-ing," he replied. "This for a high school class or something?"

"Yeah, for history."

"Seems like a great idea. Fire away."

"Umm, okay. Let's start at the beginning. When did you buy the house?" The county's website didn't list any infor-mation predating the '89 sale.

"August of '75," Holt said. "I'll never forget it. Must've been a hundred degrees on moving day."

My heartbeat picked up. The female ghost, at least, had looked to be from the time of Michael Jackson and jazz-ercise; that placed Holt as the undeniable owner of the house when she'd died. "And do you know the name of who you purchased the house from?" I continued. "Or what year it was built?" Honestly, the answers didn't mat-ter, but I'd pitched the project as a full-blown historical analysis, so it was best to keep up appearances.

"Sorry, can't help you with that," Holt said. "Of course my wife has stashed away copies of all the documents from when we bought the house, but God only knows where she's storing 'em. It was built in the twenties, that I do know, but I don't remember the exact year. Oh, we did a kitchen expansion in '83; maybe that's something you need to know. We wanted to do it earlier, but the city kept dragging its heels on letting us dig, since Avanic was so close. It was our land, but you know how it is with these big companies. They still over there?"

I snorted. "Yeah, they are." The pharmaceutical company Avanic was headquartered close to our house. An easy jaunt north through the woods behind my house would land you at a high chain-link fence, beyond which lay Avanic's sprawling complex of buildings, all slick in architecture and fronted with mirrored windows. I frowned. "Wait—why would Avanic impact the home renovation?"

"Underground utility lines. They were worried the digging might cause an electrical outage. Way I always heard it, their labs draw a fair bit of power."

I typed a few notes. "Um. So why were you living in Enville?"

"Actually I was born and raised in Enville, as was my wife, Linda. We both went to Enville High School, started dating freshman year, married at twenty. We were living in an apartment for a while. I started work as a plumber, and she was a secretary for some doctor—can't remember his name. Then we had our daughter in '74."

"What's her name?"

The answer came quieter, lower. "Becky. Full name Rebecca Anne Holt."

"Do you have any other children?"

A pause. Something unvoiced hung in the air. "No. We bought the house in 1975, thinking we'd need the space for more kids. Well, even with just Becky it felt nice to leave apartment living behind." He was right: it *was* a big house for only three people, though I'd never known it any other way. Holt cleared his throat. "We were planning on having more kids, but we couldn't."

What did you even say to something like that? Here I was, prying open people's pasts, hoping for some answers—when all I was doing was unearthing sad memories. "I'm really sorry to hear that."

His voice took on a false brightness. "Well, best to leave the past in the past." Not an option for me, unfortunately. "So we bought the house, then a year later business was really picking up, so my wife quit her job to stay home full-time with Becky."

I skimmed my notes. "And how was life in Enville while you were living in the house—normal? Any, err, notable current events?"

"Hmm." Silence on the line for a few seconds. "No, I don't think so. You know Enville… It's a pretty sleepy town."

"Why'd you move?"

"Well… I'm sorry, I should've said earlier. Becky had leukemia."

Oh. "That's terrible."

"And… sh-she died in 1985. She put up a good fight, but…" I stared at my keyboard dumbly, suddenly wanting nothing more than to hang up the phone. At last I typed out a few sparse notes as I did the math. Dying in 1985 would put his daughter at eleven years old—far too young to be one of my ghosts.

"Anyway," Holt continued, "Linda and I stayed in Enville for a few years after that, but it was hard. The house felt too big, too empty. Linda went back to work for some distraction, but she was having a real rough time. So we decided to go for a complete change of scenery. Moved to North Carolina, and we've been there ever since." The line was quiet for a moment. "Is there anything else you wanted to ask?"

I glanced at my notes. "This might sound strange."

"That's all right. Ask away."

"Did you ever see some teenagers hanging out by the house? Wandering through the woods? Anything like that?"

"You mean loitering around? No, don't think so." He sounded certain. "You know, the forest there makes for decent hiking, so people did pass by. But I don't remember anything unusual… Is this important? I could ask Linda about it."

"Sure, thanks. And just one last thing. Please don't take this the wrong way; I'm not asking about your daughter. Just… did anything spooky ever happen at the house? Anything weird or unexplainable?"

"Like ghosts?"

"Yes."

"No." His voice was resolute. "Believe me, those last few years *felt* like something was there. If you lose a child, you're always ready for them to come around the corner. You *want* some sign. Things in a different spot on the table than where you left them. A voice down the hall. Your mind plays tricks on you. They say the same thing about people who lose a limb… You feel like it's still there. But no—no ghosts, not of Becky, not of anyone."

And with that we said our goodbyes, Holt promising to get back to me once he asked his wife if she remembered any teenagers skulking around in the woods.

I'd reached a dead end, with nothing to show for it besides a sparse document of sad, useless notes.

Chapter 4

A DEAFENING CLAP of thunder served as my alarm the next morning. I bolted upright, knocking *Ghosts and Monsters* to the floor—I'd fallen asleep reading—and performed my newly habitual scan of my room: closet, window, door, even a quick, reluctant peek over the side of the bed. My search revealed nothing, but I still shivered when seconds later a flash of lightning lit the room in brilliant light and shadow.

I shook my head as I got out of bed. Logically, there was no point in being spooked. I'd seen no sign of the ghosts since Tuesday, and though my sleep last night had been restless, I'd also had no ghostly visitors. My parents had said I'd struggled with the nightmares in third or fourth grade, and I was no wizard with numbers, but if my calculations were correct that meant I'd be due for my next haunting in roughly seven years.

A knock on the door. "Lanie?" The rain outside was so heavy it was hard to hear my mom's voice through the door.

"Yeah?"

"Is the power on in there?"

I flicked the switch on my bedside lamp: nothing. "No."

"Ugh, all right. It's out for the whole house then. I'll call the electric company. Want us to drive you to school, honey? It's really coming down out there." Just perfect. A street in the middle of the woods with only a few residents was never the electric company's top priority. I'd be lucky if the lights were back on by the time I got home from school.

"I'm good, Mom, thanks." What was a little rain? The minivan might handle like a boat, but it was definitely waterproof.

"All right, then Dad and I are off. Traffic's probably going to be awful. Oh, remember we have bagels downstairs."

"O-okay." All my reasoning about how I had seven more years until my next encounter with the supernatural evaporated at the prospect of being alone in a house with no power; it was the perfect setup for the return of my ghosts. It's so easy to mock characters in horror movies for splitting up or venturing into the creepy basement, and here I was, following in their same, dumb footsteps. How stupid could I get?

"All right, honey, love you! Bye!"

"Bye..."

I quickly went through the motions of getting ready, opting for a pair of slate gray biker jeans and a plum *Munsters* T-shirt, soft from many washings. Normal clothes, but these ones always hugged me in the right places. Today was my library date with Ryan, so I needed to look some semblance of presentable. Ridiculous, how you can find yourself caring about the small things even when there's a vague threat of danger. Like fumbling around with your phone to change the song when driving on the highway. Or trying to look good for a boy when ghosts might be lurking in the shadows.

In the dim bathroom, with just one little window for light, I was all angles in the mirror—my shoulders sharp and jutting, my cheeks hollow. I tugged at my jeans and frowned; they hung looser than usual around my waist. The circles under my eyes were dark and bruise-like—the result of three days' non-stop worrying. Not even the world's best concealer was going to help that situation, so I skipped it and opted for just blush and mascara.

Hair was the real problem. My brown-black hair tends toward frizzy curls on the best of days, much to the chagrin of my younger self, who'd had an odd fascination with Morticia Addams's dark, silky locks. A few years ago, I'd learned to tame my mane with ample quantities of several products, carefully culled from beauty guru recommendations—but on a rainy day like today, there was little to no hope.

So I wrangled my hair back into a fishtail braid, sighed at my dark reflection, and trooped downstairs. Shoving my feet into my combat boots, I grabbed a bagel on the way out the door, not even bothering with cream cheese. Maybe I was just building things up in my head, but as I dodged puddles on my way to the minivan, I could almost *feel* the house behind me, like some animal poised to pounce.

The roads were terrible, just like my mom had predicted.

The traffic light outside the school was out, and even once I made it through the intersection the parking lot was a clogged mass of students and cars. A few teachers stood outside with umbrellas, talking to some parents dropping off their kids. I squinted, watching as a teacher waved one of the cars on. Something was going on; nobody was going into school.

A sharp rap on my window made me jump. Ryan smiled at me from outside the minivan, his face blurred by the water sluicing down the window. I pointed him around to the other side, and he hopped in. He was completely drenched.

"Hey, thanks."

"No problem. Why's nobody going in?" I started maneuvering the minivan around confused students and parents toward the back of the parking lot.

"School power's out. Can't have school till it comes back on—legal thing. One of those teachers told me the electric company said it might take all day. A tree went down on a power line. Big fucking mess."

"Are you serious?" Happy Friday indeed. This week may have sucked, but at least I could end it on a good note.

Ryan laughed. "Oh, I'm always serious when it comes to getting out of class."

I gave him a look from top to bottom. He was dripping puddles on the floor mat. "You look like you need a ride." Technically it was illegal for me to drive him since I'd gotten my license only eight months ago, but who was checking?

He gave a full-body shiver as he wrung water out of his

T-shirt. "Well, I won't complain. My brother dropped me off, and he drove away before I heard the good news."

"And you have some sort of aversion to rain jackets?"

He winked at me. "I'm superhuman, you see. Thought I could just sprint between the raindrops, but it turns out I'm having an off day." He tossed his sopping backpack into the back. "Oh, sorry."

"What?"

"Got your book a bit wet." He turned back around, *Ghosts and Monsters* in his hand, and brushed a few water droplets off the cover.

"Doesn't matter—the book's useless," I said, waving my hand. "Where do you live?"

"Hillock Street. Why's the book useless?"

I sighed as I inched back through the intersection. "I just… I'm researching something pretty weird, but I'm totally stuck. I was up until one in the morning reading that thing."

"More 'personal research?'"

"Yeah."

"What, just some background reading for an interview with a vampire?"

I couldn't help a laugh. This boy knew how to speak my language. "Not quite. Imaginative, though."

He flipped through the book, landing on a page emblazoned with an illustration of a glowering, hyena-like creature circling a puddle of blood—what I now knew to be the Arabian *ghul*, anglicized as English's "ghoul."

"You're probably worried a pack of these guys are

running rampant through town."

"Yeah. How'd you guess?" I gave him a smirk.

He shut the book with a snap. "So which is it: ghosts or monsters? Give me a clue."

"Not monsters."

"So ghosts. Your house is haunted. You're trying to talk to ghosts." He surveyed my face, hazel eyes gleaming.

Something about the coziness of the rain pelting down outside the car and talking with this boy I could sort of, almost, *maybe* call a new friend made my walls crumble. "Yeah. I guess. Yeah, that's what I'm trying to do."

He gave me a cool nod, then started when I looked away. "Wait, really?"

"Yup." I gave him a quick glance, but couldn't read his squinted expression. Disbelief? Fear that he was being driven around town by a crazy person?

At last he opened his mouth to speak. "Wow. I was expecting... not that. Take a left here, by the way."

"Okay," I said, putting on my blinker. "Please don't think I'm insane. I've never even watched one of those ghost hunter shows on TV. I mean, I like reading creepy stories and I watch a lot of horror movies, but I never actually *believed* in any of this stuff."

"What changed?"

"Earlier this week, I-I was sick, so I stayed home from school. And... I think I saw some ghosts."

"*Some* ghosts? Multiple ghosts?"

No turning back now. "Two of them. A boy and a girl,

about our age… And they were blue."

"Blue?"

"Yeah." I stuck my jaw out and shot him a defiant look. If I was really going to talk about this, I'd make no apologies for my ghosts' weirdness.

"Okay, then," he said, taking a deep breath. "So what kind of blue are we talking about? Sky blue? Cyan?"

"Murky," I said, remembering how the shadows had moved over the girl's body. "Like they were underwater. And they were dressed in these old clothes from the eighties."

"And you're *sure* nobody's playing a practical joke on you?" he asked. I shook my head. "Did the ghosts say anything? What'd they do?"

"The girl tried to talk, but it was all garbled. And then…" I blushed as I turned onto Hillock Street. "Then I fainted."

"Oh, wow." He ran a hand through his damp curls. "Uh, you said you were sick, right? Maybe—"

"I wasn't hallucinating, if that's what you're going to say."

Ryan snorted. "Yeah, that's what I was going to say. But…" He eyed me. "All right, so let's run with this. Your house is haunted. Why *your* house? Have you seen anything like this before?"

"No," I lied. I already sort of regretted telling him; no need to divulge my elementary school nightmares and take this to the next level of awkward. "I talked with the previous owner of the house yesterday, but he didn't tell me anything useful."

"Oh, the date with the old guy you mentioned," he said,

recognition sparking in his eyes. "It's that one there." He
pointed at a squat brown house on the right, and I pulled
into the driveway and put the minivan in park. "Thanks for
the ride."

I nodded as I ran my hands over the steering wheel, suddenly miserable. "I'm not crazy."

"Didn't say you were." We sat in silence for a moment.

"If you still want me to read your paper—"

Ryan cut me off, smiling slyly. "Wanna go hunt some
ghosts?"

My phone buzzed while I waited in the car for Ryan to
finish changing and come back: another message from Edgar Holt. I read it quickly, my heart sinking. His wife also
had no recollection of funny goings-on in Enville, nor of any
teenagers hanging around near the house.

The front door opened, and Ryan came out, outfitted in a
dry change of clothes and clutching an umbrella in one hand.
He held a large canvas bag in the other. I smiled as he came
closer; his hair was starting to dry into messy brown waves.
A cute boy who maybe liked me—and he hadn't run away
screaming when I told him about my problems with the undead. Had I fallen into some alternate dimension?

"What's in the bag?" I asked as he got in the car.

"I found a couple of those guns they use in *Ghostbusters*
in the back of the garage. Figured we had a couple stashed
away, since my dad's a big hoarder. Just make sure not to

cross the streams."

"Ha ha, very funny. But seriously, what's in the bag?" I reached over to open it, but he swatted my hand away.

"Be patient, Lanie, geez!"

"All right, all right."

Ten minutes later I turned the car down Ferngrove, the minivan sounding like it was about to break apart as it juddered over the old, buckling road. "You live all the way out here, huh?" Ryan asked.

"Home, sweet home. We're the one at the end. Pain in the ass whenever it snows, but it's gorgeous in the fall." And it *was* beautiful, our little, secluded corner of town; the trees lining the road were in their full glory, gold and ruby leaves trembling in the rain.

I drove around the last bend of the road, and the house came into view. Ryan laughed as I pulled into the driveway. "*This* is your haunted house? I was expecting a few more broken windows. Maybe the crumbling grave of old Aunt Sally in the backyard."

"Nothing so easy as that," I said, shutting off the car. "The only spooky thing is that our power's out." We dashed from the minivan to the front door, and I unlocked it and waved Ryan inside. "Guests first. Oh, make sure you take off your shoes or Josefa will kill me. And I hope you're not allergic to dogs."

"Josefa?" he asked as he slipped out of his sneakers and gave Mustard, waiting by the door, a scratch on the head. Good. Romantic relations with someone who didn't like dogs was simply a no-go.

He whistled as he walked into the living room and caught sight of our television. "Wow. I didn't know they made them that big."

I flushed. "Y-yeah. Uh, Josefa's our maid. She'll get here in a couple hours."

"So are your parents, like, CEOs then? What do they do?"

"I mean, sort of? They own their own business—the art gallery on East Street, next to the ice cream shop."

He squinted. "That French place? La… something?"

"La Belle et la Bête. It's a translation of 'Beauty and the Beast'—because their tastes in art don't match. Hence the…" I waved my hand first at one wall, then at the wall adjacent. On the first wall the paintings were normal enough—nineteenth century-style landscapes, your standard bowls of fruit. This was the kind of art my mom loved most—traditional, objectively beautiful.

The other wall—my dad's wall—was in stark, surreal contrast to my mom's, thrusting our house into a sort of artistic civil war. In one painting, a giant, bulging eyeball stared out at the viewer, its gleam of tears just shiny enough to form a blurry reflection of a woman. The painting beside it started as a normal enough landscape at the top, but in the bottom half the wooden frame swelled and thickened into knobbly tree branches, the canvas at the bottom shredded and coated with dirt and sand.

"And *that*," Ryan said, inclining his head toward the eyeball painting, "doesn't bother you?"

"After a while you sort of forget the weird ones are there."

He walked a few steps further into the living room, peering at one of my dad's favorites—a white canvas. If you stared at it from the right distance you could make out faint gray fir trees, like the artist had been painting during a blizzard. "So the gallery must sell, like, ten thousand dollar paintings?"

"Art's actually not that lucrative," I replied. "Most people only buy prints and stuff."

"Then how…?" He gestured around him at my house. I blushed redder still, getting his meaning. Our home wasn't a mansion by any means, but it was definitely beautiful—a sculpted marble fireplace, designer furniture, a glittering waterfall chandelier over the dining room table.

"We got a huge payout from Avanic when I was a little kid because of the explosion. Before that my parents both worked in insurance. They quit the second the check came in and bought the gallery the next day."

Ryan whistled. "Awesome. That's living the dream. What explosion are you talking about, though?"

"You don't know? How long have you lived in Enville?"

"My family moved here last year."

I nodded as I walked toward the kitchen. "That makes sense you don't know, then. Are you hungry? Thirsty?"

"Maybe just a water."

I filled him a glass, and we sat around the kitchen table. "So Avanic's this pharmaceutical company. Their headquarters and research facilities are about a mile that way."

I pointed out the picture window towards the woods. "When I was a kid there was an accident in one of their labs, and it sparked an enormous chemical explosion."

Ryan's eyes widened. "No way. How old were you? Did you feel it? Do you remember it?"

"I was nine. Actually…" I flipped over my hand and skimmed my thumb over my index and middle fingers. "It happened in July, so I was home from school. My babysitter had called my parents that morning to say she was running late just by a few minutes, but they had to go into work, so they'd left me alone. I was watching TV—some action movie, I don't know what. And then I heard the explosion, like some bomb had dropped. For half a second I thought it was just part of the movie…" It was always weird telling this story. I'd thought about it so many times that my memories felt more like a movie than real life—the colors supercharged, each event dramatically paced. They say that memories are more fallible than not—that a husband and wife, for example, might tell each other the same stories so many times that after a while they confuse who lived which memory. Yet what had happened to me was real. I ran my thumb over my fingers again.

"Then what happened?" Ryan asked.

"A pointy piece of metal struck the window over there." I pointed into the living room. I could still hear the splintering crack of steel meeting glass. "Punctured straight through and hit the carpet. I looked outside, and all sorts of stuff was raining down on the lawn. Ash and debris, bits and pieces of this and that. Then after a few seconds it was just dust coming down, so I opened the door and went outside. The air had this sour, burnt chemical smell. It made my eyes water, so I ran back inside, put on my school science goggles, then went back out."

Ryan's expression was incredulous.

"It's okay, you can laugh," I said. "It's ridiculous, right?"

"That's adorable."

"Yeah, and dumb. Anyway, I started walking down the road towards town—don't know why. I guess I was just panicked… I was a little kid, you know? I was thinking about my parents, wondering if they were okay, if they knew what had happened. I guess I wanted to warn them. So I'm walking down the road, and I can hear about a million ambulances in the distance. The city sirens were going off. It sounded like the world was ending. Then…" I drew in a breath. Ryan was leaning forward in his chair, waiting on my every word.

"Then I see a couple guys in white hazmat suits come out of the forest, about a hundred yards off. They're waving at me, and I'm freaking out because they look so weird." *Why are there astronauts in the woods?* I remembered thinking. "So I'm half-running, half-walking backwards away from them, trying to figure out what to do, and I trip over this twisted scrap of metal in the road. It cut my arm here…" I held out my right arm to show him a faint, curving scar roughly two inches long on my inner forearm, just above my wrist. "I had to get a whole bunch of stitches. That, and part of the metal that I touched with my hand as I fell was covered in chemicals. So *that's* why…" I wiggled my fingers. "That's why the pads on my index and middle finger are messed up. You can't tell with just a quick glance, but I got a chemical burn, and it messed up the fingerprints. And the nerves are also a bit funny; I can't feel things very well with these two fingers."

"No way," he said, eyes dropping to my hand.

"Really!"

Ryan laughed. "So say you were fingerprinted by the police…"

I nodded. "They'd think I smudged the prints or something. It would look weird."

"That's really cool. Sucks you can't feel much with those fingers, though."

"I don't really notice it, to be honest." I put my hand in my lap, trying not to blush at his attention.

"So what happened next?" he asked.

"Everyone arrived all at once—my parents, police, firemen. A guy from *The Enville Gazette*." Things in my memory became a big jumble at that point—a cacophony of wailing sirens, flashing lights making our street look like Christmas in July, my dad screaming at one of the hazmat guys, my mom hustling me past the man from the newspaper into the house, pressing a washcloth to my cut, thrusting my hand under the tap. She didn't wait for the water to warm up, and I remembered the sting of the cold water hitting my irritated fingertips. Then a blurry trip to the ER and a nurse unwrapping a blue raspberry lollipop for me as a doctor turned my arm this way and that.

"And… yeah, that's pretty much it. Avanic paid for us to move into a hotel for a few weeks while they made sure there wasn't any more dangerous debris on our land. And they also paid huge out-of-court settlements to a bunch of families on this side of Enville, with an agreement not to sue." I paused and looked out the window, in the direction of Avanic's campus. "Not a bad trade-off, I guess. A couple of weird fingers for a boatload of money. Oh, and a bunch of stickers and mugs—one of the higher-ups came by the hotel to give me a bunch of merch."

"Wow, that's crazy," he said, then started when the lights flickered on for a moment before dying once more. "Should we get to work?"

I nodded, and he set the bag he'd brought on the table with a clunk, then smiled. "Prepare to be amazed—I have everything we need. Uh, your parents aren't going to come home soon and catch us ghost hunting, are they?"

"Nah, they won't be back until after five."

"Great." He reached into the bag with a magician-like flourish. "*Et voilà!*"

I laughed at the familiar cardboard box. "Really? A Ouija board?"

"Listen, you have to start somewhere! This is just the first step in our plan of attack." He thrust his arm back into the bag. "We also have… *the tarot.*" He pulled out a battered deck of cards, Vanna White-style, and laid them on the table with a reverential touch.

"You know how to read those?" I asked.

"No, not at all—they belong to my crazy aunt. She lives in New York in this tiny apartment, so she stores a bunch of stuff at our house. Anyway, there's an instruction manual, so I'm sure we can muddle our way through."

I thumbed through the deck. Wands, cups, swords, coins—this was more than I'd bargained for. "Tarot's more for fortune-telling, though, right? What's that got to do with ghosts…?"

"Picky!" he said, snatching the deck from me. "I just grabbed everything spooky I could get my hands on!"

I chuckled. "Okay, what else you got?"

He dumped the rest of the contents out on the table: some crystals, white tea light candles, even a dried bundle of sage. I poked one of the crystals. "What's this for, exactly?"

He tilted his head. "That… My aunt told me once, but I forgot. Good energy, I think."

I squelched my burning desire to make some sarcastic comment. I was dealing with real ghosts, after all, so no sense pooh-poohing the medley of items before me.

That was actually something that had been festering in the back of my mind as I read *Ghosts and Monsters* last night—if ghosts were real, didn't that open the possibility for the whole gamut of legendary creatures to exist? My ghosts might not make another appearance, but what about vampires and werewolves and their ilk? I had half a mind to start going to church, even though my family kept to a strict Mass-twice-a-year lapsed Catholic tradition.

A dazzling flash of lightning made us both jump, and the

rain outside grew stronger, like the heavens were trying to wash the house away. If there was ever going to be a best time to summon spirits, this was it.

I ignored the crawling sensation building on the nape of my neck, then looked to Ryan. "Let's get started."

Chapter 5

It's easy to arrange a tableau of occult curios appropriate for a Six Flags haunted house. It's way harder to set the stage for an *actual* ghost, especially when you have zero experience in enticing paranormal entities to drop by and say boo.

Our final result, though, ended up looking pretty legit. We set up the Ouija board first, then placed the tea light candles and the crystals in an alternating semicircle around the board. Ryan had a lighter on him, so he did the honors of lighting the candles and the sage. The latter he handed to me, and I gamely swished it through the air like I was jousting some invisible foe, then set it down in a dish to smolder. The smoke was strong and not overly pleasant.

What was the point of sageing the air anyway? I had the vague sense that it was both a necessary preliminary step to use the Ouija board, while simultaneously a way to banish spirits. Paradoxical—yet at least we'd set the mood.

I made a note to bring up the lighter later. Either Ryan was a smoker of some substance or another or a pyromaniac—and at this point, I wouldn't blink at either one.

As for the tarot deck, I went through the cards and pulled out any that felt right, whether in name, picture, or some other, indefinite attraction, then placed my final selections with care above the board. The five I ended up with looked as viable as any other combination: the Eight of Coins, showing a sleeping man with coins weighing down his limbs; the Six of Swords, depicting a different man clutching a flying fir tree; the Moon, with two wolves in classic howling stance; Death, chosen for obvious reasons; and finally Justice, personified by a woman with magnificent antlers sprouting from her temples. She held the scales in balance, two expressionless children playing at her feet.

The last touch was a surprising suggestion from Ryan: my cell phone, with the audio recorder open to catch any EVP. (Electronic voice phenomena, for plebs not well-versed in ghost hunter pseudoscience.) *But what if?!* a voice in my mind cried as I hit the red record button. *What if?!*

As the seconds on the recorder started ticking upward, Ryan and I shared a glance, then placed our fingers on the Ouija planchette. I took a deep breath, then coughed as the smoke from the burning sage tickled the back of my throat.

"H-hello, spirits. I'm Lan— Err... Melanie Adams." Maybe formality counted for something with ghosts. "We'll be really grateful for whatever help you can give us today." I shot Ryan a look: his turn now.

"Hello, spirits," he said evenly, like he was having an ordinary conversation. "I'm Ryan Spina. We hope you're willing to speak with us today."

The planchette remained motionless, and the candle flames burned strong.

"Are there any spirits in this house?" I ventured timidly. A low snore broke the silence, and I jumped, scooting the planchette forward across the board. Mustard was curled up under the table taking a nap.

I tried again. "Spirits, please talk to us if you're here. Tell us your name." Pause. Nothing. "Who were you?" Still nothing. "Why are you here?"

One of the candles guttered, but the planchette didn't budge.

"Are the spirits among us tonight?" Ryan asked. I envisioned the planchette shooting over to *No*; that would be the sort of joke I would play if I were a ghost. Yet it didn't move even a millimeter.

Maybe a different approach was needed. "Tell us how you died," I said. "Were you killed?"

"Pretty bold," Ryan muttered, just as a flash of lightning lit the room, followed a millisecond later by crashing thunder. Mustard let out a high whine.

"That was close," Ryan said, taking a look out the window. "Could that be a sign…?"

"I've never heard of ghosts controlling the weather."

"Yeah, well I've never heard of blue ghosts, either."

Time to try one last time. There were only so many ways to phrase this plea. "Spirits, give a sign if you're here," I said, voice quavering.

All the lights in the room burst back on, and this time they stayed on, the house coming alive with the renewed hum of electricity. I heard the blare of the TV in the other room—some dated sitcom, the audience laughing in unison. My parents must have had it on when the power died.

I waited, breathless, for *something*. A disembodied voice from the beyond. A blue figure melting through the kitchen pantry. Anything.

But nothing happened—just another burst of canned laughter from the TV.

"Maybe your ghosts really like *The Golden Girls*...?" Ryan asked.

I shook my head gloomily. "I almost thought we were going to get some answers."

"Well, there's still a chance." He reached for my phone and ended the recording. "Want to listen back to this?"

I'd forgotten all about the EVP recording. "Sure."

We brought the phone into the living room, and I hooked it up to the sound system, cranking up the volume. I didn't want to miss a single whisper.

But no eerie murmurs or groans interrupted the pauses between our questions. The highlight was undoubtedly Mustard's snore, which boomed out of the speakers in full glory and earned a snicker from Ryan. I shut off the recording, and we sat in silence. The mood felt deflated, like some indefinable magic had been hovering in the air, only to fade away into oblivion just before we got a good look.

"It's sort of like when I figured out there was no Santa Claus," Ryan joked after a minute.

I nodded, though the simile wasn't perfect. This was

more like knowing for a fact that Santa was real, then sending letter after letter to the North Pole with no response.
And the Santa in this scenario was undead.

"Hey, cheer up," Ryan said. "This is good, right? We took all
the right steps. If these ghosts of yours wanted to scare us or
need help, then they missed their chance. You're in the clear."

"Yeah, you're right," I said, giving him a half-hearted
smile. "You wanna eat lunch?" We walked back into the
kitchen, and he ran the still smoking bundle of sage under
the tap as I got out chips and salsa and assembled some ham
and Swiss sandwiches.

"So," I said as I fed Mustard a piece of ham, "did you
finish *Dracula*?"

"Nope, I've been making use of some extensive online
summaries." He smiled and put a finger to his lips. "Don't
tell Mrs. Naples."

"But that sounds like academic dishonesty, sir!" I said
with mock outrage. "How could an upstanding student of
Enville High School do such a thing?!"

"Yeah, yeah." He ate the last bite of his sandwich and
stretched. "Thanks for lunch. Hey, did you want me to look
at your math homework?"

"It's all right, don't worry about it." I was still tense from
our ghost hunting earlier and couldn't stomach wrestling
with X's and Y's. "But I don't mind writing your paper."

"Wait, *writing* it? Seriously?"

"Seriously. Just give me the prompt. I like the book. It's
no big deal."

"Well, okay," he said leerily. "I won't argue with someone who wants to do my homework for me. Thanks."

"No problem." I chewed on my next thought for a moment before finally spitting it out. "Hey, can I ask you something?"

"Sure."

"What's up with the lighter? Do you smoke… something?"

A smile slowly spread across his face, and he dug the lighter from his pocket and clicked it on and off. "I'm actually an up-and-coming arsonist in central Connecticut."

"Yeah, I figured."

He kept fiddling with the lighter. *Click. Click. Click.* "Why do you ask?"

"Just curious. I, uhh, I've been sort of tense the last few days." Not untrue.

He kept his expression neutral. "You want me to hook you up with some weed?"

"Could I, like, just try some first? I don't even know what to do."

Ryan narrowed his eyes at me. "You couldn't possibly be suggesting," he said in a conspiratorial whisper, "an exchange of a boring English essay for illegal drugs?"

That seemed fairly accurate. "I suppose I am."

"Well," he said, sliding the lighter back into his pocket, "then you have yourself a deal."

We packed up the ghost hunting accoutrements, then headed back to his house to smoke. There was no time like the present, with our parents all at work and the better part of the unexpected day off stretched out empty before us.

It hardly felt real to be driving the minivan down Enville's rain-slicked streets to go smoke weed at a boy's house. If someone had told me a few days ago that that was exactly what I would be doing later that week, I would have laughed in their face. I wasn't a goody two shoes per se; contented social recluse was a more accurate label—the key word being *contented*. Whenever I was stressed or sad, it had always been enough to snuggle under a blanket with Mustard, reading a book and nursing a hot chocolate. Sure, it would have been nice to have a theoretical friend over, but I hadn't ever felt like I *needed* anyone else there. I got on fine with my parents, and vloggers and streamers were good enough at their jobs that I never felt that lonely.

In any case, "being bad" was pretty unprecedented for me. The closest thing I'd ever done was last summer, when I'd absconded with a bottle of chardonnay from storage in the basement on a weekend when my parents were gone. It was the sort of thing I knew they wouldn't notice, since they were subscribed to a wine-of-the-month club and didn't drink enough to keep up with the shipments. As twilight descended, I'd loaded the wine, a flashlight, a Stephen King novel, and a blanket into my backpack and headed toward a hilly clearing in the woods half a mile south for a night of drinking and stargazing. To my disappointment, the chardonnay wasn't at all to my liking, and I left most of it corked there on the hill, like an offering to some god.

But now it wasn't just curiosity driving me. I felt like I'd been in fight or flight since Tuesday; I craved relaxation like a wanderer in a desert craves water. Hopefully weed would be more my style than wine.

I pulled into Ryan's driveway again, parked the minivan, and was about to head out into the rain before I realized that he wasn't moving.

"What's up?" I asked.

He chewed at his lip. "We're not rich like you guys," he said after a moment.

I hopped out of the car. "Okay...?"

"Just warning you that we're the type of family who only buys art prints," he said, getting out. "And they're the shitty kind you'd see in some dorm room, not your Picassos or whatever."

I poked at a puddle with my boot, the water sloshing over my toes. "Listen, I haven't been over to a friend's house in, like... a *long* time. I'm just happy to get out of the house." I said the words before I'd even given them proper thought. I was legitimately happy to be out of the house — and not just because it might be haunted — and I'd called him a friend. Both things to think on later.

"Okay," Ryan said, looking a bit relieved. "Come on in, then."

The Spina house looked like it had been attacked by a crazed Michaels employee — miniature pumpkins in each window, fake cobwebs stretched over the staircase banister. Tchochkes and family photos crowded every surface. From the foyer I could see through into the kitchen; by the look of it, the refrigerator was more card and comic strip holder than food receptacle.

True to Ryan's words, everything on the walls was the exact opposite of my house: a hodgepodge of old photos, a framed needlepoint of goldfinches frolicking in a birdbath, another needlepoint of a quote in elegant golden script, edged in pastel blossoms. *A light heart lives long.*

"Fulfilling all the stoner stereotypes, I see," I said, pointing at a print of a Pink Floyd album cover down the hall.

"My dad's a big fan," he said as he led me upstairs to a small bedroom. It was tidy enough, though as we walked in he nudged a small heap of clothes under the bed with his foot. A boy's room—*I* was in a *boy's* room. My heart gave a nervous galumph.

The walls were painted deep indigo—though it was hard to see them for the army of posters plastering the walls. Beady-eyed trolls hurling boulders at a squadron of elves; a swaggering warrior sporting laughably massive shoulder pauldrons; a green-gray goblin with a beaky nose, eyes gleaming as he surveyed a pile of coins and jewels—all these fantasy game tropes under the same flame-red letters.

HOUR OF FATE
DESTINY CALLS

"Wow, you really like this game, huh?" I asked, eyeing one of the posters. It showed three tanned sirens perched on a rock, tittering as they sang a distant ship to a watery grave. Their skin glistened with sea spray, and their flowing tresses handily covered no doubt perky mermaid nipples. The poster's placement on the wall across from his bed didn't seem unintentional.

"Yeah, I've put almost seven hundred hours into it," he said with clear pride, then blinked and darted a nervous look at me. "I mean, that's not as bad as it sounds! I've been playing for two years, so that's, like, only an hour or two most days!"

The rising pink in his cheeks was cute, I had to say. "Sounds about as nerdy as knowing every single Hitchcock film backwards and forwards," I said, crooking a smile at him. "Right?"

"Yeah," he said, gamer hackles coming down. "Right. Well, then." He went over to his still-damp backpack and drew out a piece of paper. "Here's the prompt. The paper's due on Monday."

I glanced it over; this wouldn't take me long.

"And this," he said, pulling an Altoids tin out from the back-pack's interior pocket and waggling it at me, "is your payment."

"You smoke at *school*?"

"I know, how cool am I? I sneak off campus at lunch. La-nie, weed isn't a big deal. I bet half the teachers smoke. Open that window, would you?" While I fiddled with the window latch, he popped open the tin and pulled a bowl—this terminology was as far as my knowledge went—from the back of his desk drawer. Sage, marijuana—this adventure was making me into an amateur herbalist.

Once everything was prepared, he took a seat on the carpet. "Okay," he said, as I sat down across from him. He handed me the bowl and the lighter. "So light the bowl, hold it here, and breathe in."

"Do I hold the smoke in?"

"Yeah, but you don't have to be ridiculous about it. Watch me."

He took a hit, then passed the bowl over to me. I did just as he showed me, coughing a bit as I exhaled. The smoke stuck to the back of my tongue. We went back and forth a few times, and soon a wave of tingles enveloped my head, the front of my face going numb. Some internal tension within me was easing, a pressure that I hadn't even noticed suddenly gone. I looked up, and Ryan smiled.

"Better?"

"Yeah. Very."

"Don't start talking about how much you love my rug."

I looked down at the carpet. It was a nondescript shade of beige. "What?"

"Never mind." He pushed up off the ground. "Listen, you stay here. I'm going to go get us something to eat. Find something to listen to. A first trip without music is tragic."

Oh no. This was where it could all go wrong—what if he hated my taste in music? I flipped through my phone, eventually settling on an acoustic playlist. Better suited for a coffee shop, maybe, but it would do.

Ryan was right, though, about the music. I hadn't heard this song, and the lyrics were standard fare about a man missing his lover, but everything about the song felt *right*. The singer's voice was echoey, like he'd been recorded at a distance, but his tone was powerful as a gospel singer. The guitar chords were thick and warm, each strum like a squeeze of a blacksmith's bellows, heating the room. I took a deep breath and let it out again until there was nothing left in my lungs. It felt like I'd been sucking in sips of air for days, without a thought to exhaling.

Ryan came back a minute later, cradling an assortment of snacks, and sat down across from me on the rug. I pulled open a packet of cookies and smiled when I popped one in my mouth. Chocolate had never tasted so good.

"Thanks."

"No problem. How're you feeling?"

"Really good."

We munched our snacks in silence, listening to the music. The rain was still coming down. How much water could clouds possibly hold?

"So what're you going to do now, about the ghosts?" he asked after a bit, looking at me sidelong.

"Hmm…" I looked toward the window, watching the rain fall. The problem of my blue ghosts no longer seemed so pressing. What had they really done to me? Invaded some childhood dreams, taken a peek in my bedroom. They seemed harmless, so why worry about it? I pushed a finger into the rug and sighed, trying to ignore the echo of the ghost girl's choked, distorted cry ringing through my head. I must be remembering her wrong—more wistful than wretched, surely.

"Lanie?" he prompted.

The tones of the guitar washed over me. "I guess… nothing. We did all we could."

And I let that thought settle down within me and stay, like typing a period at the end of a sentence. Done. It was done.

I grabbed another cookie, suddenly ravenous, then sank back on the carpet like I was about to make a snow angel. I felt so light, so free. "At least this whole saga will make a great st—"

Ryan leaned over me and closed his lips over my own. There was a fluttering nervousness in my stomach, replaced with unfurling heat a second later, and I tilted my head up and kissed him back. He smelled good, like soap and sandalwood. I put tentative fingers to the back of his head, pulling him in closer, and he eagerly obliged. Every movement was new and clumsy, but in that way where you know that everything is going right, that all you need is a bit of practice.

Sometime later we broke apart. My breathing was heavy, and I could feel the flush in my cheeks.

"I'll drive you home," Ryan said, glancing at me for half a second before bouncing his gaze away. The empty space between us felt awkward. Not bad—just undefined.

"You don't have to do that," I said, standing up and surreptitiously dusting a few very unsexy cookie crumbs off my front. "I feel fine." It was true; I felt only a whisper of the weed lingering at the edges of my mind, though the calm it had given me remained.

Ryan raised an eyebrow. "Are you sure?"

"Super sure. I'll take side streets." His eyebrow twitched higher still. "I'll drive like a grandma—promise." The minivan didn't allow driving any other way, to be honest. "Besides, how would you get home then?"

"Yeah, I guess. Just text me when you get there." We'd exchanged numbers on the way back to his house. He darted another look at me. "So see you in the library?"

I met his gaze and smiled at him, equally happy and nervous. "I'll be there."

True to my word, I crawled my way home at a strict twenty-five miles per hour. Fortunately, the rain and the fact that it was one in the afternoon on a weekday meant that Enville's streets were near-deserted.

Josefa's maroon hatchback was parked in our driveway. I shot Ryan a text that I'd made it home, then sniffed my braid for lingering smoke. Nothing I could smell, but best to just say a quick hello and head upstairs for a shower.

I opened the door and was greeted by singing; Josefa always said she liked cleaning our house because we didn't mind if she sang as she worked.

"Hi, Josefa!"

She looked up from dusting, and her round face broke into a smile. *"Hola, mija, cómo estás?"*

"Un poco cansada. Voy a ducharme, okay?" She nodded and shooed me off.

In the shower, I let the hot water lull me into a half-meditation. No more ghosts for me—now there was something altogether different for me to obsess over this weekend. I resolved to start the *Dracula* essay once I toweled off. And then, I wondered, maybe it would be fun to leave the horror aside for a bit and pick up a romance or two. I could head to the library tomorrow…

I turned off the shower, pulled open the curtain, and the cozy warmth that had been cradling me crystallized and shattered.

A girl in blue, the same from before, stared back at me. Her face was inches from my own, close enough to see the smattering of navy freckles on her cheeks. My throat clenched to scream, but the air in my windpipe felt frozen, like it had solidified into a chunk of ice. Something about looking at her was making my head hurt, like patches of her face were fading in and out—not transparent, but like they weren't even there at all.

She leaned in towards my ear as I stood paralyzed, and biting cold stung the side of my head, radiating through my skull. Her words came to me as a distant shout, distorted and waterlogged.

"Melissa White!"

As she formed the last syllable, a pair of midnight blue hands sprang from nothingness in front of me, fingers tensed into claws. They grabbed at the ghost, tearing at her hair, at her clothes, then seized her arm with a bruising grip. I found my breath at last and screamed and screamed as the disembodied hands dragged the ghost away until she was gone, pulled into a void.

And then it was just me in the bathroom, naked, dripping wet, and freezing cold.

Chapter 6

A RATTLING OF the doorknob—I'd locked it—then a panicked pounding on the door: Josefa. "Lanie! *Qué pasó?! Déjame entrar, déjame entrar!*"

I swiveled towards the door, my wet feet slipping on the porcelain. "I, uh, spider!" How the fuck did you say spider in Spanish? "Spider *muy grande!*" What were the chances she'd believe me? I kept babbling. "Climbing on *mi pie.* I, umm, squished it, but I think it bit me."

"Estás bien? De verdad?"

"Yeah." No, not okay in the slightest—but I couldn't tell her. I could see the progression clearly: a whole horde of disbelieving, concerned adults. Staring up at the cold, coffin-like inside of an MRI machine. A frowning doctor tapping notes into a computer. A nurse handing over a psychiatrist's business card to my dad, my mom's face drawn and worried. Then a rattling bottle of psych meds, like the proverbial pot of gold at the end of the rainbow—only this was the world's shittiest, scariest rainbow, all shades of shifting blue.

I knew what was happening to me was real, and God

help me, I was going to figure out how to fix it.

Josefa's footsteps padded away a few seconds later. I toweled off, then reached for my phone. My hands were shaking so badly it took almost a minute to type two simple sentences to Ryan.

> I saw one of the ghosts again. I think her name is Melissa White.

My thumb wavered over the send button. This felt like going backwards, like I was throwing some hopeful sapling into a wood chipper.

Screw it. My ghosts took precedence over some kissing, and I needed all the help I could get. Ryan had seemed to believe me before, so why not now? I hit send, braced myself, and opened the bathroom door, ready to run through a gauntlet of ghosts on the way to my bedroom.

The hallway was empty. I darted into my bedroom—also seemingly empty—then shut the door behind me with a firm click.

"All right." I turned around in a slow circle. "Anyone here? Melissa? Come on out."

No answer. All I could hear was the faint sound of Josefa's singing filtering through the door and the heavy rain outside.

"You sure? Nothing else you want to tell me?" I tried to muster ferocity as I stared at the closet, at the shadowed depths under the bed, at the mirror. As if I would be intimidating to some ghosts clad in just my towel.

So I got dressed, combed my hair, went through the motions—even threw on a coat of nail polish. Anything to feel normal for half a second. My phone buzzed a few times, but I let it rest facedown on the bed. At last, I blew a thin stream of air on the drying polish and gave myself a countdown: ten more breaths of normal. I kept them calm and deep, even though my nerves were humming.

Three.

Two.

One.

I grabbed for my phone.

One text from my mom:

> Heard school was canceled!!! I'm ordering a pizza for dinner. Pepperoni and mushrooms sound good?

And two from Ryan:

> Holy shit, are you ok?

> You need to look at this.

He'd included a video link, and I tapped it open.

Music blared, something copyright free and low-key creepy. Green words floated on a black background.

The Mysterious Disappearance of Melissa White

The text spun away, replaced by a girl's smiling picture—the generic kind you'd see in a high school yearbook. The kind you might see on the back of a milk carton.

It was her, rendered in shades of living color. Wide-set gray-green eyes, lined with eyeliner. Those same freckles—now beautiful brown, instead of navy—and a glow to her skin that spoke of languid days in the sun. Blond hair curled and teased just so, obviously primped in front of a compact mirror just a minute before. A wide grin, more than just a smile, almost insolent. She'd tilted her chin up a bit, as if daring the cameraman to ask her to tone it down and stop treating her school picture like a goddamn private photo shoot.

The music faded, and a microphone crackled on. "Hi, everyone, welcome to my channel." It was a man's voice; I pegged him as somewhere in his forties, but the sound quality made it hard to tell. As he proceeded to go through the usual plea to like, comment, and subscribe, I scrolled through his channel and the video statistics. D_plexippus, as this guy had christened himself, had uploaded less than ten videos, half of them dedicated to missing persons cases, the rest your standard conspiracy videos. The Melissa White video, uploaded in 2011 and with a whopping eight views, was his most popular one of the lot. It didn't have a single comment.

D_plexippus finished his spiel at last. "All right, so this is the case that got me into this whole scene. Melissa White, from Lanster, New Hampshire."

I drew back. New Hampshire? What the hell was her

ghost doing in Enville, Connecticut, then?

"I actually knew Melissa," he continued. "Not very well, but I did. She was my babysitter fairly often when I was a kid, up until halfway through the summer of 1985, when I was nine years old."

Some lines of text popped up on the screen beside her picture.

Full Name: Melissa Mary White
Date of Birth: February 2, 1969
Place of Birth: Lanster, New Hampshire
Missing Since: September 22, 1985. (Sixteen years old)
Height: 5'4" (At time of disappearance)
Weight: 115 pounds (At time of disappearance)
Race: Caucasian
Hair: Blond
Scars and Marks: Freckles; ears pierced; navel pierced
Clothes and Jewelry: Unknown

The school picture flipped to another photo—Melissa standing by a beach dressed in a pristine white bikini. There was a grainy silver glint at her belly button—her piercing. She was half-smiling, half-smirking at the camera, though her eyes were hard and shuttered. She was a knock-out, but a sad aura hovered around her, like some young almost-Marilyn Monroe.

"And that's pretty much all I remember," D_plexippus said, "except that she was on the phone all the time with her friends when she was over babysitting. And twice during the summer of '85 she made long distance calls from our house to New York. My mother was livid—fired her for good the second time. I don't remember any real details of who she was talking to, unfortunately. I was always watching TV in the other room."

The picture of Melissa in the bikini and the text spun away, replaced by a full-screen black and white photo of a woman in a clinging dress lying on her stomach on a carpet. She was reading a book; feathery blond curls cascaded over her shoulder to shield her face from view—though they did nothing to hide her generous breasts. A sunbeam tumbled down on her from an open window, lighting her up like an angel. It was Melissa—but Melissa through the eyes of a photographer, and what looked like a professional at that. The angle of the shot, the pose, the get-up... She looked much older than sixteen.

"So," D_plexippus said, "this is one of several photo prints found hidden in Melissa's room after she disappeared. As you'll notice, all of them are black and white, and all of them obscure the model's face. A few people on the boards have posited Melissa kept the photos because they starred a model closely resembling her..." Another photo cut in: the camera lens was peering down the middle of a spiral staircase, a blond woman's blurred, shadowed form descending the steps a few floors down.

"Yet I think we can safely make the leap that Melissa *is* the model, given that they all feature the same blond female and were *hidden* in Melissa's room. Why hide them if she just admired them?" I nodded; his logic made sense, even though this video was unabashedly creepy. I was onboard, so long as D_plexippus didn't start blaming Melissa's disappearance on the Illuminati.

Another photo filled the screen, this one of the blond figure hurrying away from the photographer down an alleyway. A puddle reflected her form in distorted ripples.

"After Melissa's disappearance, they published these photos in the local newspaper, hoping someone would come forward with information. Her parents had no idea who'd taken them. And something about the photos really struck me, so I clipped them from the newspaper and kept them for years and years. Just a weird thing to remember her by, but the kind of thing a kid does. I *was* a kid. And I'd always liked photography, plus my dad was an amateur enthusiast, so he let me use his cameras a lot. Sort of a bonding thing between the two of us."

D_plexippus cleared his throat. "Sorry for the side tangent, but it's just to say that I had a bit of a background in photography. Once I got to college I took some photo electives, got a bit better technically. So one weekend I took a trip to Boston, popped into an art gallery, and saw an exhibition by August Rufner. And his work reminded me deeply of the pictures of Melissa I'd kept all those years."

A collage of photos wiped away the image of Melissa in the alley, each one rendered in dark shadow and creamy light, each one featuring a woman caught in candid action, her face hidden by shadow or positioning. I paused the video, studying every photograph in turn. D_plexippus was right; something about the styles was similar, a raw, melancholic energy suffusing every scene. The previous shots of Melissa fit right in.

D_plexippus launched into a long explanation about the technical parallels: lack of dodging in and burning, comparable focal length, similar composition styles. It all went over my head, but it sounded like he really knew his subject. I was just about to search for more details about the photographer when D_plexippus beat me to it.

"Some background on Rufner is in order. He was born in 1961, making him twenty-four when Melissa was sixteen. At that time he was doing a Master of Fine Arts in photography at Dunn College in upstate New York. He found a modicum of success in the art sphere in the mid-eighties through the mid-nineties. Mostly faded from the public eye after that, and now he teaches at Wincrest College of Design, also in upstate New York.

"Here's the timeline you need to focus on. Melissa's parents just so happened to attend Dunn College as undergraduates, and the whole family had taken a long weekend earlier that summer in '85 to go to Dunn College for their twenty-year reunion. Two long distance phone calls later that summer from my house to New York. Now here's the fun part..." I frowned. Fun? Weren't we talking about a teenage girl's inexplicable disappearance?

"Rufner's very first gallery exhibition opens in the local

Teutsch Gallery on Friday, September twentieth, 1985. Melissa goes missing that very same day, and the official missing persons report is filed that Sunday. According to the newspaper, her parents said she told them she was staying the weekend at a friend's lake house, but that girl hadn't made any plans with Melissa.

"So, my friends, I'm wondering if she didn't make up a story so she could travel down to see Rufner, congratulate him on his exhibition, maybe even see the photographs of her there. Unfortunately, I can't find any art book or prints from Rufner's first exhibition to verify those three photos were included. Yet the photos from the other collage I showed earlier were from the Teutsch Gallery showing, re-released later in a book of Rufner's collected works."

His voice grew lower. "But even absent proof, isn't it too much of a coincidence for both Melissa and Rufner to have been in the same town at the same time and those photos to have such a similar style? This is how I envision events went down: Rufner and Melissa meet at the reunion while her parents are off somewhere else. Forbidden fling, young girl taken with the older, artsy guy, that sort of thing. Rufner takes her picture, gives her some prints, she's flattered. She keeps in touch with him off and on. He decides to display her photos in the gallery, she goes to see him and the photos. And then… then we don't know. Maybe he kills her. Maybe something else. I mean, for one thing, how did she travel to New York—bus? Hitchhiking? Melissa didn't have a car. New Hampshire to New York is a ways to go for a sixteen-year-old without their own transportation.

"Okay, so now she's officially missing. Maybe Rufner has something to do with it, maybe he doesn't—no way to know. Let's presume innocence; he might not even know she's gone missing. Who in New York is going to know that some girl all the way up in New Hampshire has disappeared? Perhaps he finds out later; what would he do? He surely wouldn't come forward and say anything about it, since he'd be the primary suspect, no question. Young, gorgeous girl with some secret, older photographer boyfriend doesn't look good. The age of consent might be legal, I'm not sure, but the optics are terrible. So that's my pet theory."

D_plexippus let out a hum, then fell silent for a moment. "In any case, leave a comment here or on the boards and let me know what you think. See you next time." I stared at the screen, dumbfounded, as the creepy music ended abruptly and the next video queued up to play.

There was no doubt it was a stretch. But… I shook my head. No, it couldn't be true. This was so far-fetched as to be insane—sprawling theories spun from gossamer-thin clues.

Even so, I pulled up Wincrest College of Design's website. Navigating to the faculty page, I shivered as I scrolled to the R's and spotted August Rufner's name straightaway. He was still teaching at Wincrest. I clicked open his profile page.

There was a picture. Rufner was a gaunt man, his cheekbones high, his eyes sharp. His hair was long and dark as well, its messiness deliberate-looking. If there

was a physical stereotype of snooty photography profes-
sors, Rufner fit the bill.

Yet even though he didn't look particularly nice, I still wasn't convinced he was actually involved in Melissa White's disappearance. Innocent until proven guilty and all that.

Did Rufner know about this video? Was one of these eight views—now nine—his? How strange and terrible it must be to have some half-formed accusation of murder posted on the Internet for all to see, obscure though the video was.

One last thing to check. I opened a new tab.

Lanster, New Hampshire to Dunn College, New York.

The suggested best route between the two cities passed right through Enville.

Chapter 7

I JUMPED WHEN my phone vibrated—Ryan, of course.

Did you watch it? Is that
her? What do you think?

It's her. I believe it. Look at this.

I sent him a picture of the route between Lanster and Dunn College, and his reply came a second later.

Damn.

I heaved a sigh. What now? I reached for my laptop and drummed my fingers on the keyboard, thinking hard.

Melissa's ghost was haunting *my* house, not some creepy photographer's old apartment in upstate New York. So that seemed to exonerate Rufner unless he'd personally driven to New Hampshire to pick her up then driven straight back—an eight-hour round trip. Not likely, especially on the day his exhibition opened.

I played the video again, listening carefully. What did D_plexippus mean when he mentioned "the boards?" He'd said that twice. Some forum? I bit at my lip and, with a prayer to the Internet god that was Google, searched his username.

And blinked when hundreds of thousands of results came back. Showing results for D. plexippus. It was the Latin name—*Danaus plexippus*—for the Monarch butterfly.

I sighed as I scrolled through the results. Overviews of the Monarch butterfly species, scientific papers, learning modules for little kids—how the hell was I supposed to find him in this mess? Even my search for "*D_plexippus Melissa White*" only turned up more web pages about butterflies; about a million butterflies had "white" in their name, and there was another dainty, azure variety called the Melissa blue. Infuriating.

At last I slammed my laptop shut and sank back on my bed, staring blearily out the window. The weak sunlight had ceded to gray-blue twilight, the moisture-clogged air blurring the trees outside the window like a cloud had enveloped our house.

"Think," I whispered. "Think."

But no epiphany graced me with its presence. I let the room sink into darkness as the found photos of Melissa flitted through my mind, one after the other.

I'm in a room of dim red lights and shadows, stinking of chemicals—a darkroom. Liquid sloshes somewhere from the left, but

when I turn all I find is deeper gloom within the darkness. The shadows squirm and slither over each other, convulsing, writhing. A gasp escapes my lips against my best intentions, and the shadows pause, black coils turning to me as one, poised like snakes ready to strike.

I try to take a step back, but my body is heavy, as if anchored to the floor with tree roots. Every muscle strains, but I can't move.

And then with the click of a camera and a flash of brilliant white, I see Melissa's figure illuminated in the heart of the darkness. She's clad in the dress from Rufner's picture, and shadows wriggle under her skin like maggots. She cowers as the light dies.

Flash!

She's turned away, tensing to flee, lustrous blond curls hanging like a waterfall down her back. The light dies again.

Flash!

She's sprinting away, but she takes a look over her shoulder back at me. Her eyes are inky holes.

The light dies for the final time.

No transition—I'm on the rug in Ryan's bedroom, in his arms. Warmth, happiness. I let him kiss me, and I kiss him back. Not sloppy, not tentative—just right.

Then he's gone, too. I'm looking up towards where the ceiling should be, but there's a clear sky instead, like I'm in a dollhouse and some giant child just lifted off the roof.

The sun beats down on me, and I smile. Warmth, happiness. The four walls around me fall away, the whole backdrop vanishing. The only things left in the world are me and the sky, and the longer I look up into the sun-flooded cosmos, the smaller I'm becoming.

A shiver races over my body, partnered with the rustling of hundreds of paper-thin wings. I tear my gaze away from the sky and look down. My whole body is covered with butterflies of every variety—big as a robin, small as a fingernail, glimmering scales, dusty wings, crimson, aquamarine, lavender, tangerine, fuchsia, cerise. I raise my arms in wonder, moving slowly lest I jostle their delicate bodies.

There's a low murmur from behind me—a breathy, female voice. "Lanie, can you hear me?" I turn my head: no one there.

Another whisper—my name once more. "Lanie!" This time when I turn to look I catch a flicker of blue. The butterflies, the sky, my hands, everything else has faded to gray, like I'm in a movie that's just flipped to black and white, a reverse Wizard of Oz moment.

Knock.

"Go away!" My voice is high, kiddish. I know Melissa is here, watching me.

"Lanie, please!" she says. "I—"

Knock.

"Go away!" I shriek at her. "Go away, go away, g—!"

"Lanie?" I jerked back awake with a gasp. My mom had cracked open the door, the light from the hallway outside piercing the darkness of my bedroom. I blinked and couldn't help a glance down at my arms. Not a butterfly in sight. Just a dream.

"H-hi, Mom." I raked a hand through my hair to find it damp with sweat. "Guess I fell asleep."

"Sorry to wake you, hon. The pizza's here, so come down and eat when you're ready."

"Cool, thanks." I shuffled to the bathroom to put my hair up in a ponytail and splash some water on my face. Taking a glance in the mirror, I shuddered; it reflected back a drained facsimile of myself, skin wan, eyes bloodshot. Were the eyes just a product of the past few anxious nights—or the weed?

Speaking of anxious nights, what about that dream? The details were slipping away fast—something about butterflies—but the end stayed sharp. The whispering and that elusive blue hovering just out of sight *had* to be Melissa. How was I supposed to sleep, knowing that at any moment Melissa the over-eager ghost might drop into my head for a watery chat?

"Lanie, it's on the table!" my mom called up the stairs.

"Yeah, okay." My voice was low and shaking. I joined my parents in the dining room, feeling nauseated.

"Had a nice nap?" my mom asked.

"Yup." Best to keep up a normal act.

My dad sniffed. "It smells kind of smoky in here. Do you smell that?"

I dropped my eyes to my lap. That would be the sage we'd burned. "Yeah, I made tea a few hours ago, and the burner started smoking like crazy."

"I'll clean it out later," my dad said. "Heard you got the day off. Three-day weekend, lucky you!"

"Yeah, the power was out at school."

"Well, I'm glad you got the day to relax," my mom said, reaching for another slice. I'd still hardly taken a bite of my own. "You've seemed stressed these past couple days."

She didn't know the half of it. "Just had a lot of home-work," I mumbled.

"That history project?"

"Yeah." I plucked a piece of pepperoni from my pizza slice and tossed it to Mustard, who was begging at my feet. "It's interesting, but the research is killing me."

That night I didn't sleep. Not of my own volition — my unconsciousness was working against me, fear bristling in the back of my mind every time I closed my eyes.

Hadn't I *wanted* to talk to the ghosts? To ask them what their problem was? But that had been before I'd seen those dark hands materialize from thin air, clutching at Melissa's ghost. Now who could say what I was dealing with? Some other malevolent force, perhaps. Logically I knew there was no solution in not sleeping, but my nerve-wracked brain wasn't listening to logic.

So I stayed awake, scrolling through occult web pages that looked like they were constructed pre-2000 for infor-mation about detached, ghostly hands. When that didn't pan out, I started another futile search for D_plexippus. I gave up somewhere around six in the morning and put on a romantic comedy for distraction. Yet my overtired brain, running on the fumes of a second wind from God knows where, refused to be lulled by the mindless entertainment. The male and female leads were embroiled in some overwritten misunderstanding—easily solvable, if they'd both quit hanging up the phone on each other mid-sentence. It was ridiculous, and moreover, it was too happy, too normal. How could they fret about love when there were real, live ghosts afoot?

I snorted. Real, *live* ghosts—what was wrong with me? Black night was brightening to gray. How long could a person stay awake? A few days at most, right?

I gave all four walls of my bedroom a long, mean look, then added a middle finger for good measure. "Fuck you, if you're here!" Then I dragged my comforter over my head, breathing in the warm, soupy air, and was dead to the world seconds later.

No dreams, thank God. But in those scant, blessed hours of sleep, somewhere at the edges of my mind I swore I felt some dark presence creeping.

Chapter 8

My mom let me sleep until noon; it was Saturday, after all. But no later—she'd invited my grandma over and she'd get here in a few hours and I couldn't sleep the whole day away and could I please run to the store and grab some milk and zucchini?

"And how will you possibly manage when I go away to college?" I asked, yawning as I slipped on my boots.

"Community college is always an option!"

"Yeah, sure," I said with a smile and a roll of my eyes. Joking aside, there was no chance in hell I'd be going to community college; my mom would never stand for it. Not that she had her sights set on me getting into an Ivy League school, but she was a big stickler on keeping up my grades so I could go somewhere good.

Which meant I would really have to do something about math… But that worry could wait until another day.

My mom pressed a twenty into my hand. "Bring back five bucks."

The day was cold and gray, but at least the rain had

ceased. Back in the minivan, I put on the Black Keys, all drums and blown-out vocals, and raised the volume to a tick below deafening. Every second breathed life back into my bones, beat by beat.

You can do this, I told myself as I shifted into drive. What I didn't know about my ghosts still outnumbered what I did, but I was getting somewhere.

I drove around the bend and smiled when I saw 2 Ferngrove. One of the family's kids was playing with some toy trucks at the side of the lawn, and he waved to me. I slowed down and waved back, taking the extra second to ogle their Halloween decorations. The people in that house always went hard on the holidays, and this year was no exception. Their front lawn was studded with a newly erected styrofoam graveyard, the bushes strewn with fake cobwebs and foot-long plastic spiders. The latest addition was a huge, inflatable Frankenstein placed front row center.

I couldn't see myself getting into the Halloween spirit this year, but it didn't mean I couldn't admire my favorite holiday from afar.

I was back forty-five minutes later, toting the groceries, five bucks change, and a caramel apple latte monstrosity (with extra whipped cream) from the Dunkin' Donuts by the grocery store. The sugar and caffeine were hitting me like a shot straight to the bloodstream. I almost felt like a person again.

Grandma Ruth showed up right on time—an hour and a half after she'd said she would. My grandma ran on

"Ruth-time," as my mom sometimes called it lovingly, and the relaxed aura that floated around my grandma and her practiced, wrinkled smile seemed to make everyone else run on Ruth-time, too.

We sat around the kitchen table chatting and munching on snacks as my mom worked on dinner. It was a comfortable, familiar scene I'd lived a thousand times before. I could almost forget that just yesterday Ryan and I had bedecked this same table with occult knickknacks.

Almost.

My dad got up to put on the Red Sox game in the living room, and I winced internally. Again, I'd been here a thousand times before and knew what was coming.

My grandma pounced as soon as my dad was gone. "So, Lanie, any new boy toys?" She waggled her eyebrows at me, eyes dancing. She asked me every time I saw her, and it had become a bit of a joke between the two of us, me acting the red-faced teenager and her the over-prying septuagenarian. I didn't mind it, really. She was from an era where people met their sweethearts at sixteen, went steady at seventeen, and got hitched at eighteen; that had been her love story with my late Grandpa Douglas, after all. Nothing wrong with jokes and a bit of vicarious living.

Except now I did sort of actually have a "boy toy," as she put it, and no desire to come clean. I bowed my head in dolorous fake-sorrow. "Not yet, Grandma."

"Oh sweetie, you'll find someone—someone who will take one glance in those big blue eyes of yours and won't find their way out again." She patted my hand, then went to help my mom in the kitchen.

Soon the smell of garlic and melting butter was filling the whole downstairs, my dad was lighting a candle for the middle of the table, the Sox were safely ahead by three points, and dinner was served. We said grace to make my grandma happy, clinked glasses over the table (theirs sauvignon blanc, mine some sparkling white grape juice I'd found stashed in the back of the fridge), then dug into dinner.

Bzzz.

"Lanie, no phones at the table." My mom shot me a glance, and I blushed as I fished my phone out of my pocket and put it on silent.

"Sorry, sorry." A wave of chills washed over me. Even with the half-second glimpse I'd gotten at my phone, I'd read Ryan's whole message.

We should call Rufner.

I pushed a piece of chicken around on my plate. Call Rufner? I'd been banking on the theory that Melissa hadn't made it to him in New York; hypothetically, he wouldn't know anything about how she'd disappeared. But what if he *did* actually know something?

Or worse, what if he was involved? I stabbed at the piece of chicken with my fork. It was too risky to talk to him.

"Lanie?"

My eyes stuttered up from my plate. They were all looking at me. "What?"

My dad shot me a quizzical look. "Didn't you hear Grandma talking about the movie?"

"Uhh…"

"That's okay, dear," my grandma said, swooping in. "So like I was saying, you know how we sometimes go to those musicals at the Old Town Theater?"

Did I. My grandma was always talking about how she could have been an actress on Broadway, belting out show tunes with the best of them. A few times a year, at her behest, we all went to see whatever the Enville theater troupe was putting on. They did a decent job for community theater, but the microphones were always buggy to the point of distraction, the sets little better than a middle school art project. The spring performance last year had been the best of the lot; they'd veered away from the usual kid-friendly fare with *Sweeney Todd*. Yet the production of *Annie* we'd gone to a few months ago had been sheer torture, the orphans' screeching rendition of "It's The Hard Knock Life" necessitating a *long* bathroom break.

"Well, I was thinking," my grandma continued, "that since *Annie* was a bit… much, that maybe we should branch out from the musicals. The theater's doing some screenings of *Psycho* in the run-up to Halloween" —now she had my attention—"but they're special showings. They have a copy of the film without the soundtrack, so a live orchestra from the community college is going to perform alongside the movie. Can you imagine that? All those violins? I thought it might be a fun night out."

"Yeah," I said, bobbing my head, "let's do it."

"And I knew you'd say that, Lanie, so I already bought the tickets!" She beamed at me. "I thought they might go fast."

"Wow. Great." Hopefully the orchestra would put on a better show than the community theater. Enville wasn't the biggest town, so the talent pickings were slim.

"The tickets are for Saturday the thirtieth," my mom said. "The day before Halloween."

"They had ones for Halloween day itself," my grandma said with a wink, "and you're probably past trick-or-treating, but I figured you might be going to a party or something."

"You *should* go to a Halloween party!" my mom chimed in, her tone too bright. "Or we could even have one here, and you could invite people!"

I studied my fork intensely. I hated when she got too worried about the no-friends thing. "Yeah… This year I'm going to stay in. Some terrible B movie, all the leftover candy corn that none of the kids want. A tradition's a tradition, you know!"

"But what if—"

"Michelle," my dad cut in, the barest edge of sharpness lacing his tone.

"It was just a thought," my mom said with a look at my dad. "But candy corn and a movie sound fun too." With that, she dropped it, and dinner was over.

My parents took my grandma into the living room to peruse the portfolios of some artists they were considering signing to the gallery, and I started clearing the table. As soon as they were out of the room, I looked at my phone.

Whoa. This was getting real serious, *real* fast.

I bit my lip, thinking.

As I was formulating the proper, exasperated response, my phone began to ring in my hand. Private number—there wasn't even an area code listed. I declined the call and stuck my tongue out at the screen.

Or whatever was enough to make my pulse pick up. Then he sent me a leaf emoji and a question mark a second later. I felt a whisper of disappointment. Was that all he meant—or something more?

Even so, I wouldn't mind smoking again—could use some now, in fact. This whole talk about calling Rufner had made me nervous.

I'd tell my mom I was heading to a classmate's house to work on my concocted history project. She'd practically push me out the door.

I blew out a breath. This was no big deal; it was just a phone call—right? Yet my palms were clammy, my mouth dry. I sighed and reached for my half-full glass of grape juice, took a sip, then blanched when the bite of alcohol hit my tongue. Gross—I'd mixed up my grandma's unfinished wine glass and my own.

I started towards the sink to spit it out, then thought better of it. She'd never notice, and I wanted more than anything to sink back into easy, distracted calm. It was the weekend, after all; couldn't I put the ghost stuff on pause for a little while? So I swallowed it down with a grimace, then downed the rest for good measure, doing my best not to gag.

I set the glass down quickly at the sound of approaching footsteps.

"How's it going in here?" My mom poked her head through the door, and her eyes crinkled when she saw me pulling on rubber gloves to do the washing up. "Oh, hon, you want me to do that? So you can go watch the game and talk to Grandma?"

"Sure. Thanks, Mom."

I joined my dad and grandma on the couch. The top of the seventh was almost at a close, and the opposing team was looking dejected; the Sox had widened their lead by two more points during dinner.

"I really think this might be their year," my dad was saying.

"You know better than to talk like that," said my grandma, knocking on the wooden coffee table.

My dad scowled. "I can't stand those superstitions. Ideas like that get in the players' heads, especially this late in the season. Messes them up." He leaned forward as the pitcher went through his pre-pitch ritual: smoothing the dirt on the mound, a touch to his glove, a deep breath. And then the pitch—a perfect strike—and the batter was out, just like that.

"And we're on to the seventh-inning stretch!" said the announcer jauntily. The screen cut to an old man in a baseball jersey holding a microphone—some retired player I'd never heard of. The organ music swelled, rallying the crowd, and I grinned as my grandma joined in.

"Take me out to the ball game!" For all her big talk about Broadway, she *did* have a decent voice, especially for a woman her age. "Take me out to the crowd!"

I could already sense the effects of the wine. My head felt light and my movements quicker, like all my joints had spontaneously loosened. I recognized the feeling from when I'd drunk a few swallows of the pilfered chardonnay on the hill last year.

"Buy me some peanuts and crackerjack…"

I drew my knees into my chest. This wasn't a healthy way to deal with the stress, I knew. Sure, it was just a few mouthfuls of wine, barely half a glass, but I'd been through enough mandatory health classes to know that what I was doing wasn't ideal.

"I don't care if I never get back!"

I'd try some other form of stress relief next time. Maybe yoga or medita—

What was that?

A shadow beside the TV was shifting and deepening. In the space of a breath, it swelled like a dark, amorphous tumor, as if to spite the lamp above it, light bulb blazing bright.

"'Cause it's root, root, root for the home team…"

As it grew, I saw now that the shadow wasn't black at all, but rather a dirty, gloomy blue, like water thick with silt at the bottom of the ocean. And then the darkness resolved itself into a skulking figure, too shadowed to see anything but the silhouette: spindly limbs, as if they'd been stretched on a rack; a body emaciated and skeletal; a nest of matted hair; those familiar hands, long and grasping, fingernails coming to ragged points. And where the eyes should be burned a commanding darkness, like two black holes.

"If they don't win it's a shame!"

I thrust backwards into the couch, every instinct screaming to run. And my grandma kept singing, my dad nodding his head along with the song. It was right there, a hulking, spectral demon smack dab in the middle of our living room, and they couldn't see it at all.

"For it's one… *two*… *THREE* strikes you're out at the Old! Ball! Game!"

What the hell was happening? What the hell was wrong with me?

Chapter 9

THE GHOST—the monster—slunk a step to the side to block half the television screen as the crowd burst into cheers. In transfixed terror, I watched as it cast its face around the room, seeming to pay me no mind—first to the left, then to the right, like a guard dog on the lookout for something.

Or somebody—Melissa?

Not the time to think about that. I had to get away—had to get *it* away from my family, at least. But there was nowhere to go, no reasonable excuse to make.

"Lanie? You all right?" My dad was peering at me concernedly. "You look ill."

"I…" The monster took another few steps, its movements lithe and predatory, nearly rounding the coffee table. It paused less than a foot away from my grandma. Cold beads of sweat sprouted on the back of my neck as I heard a throaty growl issue from the shadowed space where its mouth should be. What was the darkness concealing there? Row upon row of spiked teeth, aching to rip and tear? A slavering tongue, licking grinning lips?

"I-I'm going to go upstairs. Lay down. Y-yeah…" I stood up from the couch on wobbly legs, feeling like I was about to throw up.

"Do you need help, sweetie?" I heard my grandma's voice as if from a distance. I waved her off weakly, stumbling a bit. The buzz from the wine wasn't helping matters.

The wine…

The wine. My heart thumped a staccato beat against my ribs.

No time to hypothesize. Get upstairs, away from the others.

I heard another of those low, rumbling growls, somewhere close behind me to the left. It was following. My vision tunneled as I climbed the stairs. This must be what it felt like to be a prey animal—an antelope, perhaps, bounding across the savanna as a lion with razor-sharp claws closed in. I threw a glance behind me as I arrived at the landing.

The monster was two steps behind me. Tailing me. Hunting me.

But couldn't it have killed me by now? I'd given it ample opportunity. I reached my room and strode to the middle of the floor, then wrenched around to face the demon. I almost couldn't look it straight on. Didn't they say not to stare a bear in the eyes?

Yet I forced my gaze upwards anyway, meeting its hollow black gaze. The monster loosed another growl, this one louder, almost a snarl. It—or she? For now that I was looking at the demon head-on, I had the sudden suspicion that it was female—something about its hair, the way it moved…

Okay, I'd made it this far. Now what?

I sidled around the edge of my bedroom back toward the door. I kept my steps measured and steady, my front facing the monster at all times.

Two more steps. One more step.

With my eyes still fixed on the monster, I reached my hand out, fingers trembling as I felt for the doorknob. I found it after a few bumbling, terror-soaked seconds, my sweating palms slipping on the metal.

Steady… Keep it slow…

And with one easy, leisurely movement, I closed the door, sealing myself in with my phantom stalker.

Even so, I suspected a door was not likely to keep this demoness. I remembered the lamp I'd thrust into Melissa's stomach and the biting wash of cold as I'd vaulted straight through the second ghost. These creatures might look solid, but they were incorporeal; the four walls of my room would be no container.

The demoness crept a step closer, the distance between us now a mere three feet. I stood my ground, envisioning myself as some other predator, hackles raised, lips drawn back to expose long canines.

"All right, you bitch," I murmured. "Let's chat." Just brave words, but false courage was better than nothing, right?

I moved away from the door. Let her forget the rest of the house existed. Let her forget everything except me.

She rocketed forward quicker than I could scream, her shadowed face coming to rest inches away from my own, blocking the rest of the room from my vision like an eclipse over the sun. She smelled of something sharp and rotting. Now that she was so close, I could at last make out some of the details of her murky darkness: a shriveled, sunken nose; a mouth too wide; her skin a pitted ruin, hanging in shreds around the spaces where her eyes should be.

My skin prickled with cold. It felt like the temperature in my room had dropped to single digits.

Her lips cracked open, revealing more of that inky inner void.

"Leave ussss… ALONE!"

Her words were distorted but undeniable. And then she *roared*, an otherworldly howl of rage that climbed to an ear-piercing shriek. I staggered backward towards the bed, cowering, my brave front dissolving in an instant.

But at last the roar ended, leaving only a hollow silence. I pushed off the bed and faced her again, letting the seconds tick by. I could hear the muffled chatter of my family downstairs. One minute passed. Two. The demoness's stance shifted, back on the prowl again, her gaze leaving me as she scanned the room. She was acting the guard dog once more.

"Yeah, that's what I thought," I said under my breath, more to myself than to her. "Okay. You're okay. Here we go."

I settled back down on the edge of the bed, clenching my fists to keep from shaking. My nails dug half-moons into my palms. How long had it been—fifteen minutes? Half an hour?

There.

Whole pockets of her darkness were fading out: her left

shoulder, three of her clawed fingers. It was like some godly eraser was rubbing her away. And now larger chunks: her jutting, skeletal hip, her entire right arm.

The last part to go were her eyes, those empty holes of darkness still searching the room.

The wine, the weed, the dreams—and the high fever that had started it all.

I was seeing ghosts—and my new demonic friend—whenever something altered my consciousness. Not every time—but it was possible under those circumstances.

I'd wondered why the ghosts hadn't responded to any of our attempts to make contact yesterday. But maybe Melissa had been trying to, as we fiddled around with the tarot cards and the Ouija board and all the rest. Maybe she'd been *right there*.

And then I'd smoked at Ryan's house, the effects of the weed nearly gone by the time I got home—but not gone entirely. I remembered Melissa's face, dappled with patches of nothingness. And then the sudden blossoming of the shadow monster, just when I was starting to feel the effects from the stolen swallows of wine.

All I'd had to do was wait out the buzz, and goodbye ghosty.

But was she really gone—or just invisible to me? I shifted uncomfortably on the bed, envisioning the monster continuing her skulking circuit around me, maybe coming in close to bellow in my face again.

Leave ussss… ALONE!

The phrase was just one more uncertainty to put with everything else.

But what *did* I know? For one, these paranormal entities didn't seem like they could hurt me. The most they did to me physically was make me feel like I'd just taken a long, luxurious ice bath.

They were all blue, too, though this latest apparition was darker than the others, and their voices were garbled, like they were shouting at me through water. Some sort of mass drowning, maybe in the Enville River? But the thought of anyone perishing in the Enville River, let alone multiple someones, was laughable. The "river" had been charitably named, more a merry little stream than anything else, often drying up to little more than a trickle in the listless days of summer.

A final observation: it wasn't just my dog that couldn't see them, but my family members as well. I was no mathematician, but even I could pick out the common denominator.

I shivered. My sweat-soaked clothes and the lingering chill from the demoness were doing my body heat no favors, so I stripped off my clothes in favor of the fluffiest, warmest pajamas I owned. The last thing I needed right now was to get sick again and bring on more fevered visions of the dead.

Chapter 10

"AND SHE SAID *what?*"

I was lying back on Ryan's rug, unloading like I was at a therapy session. My nightmares, the wine, the stare down, the demoness's final fade into oblivion—I let it all come out, sometimes easy, sometimes halting, sometimes jumbled. And though it felt good to unload, it also didn't *solve* anything.

Now that Ryan had heard the whole story, he was doubling back to the real sticking point, the thing that I, too, could not get out of my mind.

"She said 'Leave us alone.' *Leave us,*" I repeated, spitting the words out. "Like *I* am harassing *them*. Like all this is… is *my* fault! Like I'm trying to be haunted by a *gang of goddamned undead groupies!*"

"Okay, okay!" Ryan said, interrupting my tirade. "But what do you think she actually meant by it?"

"I don't know. Or maybe…" I pursed my lips, thinking. I'd been mulling over the little I knew about Claw Hands, as I'd internally christened her, over the course of the past day. I cleared my throat and started again. "It was Melissa who spoke to me when I had the fever, not the boy ghost. And then it was her I saw in the shower, not the boy. Melissa seems proactive, like she has some sort of a message. Claw Hands pulls Melissa away before she can do or say anything else…"

"Because she doesn't want Melissa talking to you," Ryan supplied.

"That's what I've been thinking too. And now…" I trailed off. "I wish you could see the demon. I think she's guarding me *against* Melissa, trying to keep her from getting near again. '*Leave us alone,*'" I repeated once more. "It sounds protective, right? I think whatever Melissa's trying to do is making Claw Hands majorly unhappy."

Ryan took a look around his room. "Do you think she's here now?"

I brought my hands to my face, rubbing my eyes with my palms. "Maybe."

"So I take it you don't wanna smoke?"

"Yeah, I'll pass," I said, unable to keep the bitterness from my tone. Not that I *wanted* to smoke, but I was rather attached to the idea of being able to do whatever the hell I wanted, without sparing a thought for the supernatural. These ghosts were going to make me into the world's biggest advocate for sobriety.

Or, I mused, I could just resolve myself to seeing my demoness every now and again. As long as Claw Hands stayed harmless, that held a certain hardcore allure.

Ryan stretched. "It's just that I was thinking about this from a scientific perspective."

"What do you mean?"

"Well, there are about a billion experiments we could run—so many things that we don't know about this… situation. You're an only child, right?"

I nodded.

"One thought I had is that maybe only younger people can see the ghosts." His eyes lit up. "Here's another one. You smoked here the other day and didn't see Melissa, so she seems to have a range. Perhaps your demon has one, too."

I felt a piece of the puzzle slide into place: the chardonnay on the hill last summer. Nothing had happened to me that night—but that hill was half a mile south of my house.

My mouth fell open. "We could map out their territory." And naturally, whatever lay at the very center of that territory must hold some clue—could maybe even put Melissa and the others to rest.

He leaned in towards me, a glint in his eyes. "So what do you say? Wanna prank call a university professor, then go get high?"

But unfortunately, both those things would have to wait. It was Sunday, so Rufner wouldn't be at school.

Even so, we jotted out a bunch of notes for us to use when we called him later. They read like lines to be slung by a scowling cop at a suspect in an interrogation room, a single-bulb lamp dangling overhead.

Where and when was your first gallery showing? What was

the theme of the pieces in the exhibition? Have you by chance ever heard of a girl called Melissa White?

"He's never going to answer these," I said.

"But he might!" Ryan protested. "If he's innocent, why would he mind answering a few questions? I think we'll be able to tell if he's innocent or guilty just by asking. He'll get all cagey if he did it."

I raised my eyebrows. "I didn't realize I was sitting next to some prodigy boy detective!"

My phone vibrated: a text from my mom to be home soon for dinner. Yet a quick kiss from Ryan convinced me to linger a few minutes longer. And it felt good to steal those minutes—but not as warm or melting as last time. I couldn't shut my mind off, couldn't lose myself.

Then it was truly time to go, and I stumbled out of his house, telling him I'd see him tomorrow in the library. I drove home in a daze, hardly even realizing I was home until I stopped the car.

"Finish it up?" my mom called from the kitchen as I walked in the door. My head spun for a moment. What was she talking about?

Oh, right. The history project.

"Yeah, I think I'm pretty much done. Hope I get a good grade."

"I'm sure you will, sweetheart—but what was the verdict? I've been on pins and needles. Did anyone, you know… *pass away* in the house?"

I squirmed, knowing what we planned to do tomorrow.

"No, not as far as I could find…" *Yet.*

She gave a pleased nod. "Whew, that's good. Well, dinner's in fifteen, okay?"

"Okay." It smelled good, but I couldn't get excited. School, homework, family dinners—they all ate up so much time, all stalled me from uncovering the truth. I felt a flicker of annoyance when I remembered I still had to write the *Dracula* essay for Ryan—not to mention my own homework. How ridiculous, to have to worry about school when Claw Hands was likely my silent, unseen house guest at this very moment, close enough to reach out and touch.

So I pushed my dinner around on my plate, then went upstairs and banged out five serviceable paragraphs. *Stoker employs the figure of Dracula as a counterpoint to late nineteenth-century London's blah blah blah. The blood ever-present throughout the story displays Stoker's foreboding of a forthcoming conflict between blah blah blah.* Not that I was writing drivel—I couldn't see Ryan getting anything less than an A minus. My heart just wasn't into it.

I sent him the essay, then spent the rest of the evening wallowing in listless boredom. Every now and again my gaze drifted over to my backpack, but I couldn't manage to get off the bed and open my textbooks.

Instead I put on some music, low enough to still hear the chill October wind blustering outside, and let the combination of the two lull me into… not daydreaming, not reverie, but a wishing almost like prayer.

Let me find out why. Why Melissa and the others. Why me.

Because I was so, so tired of having the constant apprehension of danger pricking the back of my neck. Because I so desperately wanted the lights around our dining room table to seem just as bright as they'd used to, for food to taste right again, for a kiss with a boy I liked to not feel like a waste of time.

I wanted the details of life to matter again, to seem like more than dust and refuse littering a long, desolate street to who knows where.

Yet the scariest thing of all? I found that I was bearing the loss of those details. I wanted all those things, yes—but I didn't *need* them.

How long could I keep traipsing down that road before something snapped at last?

I woke up the next day in better spirits, almost invigorated. All I had to do was get through the roadblock of school, then we could go back to my house and map the ghosts' territory. When was the last time I'd felt this awake on a Monday?

That lasted until Ryan sent me a text during history.

Out sick. Don't do anything without me!
I wanna see if I can see the ghosts too.

I sent him a quick reply when Mr. DeBraav turned his back.

Ok :(Feel better!

A whole day to make no progress. I trudged out the door as the bell rang, all my newfound energy completely squashed.

Math was terrible. Mrs. Morrie took the start of class to do a surprise notebook check.

"And you still haven't made up that unit test," she said as she noted my lack of completed homework. The look in her eyes added a whole host of details.

Damn. I'd hoped she'd forgotten.

"It's been nearly a week since you were out," she continued. "Surely you're over-prepared by this point. Tell you what—let's have you take it out in the hall this period. You won't get much out of today's class anyway, since you don't have your work done." Oh, how I hated her and her stupid subject. When I turned the test in fifty minutes later, much of it still blank, she even had the audacity to give me a thin-lipped smile.

"Thanks, Lanie. I'll have it graded by tomorrow."

Of course she would.

At least study hall was next. As soon as I got up to talk with the proctor she was tearing me off a pass. "Library?"

"Yeah. Thanks." Back at my regular desk, surrounded by the thick bookshelves and the librarian-imposed quiet, some of my bad mood seeped away.

All right, time to get back at it. I pulled out my laptop, determined to use the period to track down D_plexippus.

Yet I could find nothing, *nothing*, amongst the endless websites about butterflies. After half an hour, I pushed my computer away with a silent snarl and sank my head to the desk.

"Bad day?" The librarian had wandered over. Her brown eyes regarded me shrewdly from behind the shield of her glasses.

"Not the best."

"Where's your friend?"

She didn't miss much. "He's out sick."

"Well, if you need help finding something, let me know. We have a whole shelf on insects." She gave a pointed nod toward my computer screen, which I'd left open to my latest D_plexippus search. I was on the twelfth page of results.

"Thanks," I said as she padded away. Then, on a sudden impulse, I called after her. "Wait."

She turned back. "Maybe, uhh..." My thoughts swung wildly. How to phrase this? "I don't think a book will help me. I'm looking for a particular website about butterflies. I, um, cleared my browser history, and now I can't find it again. But here's what I remember about it: it had a particular spelling on one of the pages. Sort of a misspelling, actually, but my search results always auto-correct." I scrolled up to the top to show her what I meant. Showing results for D. plexippus. "And I *also* remember the name of the, uh, web page designer who made the page. But she has a really common name, and that's sort of confusing the results, too..."

The librarian's forehead was furrowed. I was sure all that had come across as straight-up gobbledygook.

But then I saw her eyes gleam behind her glasses. "Ah, a classic problem. These computers are so wonderful, but the information they offer us is overabundant, wouldn't you agree? Less like finding a needle in a haystack than a grain of sand in an ocean." I gave a noncommittal hum as she drew up a chair. "It sounds to me like you need a Boolean search. You know, every fall we haul in the ninth-graders from their English classes and talk to them about the library databases, how to search our catalog, Boolean searches, that sort of thing. But do they listen? No, of course not. It's dry stuff, but goodness me, it would save everyone so much time if they *paid attention*."

"What's a Boolean...?"

"So let's take your first problem," she said. "The misspelling. We'll put it in quotes, so your results stop being so squirrelly and you actually get the underscore. And do the same thing with the designer's name. No, in a separate set of quotations. There you go. Last thing's last, let's ensure we actually search for *both* of those phrases together in the same page by putting in a capital AND."

I typed out her instructions and hit enter.

"Hrmm," the librarian said, tapping a finger on the desk. "Is that what you were looking for?"

I smiled shakily. "That's... yeah, well, that's not it. Like I said, I'm researching butterflies. You know, maybe I'm remembering something wrong. Anyway, thanks for your help."

"Anytime, dear," she said, her knees cracking as she got up from the desk. "And let me know if you need me to show you that section with the insect books I mentioned. It's right over there." She pointed toward the end of the stacks.

I paused for a long moment, allowing her time to get back to her desk across the room, then angled my laptop away to make sure she couldn't see my screen. At last, I clicked the result that the search engine had spit out—a long title that set my heart beating fast.

Missing Persons - Melissa White pics theory posted by D_plexippus 04-22-11, 9:28 PM - Uncle Ed's Forum of the Weird, Secret, and Inexplicable.

Chapter 11

My browser took a few interminable seconds to think before loading the page. Uncle Ed's Forum hadn't been crafted with beauty in mind; the layout was in an old-school design style, the background a dark, stormy gray and the text in bright, contrasting red. I snorted at the graphic emblazoned on the top of the page: a goofy-looking cartoon of a man peering through a magnifying glass, his cheeks florid and dark mustache bristling. No doubt this was the eponymous Uncle Ed.

And then I started reading. The opening post, a lengthy stretch of text, had been written by D_plexippus himself, his avatar the image of a monarch butterfly resting on a twig. The information was all old news to me, exactly the same story as D_plexippus had laid out in his video, save that August Rufner's name was only written as the abbreviated "AR." I skimmed through, looking for anything new in vain, then scrolled down to read the replies.

There weren't many, not even enough for a second page.

MyLongKatana, 04-22-11, 10:27 PM: Cool theory, bruh.

GgBb, 04-22-11, 11:08 PM: Yeah, idk… It's a stretch, but I could believe it. Be careful with the names, might get flagged for doxxing?

Uncle Ed [moderator], 04-22-11, 11:11 PM: D_plexippus, please abbreviate the photog's name. Thanks.

D_plexippus, 04-22-11, 11:16 PM: Done, sorry.

AJ74, 04-23-11, 01:14 PM: Hey, I would take a peek over in MFSK if I were you. There's a central Connecticut 1980s thread in there from a while back. Seems like she would have passed right through that area, and the timing's right.

D_plexippus, 04-23-11, 03:20 PM: Wow, thanks! I had no idea. I spend most of my time here or talking Project Monarch.

Of course he did—hence the name and the avatar.

There were no further replies. I frowned. MFSK—what was that supposed to mean? I clicked over to the forum directory, scanning through the myriad sub-forums. It was hard to pick a favorite; each one was its own delicious flavor of absurdity.

Aliens, of course! (ALL LIZARD PEOPLE THREADS
GO IN THE REPTILIAN FORUM!!!)

Beyond the Veil: lucid dreaming, psychedelics,
near-death experiences, sensory deprivation, etc.

CIA Programs: MKUltra, Project Monarch, front
organizations, etc.

Creature Feature: Bigfoot, Loch Ness monster,
chupacabras, etc.

My Favorite Serial Killer (CHECK THE STICKY INDEX,
REPEAT THREADS ARE AUTO-BANNED)

Reptilians (ALL are welcome, please join us, we won't
bite!)

Secret Societies: Illuminati, Ordo Templi Orientis,
Bohemian Grove, etc.

It took me a moment before I realized I had scrolled right past what I was searching for—My Favorite Serial Killer, which had to be what MFSK meant. I flinched a bit as I clicked the link, envisioning... I don't know what, but something utterly gruesome.

To my relief, the page within looked about as ordinary as

any sub-forum dedicated to serial killers could—more a hub for discussion and amateur Internet sleuthing than actual serial killer fan clubs. ZODIAC KILLER MEGATHREAD!!! the top post screamed, the replies numbering in the hundreds. I typed "Connecticut 1980s" in the search box.

And there it was, just as promised, posted in January of 2011: MOVED from Missing Persons: Suspected 1980s central Connecticut serial killer.

I opened the thread, written by someone calling themselves OGKushGod69, my eyes widening as I read.

Edit: Mods, thanks for moving this. Hi everyone, thanks for reading and please leave a reply with your thoughts! :D

Edit 2: Added one possible victim to the list.

To start things off, YES, I have done a bit of research to see if the police/FBI have publicized any sort of theory about a serial killer operating in central CT in the 1980s, but I cannot find anything suggesting they have. If anyone discovers anything to the contrary, please let me know!

Basically, I've always been pretty interested in the Pamela Billings missing persons case, since I live near the area where she disappeared. Real brief summary: she was born and raised in Sutton, CT; reported missing May 30, 1983 at age sixteen; ordinary teenager as far as anyone could tell; no known romantic relationships.

A chill raced over me. Sutton was only one town over from Enville.

As far as the police could piece together, here's the timeline of events on May 30. That was a Monday, Memorial Day, and Pamela had school finals all the next week. She drives over to a classmate's house to study and leaves her friend's house around 8:30 PM. The police find her car the next morning on the side of the road, locked with the keys gone, out of gas. She had mentioned to her classmate when she was leaving that her tank was low and she needed to fill it, but she thought she could make it home.

The police's working theory, which I think very plausible, was that she ran out of gas and started walking towards the nearest gas station to get some help, about two miles down the road. They had no other clues to go on, and as far as I can tell there were never any accusations or suspects, nor any real headway made in the case.

Okay, so that's the first bit. I've been hanging out in Missing Persons for years. I don't know, it's just my favorite spot on the boards. And I always make a bit of a mental note if there's a hitchhiker case where people think they passed through the area by my house. What I've noticed is that a few teenagers, mostly girls, all of them ages sixteen or seventeen, disappeared around the same time (1983-1988), and it looks like ALL of

them could have passed through the Farmdale Valley
area of CT. I'm naturally wondering if there was a serial
killer operating in the area picking up kids off the street.

Here's the list:

Pamela Billings

Anna-Marie Booth

Scott Hartman (Not sure about this one, since I think
serial killers normally stick to a profile for their victims,
and he's the only boy… Feel free to correct me on this if
I'm wrong!)

Tina Hoff

Melissa White (this one's more of a maybe than the
rest)

Anyway, let me know what you guys think.

Five names, yet I'd only encountered two ghosts. Odds
were good that Scott Hartman was the boy ghost… Was I going to bump into Pamela or Anna-Marie or Tina any day now?

The bell to end the period made me jump and bang my
knee on the desk. I couldn't help shaking as I gathered my
things together; it was not lost on me that I'd called the previous owner of my house last week and casually asked if he
remembered any teenagers hanging around near the house.

As if a serial killer would give me a straight answer to
that question.

Over the past few days, I'd been working on coming to

terms with the unfortunate possibility that I might see ghosts and demons every so often for the rest of my life. I'd been pitching it to myself like I had a front row seat to a personal horror movie—and didn't I love horror? As long as the ghosts stayed incorporeal and didn't actually *do* anything to me, I might be able to handle that.

But how to handle a real, live killer, who I might have unwittingly contacted and tipped off to my fledgling suspicions, who, if that were true, knew my name and precisely where I lived? *That* was a different thing altogether.

If all those suppositions were correct, I was, in a word, *screwed*.

Edgar Holt—who was he, really? Had all that talk of a normal, if tragedy-stained, life just been some tale spun to me over the phone by a psychopath? Or maybe every word was true, and he lived a double life?

I sent Ryan a text during lunch, including links to the forum posts.

> Major breakthrough. I'm scared. Remember how I said I talked to Holt last week? If he's the guy and suspects that I know anything…

His reply came during Spanish.

> Ok, don't panic.

I stuffed my phone in my pocket and raised my hand. *"Puedo ir al baño?"* The teacher sighed and waved me out.

Perched on a toilet in the dim, smelly girls bathroom, I got out my phone just as it buzzed with another text.

What day did you talk with him?
Where did he say he was living again?

Last Thursday. North Carolina.

So it's Monday. He could have already come up here from North Carolina if he thought you knew anything.

Or he could be coming up here right now!!! Should I call the police or something? What would I even say to them??

I stared daggers at my phone, hoping for some miracle answer, not convinced in the slightest that I was going to get one.

Dead. I was so dead.

My sweating hands almost dropped the phone as it buzzed again.

Don't call the police! There's no evidence you can give them that links that list of names to Holt. And that's a good thing! It might not even be him.

He did have a point. Maybe some unknown sociopath

had used the woods around my house as a setting for their gruesome pastime, the Holts blissfully unaware of the murders taking place just beyond the borders of their backyard.

I fiddled with a curl of hair, thinking, then sent him another text.

The shadow of Edgar Holt dogged me for the next twenty-four hours. I wasn't sick, but I might as well have been, a knot of worry squirming in my gut, my skin crawling with invisible spiders. Whether I was walking down a congested school hallway, driving in the minivan, or sitting alone in my bedroom, I couldn't get Holt's smiling, sunburned profile picture out of my mind. I imagined his likeness in strangers' faces, hiding behind trees, crouched in the darkness of my closet. I checked the locks on our windows, shut the blinds at the first hint of the setting sun, and even rustled up an old baseball bat from our basement, which I stowed at the ready by my bed.

What a luxury that this past week I had only been scared of *being* scared. Now I actually had to worry about dying.

But twenty-four hours came and went, and Holt made no grand entrance. Nor was Ryan back at school; the "stomach thing," as he'd put it, had unfortunately persisted, but he promised to be well enough to map the ghosts' territory after school. Thank goodness—if the demoness's range extended beyond the confines of my house, there was no way I was tramping through the woods alone trying to mark the borders.

I drove straight to Ryan's house when school let out. We didn't talk much on the drive back to my house. Ryan's face was wan; he looked like he hadn't slept much.

"You're sure you're up for this?" I asked.

His eyes slid over to mine, and he gave me a short nod. "Never felt better."

Before I knew it, we were back at my house, Ryan slipping out of his shoes and patting Mustard on the head like he'd been here a million times instead of just the once.

"So," he said, looking to me, "where should we start?"

I bit at my lip. "My room, I guess, since that's where I last saw the demon. Even though I'm betting she's here, somewhere, right now." I gesticulated vaguely around me. "We can work outward from there into the other rooms. Then we'll see if she can go outside."

We trooped upstairs. It was surreal to be pushing my bedroom door open for a boy, beckoning him inside, watching as he took in all the details of the room, of *my* room, of this space that formed my comfy introvert's cocoon. The packed bookshelf, a few disorganized piles of books stacked at the side. The ill poinsettia on my desk, bought with good intentions last Christmas and now eking out a sad existence in its too-small pot. The numerous Hitchcock posters tacked to my walls, a few from *The Addams Family* and *The Twilight Zone* thrown in for good measure.

He walked over to my dresser, peering at the framed photographs I kept displayed on top. I blushed when he leaned in closer to one of the photos; it was a picture of seven-year-old me outside in our backyard, covered in dirt and beaming at the camera. "Pretty cute," he said, picking up the photo and looking from it to me and back again. He gave me a wry smile. "Haven't changed a bit."

"Thanks," I said dryly.

He carefully set the photo back down. "You ready?"

"Yeah, guess so." I sat down on my bed. My mouth had gone dry. *Personal horror movie*, I reminded myself. *That's all this is—no need to be scared.*

But I could still feel my pulse picking up as Ryan got out the lighter and prepared the bowl. He made to pass them both to me, then noticed my shaking hands.

"Listen, you sure you want to do this?"

"Yes! No. I mean, I have to. I don't have a choice."

"That's bullshit. You always have a choice."

I shot him a miserable look. "You know what I mean. What, I'm just not going to drink in my house, *ever*? Live in fear of getting a fever? What about the serial killer who may be planning a fun weekend jaunt up from North Carolina to knock me off? But if we can find some remains or something and give the police actual evidence—"

"Okay, I get it," Ryan said, cutting me off. "I'm just saying that you don't have to do this right now if you're freaked out. We could just sit and talk, or—"

I plucked the bowl and the lighter from his hands, my own now as steady as they were going to get. "No. Let's— let's do it."

And I took a hit before he could say another word—and before I could second guess myself.

Personal horror movie. Personal horror movie.

"Remember," he said, "there's a possibility I can see Claw Hands too. And... You know, Lanie, if I could, I'd take this away from you. No one deserves this."

"Thanks," I said, then took another hit, sucking the acrid smoke deep into my lungs. "You're not just saying that because I wrote you an awesome *Dracula* essay? Buttering me up so I agree to dress up as you and take your final exam or something?"

Ryan laughed a little. "Good idea, first of all. But you're way too pretty to pass as me, I'm afraid."

And as I waited for the calm of the high to steal over me, he took my hand in his own, holding it until I heard the demoness's low growl from behind me.

Chapter 12

RYAN FELT MY grip stiffen, and his face fell. "She's here?"

I winced as I turned to look behind me. There she was, Claw Hands herself, magnificent in her glowering darkness, standing right by my bedside table.

"Yes. R-right over there," I said, pointing. My hands were shaking again. The demoness rumbled another louder growl, then cast her head around the room, still on the lookout for Melissa.

Ryan squinted in the direction I was pointing, then extended a hand and waved it around, his fingers passing straight through her. He shook his head, and my heart sank. He couldn't hear nor see nor feel her—which meant the ability to perceive ghosts and demons wasn't an age thing, but a me thing.

Lovely.

"All right, time to move," I said, then stood up from the bed on trembling legs and tripped over my own feet.

"Whoa, careful there," Ryan said. He draped an arm

around me. "Let's go, and take it slow."

So, at an unhurried pace, we went on a room-by-room tour of the house, Claw Hands accompanying us—or rather me—everywhere we went. And just as she kept watching for Melissa, so did I keep my own close attention on Claw Hands herself, watching her loping, shadowy form for flickering or fading. This was harder to do than it sounds; she was so fearsome-looking, so *wrong*, that it was hard to look at her.

She didn't dim for a second.

At last we had checked every room of the house. "Anything?" Ryan asked, pale-faced. He wasn't looking good, either from the food poisoning or the knowledge of the demoness lurking in our presence.

I let out a shuddering breath. "She's still here. Let's go outside." I led him out into our backyard, Claw Hands at our heels. "Last summer I took a bottle of wine out to a hill half a mile that way," I said, pointing south, "and nothing happened. So I say we head that way and see if she leaves."

Ryan peered towards the tree line, a dubious look stealing over his face. "Sounds good, but is there a trail? I'm useless if we get lost—never did Boy Scouts or anything."

I gave him a faint smile. That, at least, would be no issue. "Just follow me. This forest was pretty much my playground growing up. I'll know exactly where we are up to two miles out or so."

"After you, then," he said, waving me onward, and I took a few steps before a sudden thought crossed my mind.

"Wait just a second." I darted back upstairs to my bedroom

and grabbed the baseball bat. "Just in case Edgar Holt shows up," I said, choosing to ignore Ryan's amused expression.

"I really don't think he's—"

"Just a precaution," I said, then started across the lawn, the leader of our ragtag band of three. We walked slowly; I was expecting—*hoping* for—the demoness to leave any second. Yet she trooped steadily alongside me, her too-long-too-thin body an umbral darkness at the edge of my vision.

In the woods the towering trees were rustling with crisp fall leaves, the ground soft under my boots from the downpour a few days back. I guided us along the usual path I took to get to the hill, through the dense grove of ferns that gave our street its name, our trajectory heading towards the thirty-foot drop-off that formed a natural wall between our house and the southern clearing. From there we would skirt the cliff west until the ground below and above finally met.

Once, when I was eleven, I'd made a bet with myself that I could climb down that cliff. And I'd almost done it—then my nerve-damaged fingers had slipped ten feet from the bottom. The stumbling journey back home—both knees of my jeans ripped beyond repair, my face a mess of dirt and blood, my wrist sprained from the fall—had been a shameful, humbling experience. Luckily that was the extent of the damage; I could easily have broken a leg, or worse.

The real punishment for braving the cliff was that I'd never heard the end of it. To this day, whenever I told my mom I was going out in the woods she gave me that patented motherly stare and warned me not to fancy myself a rock climber.

Fifteen feet before the drop-off, Claw Hands snarled and stopped short. Ryan saw me tense up.

"Is she…?"

I turned and faced the demoness, then took a purposeful step backward towards the cliff. She stayed rooted in place. Ryan watched me anxiously, unsure what was going on. I took a few more steps back, putting a good ten feet between us.

She didn't move an inch. "This is the edge," I said, tracing a line in the dirt with my foot. "*Her* edge." We had come unprepared; I should have brought something with me to mark the ground, but I hadn't expected the demoness's territory to extend out this far.

"Okay then," I muttered, my nerves settling a bit. Best to think of this like a scientific problem, just like Ryan had suggested—a set of paranormal laws that would help us solve the puzzle.

First Law of the Paranormal: The ghosts and Lanie's constant demoness companion can only be sensed by Lanie herself.

Second Law of the Paranormal: Said ghosts and demoness only manifest under altered mental conditions.

Third Law of the Paranormal: Said ghosts and demoness have hard territorial boundaries, à la an invisible electric dog fence.

Postured Fourth Law of the Paranormal: Whatever the hell is at the center of this territory will solve all my problems.

I squinched up my face, trying to envision the woods from above, then picked up a stick and began scratching a rudimentary map in the dirt instead. "So we're about, say… a third of a mile out from the house right now —almost directly south, I think. I'm assuming their territory is radiating out in a circle from some point —a grave site or something." Let's hope that were the case. If the territory were in some odd shape, all bets were off about finding the source of my haunting.

My haunting. It sounded like some feel-good, hippie phrase. *Claim your haunting! OWN it! With just a simple change of phrase, this unfortunate state of affairs becomes more manageable!*

I shook my head —just like me to get distracted when I needed to buckle down and do some math. But this was no dry word problem; for once I was faced with a real-life math problem of the utmost importance. "Here's Ferngrove Lane." I drew a line from the west leading to the dot denoting my house. "That means…" I checked it again in my head. "That means that if we find the edge of the territory bisecting Ferngrove, that we can plot two points on the edge of the border. But you can't plot a circle with only two points, right?"

Ryan nodded. "We'll need at least three. Maybe more for accuracy, since we're doing all this on foot. A point to the north would make it easier. Is there anything up there we can use as a landmark?"

"Avanic. Hopefully there's a border somewhere over

there." The sky was darkening; we wouldn't have time today for the northern hike. But we could at least find the point on Ferngrove Lane.

I pointed at a copse of firs over to the left. "Let's head that way. It's a straight shot to the road."

Ryan grimaced, then cleared his throat and hawked a spit ball on the ground, almost hitting the demoness's left foot. "Sorry. Gross, I know. Umm, I'm feeling sort of terrible right now. Can we head back to the house instead?" He was looking paler than ever, his eyes glassy.

"Yeah, of course." I swallowed, knowing this meant crossing back towards the demoness. It had been such a relief to put these scant few yards between us, to realize I had some semblance of power in this unwilling relationship.

I gritted my teeth and marched back across the boundary. The demoness's head tracked me as I approached, and as I strode past her she uttered a rasping hiss.

Ryan saw me bristle. "What's wrong?"

"Nothing," I spat, staring Claw Hands in the face.

We trekked back to the house in silence. I held the baseball bat with one hand and Ryan's hand with the other. Though his palm was cold and clammy, it didn't matter to me; he couldn't help being sick, after all, plus my thoughts were in another place altogether. Could I convince my parents to move across town? Even if we couldn't find the epicenter, moving would solve the problem — right?

I was so lost in thought that I hardly registered we were out of the woods until we were halfway across the backyard lawn. Ryan let go of my hand and hustled past me towards the porch, taking the steps two at a time. "Bathroom?" he grunted through clenched teeth, face white, as he wrenched open the door.

"Down the hall on the le—" I almost crashed into his back. He'd come to an abrupt halt in the entranceway.

"H-hello…" I heard him say.

"Who—?" My mom's voice. *Oh no.* "Lanie, who's this?" Why was she home early from work?

"Uh, this is Ryan, from school," I called, then followed him into the living room. My mom looked from Ryan to me quizzically before her eyes dropped down to my hand. I was still clutching the baseball bat.

I frantically scoured my brain for a lie. "We were—"

But I was cut short by Ryan doubling over and throwing up all over the carpet.

Chapter 13

I'D BEEN TOYING with the idea of someday soon disclosing to my parents that I was sort-of-kind-of seeing someone. If things between us became more official, I'd envisioned Ryan sitting down with us for dinner, something nice and casual like spaghetti and meatballs, then the two of us heading to a movie.

Of all the first impression scenarios I'd imagined, this had not been one.

"Oh my God!" my mom cried, stepping out of the way just in time.

Ryan raised his head, mumbled an apology, then took off running down the hallway. I flinched as the bathroom door slammed shut.

My mom and I stared at each other for a long moment, her gaze prompting me for some explanation. This was too much to handle; the sharp scent of vomit hung in the air, and Claw Hands hovered at the corner of my vision. I looked away first. "I'll clean this up."

She followed me to the closet, watching as I pulled out

some rags and cleaning spray. "So… Ryan from school, huh?" Something about her tone was off, though that could be blamed on the unexpected vomiting guest.

"Yeah. He's, umm, a good friend." As I walked back to the living room I let my hair fall in a curtain to block my beet-red face.

"That's nice. What's with the bat?" And this time I could hear for certain that something was wrong.

"That's… hard to explain," I said, making to kneel down on the rug, but she grabbed my arm and stopped me, then brought her face in close to my own.

"Lanie, are you…?" She peered into my eyes, then took a long sniff. "Are you *high*?"

A low, demonic snicker came from behind me. I grasped for words and came up short. My reddened eyes and the smoke clinging to my breath and my hair had already said it all.

"You *are*." She drew back with a gasp.

"Mom, I—"

Her eyes bored into my own, her lips pressed tight into a line. "I am going to drive that boy—Ryan—home. *You* are going to stay right here and do some hard thinking. And then I am coming right back, and we are going to talk about this. Got it?"

I dropped my gaze. "Yeah."

"Oh," she said, "right. You are also going to give me a real clear explanation about your grade in math. I got a phone call from your teacher an hour ago about your test—

that's why I came home early. Forty-two percent, Lanie? She says you're almost at a C minus in the class. What is going on with you?"

I sank onto the couch, numb, only half-aware of her footsteps padding away. A minute later, two pairs of footsteps approached again.

"Bye, Lanie," I heard Ryan say. "Sorry about... Well, anyway, bye."

I dipped my head, not wanting him to see my mottled red cheeks and the moisture threatening to overspill my eyes.

And I sat still on the couch, even when I heard the slam of the car door and the garage door going up and down again. I counted to sixty in my head, letting them get a distance away from the house, trying to deepen my shallow breaths.

When the minute was up, I stood in one swift movement. "Time to go, bitch," I said to the demoness in a trembling whisper. Who knew when I would next get a chance to map her territory?

We marched side by side right down the middle of the road. Every few seconds I flicked my eyes toward her, expecting her to have stopped. Yet we'd rounded the bend and almost reached 2 Ferngrove by the time she halted.

I snorted at the contrast between the house's goofy Halloween decorations and Claw Hands's own monstrous figure, then looked around, marking the area. Oak tree to the left, large rock, almost a boulder, to the right—it was enough that I should be able to find the spot on a satellite map. That was two points, then, out of three to make my circle.

"Can't do it, huh?" I called to the demon, sweeping my arms out to the side, daring her onwards. "Think you're so big and scary. Yeah, but you're trapped in a cage—some demon."

She loosed a grating bellow, but that was all. This time when I crossed back over to her side of the boundary I didn't flinch at all. She stayed a pace behind me as we walked home, like a sulking dog.

I spent the rest of the time until my mom came home cleaning the vomit out of the rug until it was just a conspicuous wet stain, all while Claw Hands lurked silently in the corner. I could have worked on concocting some elaborate lie or maybe an attempt at the perfect apology, worded and timed just so, but I didn't. My mom wasn't stupid; I knew she'd see right through me.

Just when I looked over to Claw Hands, only to discover she'd faded away, I heard the clank of the garage door opening. A surge of that numbness coursed through me again.

My mom walked in a moment later with a sigh and came over to sit beside me. "All right, let's talk."

"I'm sorry, Mom," I blurted preemptively.

She gave a quick little nod, her eyes still flinty. "That's a good start, but I need more than that. Pot, Lanie? How did this start? And don't think for a second that I'm going to keep your father in the dark about this."

"Th-that's okay." I had already figured on that. If I had to guess, he would take it better than her; I was fairly certain he'd smoked in college. "I've been feeling stressed lately. A lot of homework. That's why I did it."

Her eyebrows rose. "We'll come back to that in a second. Who gave you the pot?"

My answer was so low as to be almost inaudible. "Ryan."

"Good. That's what he said, too."

Anger rippled through me. "You asked him that?"

"Sweetheart, if I come home and find some boy I've never met hanging out with you, the both of you high, then I'm going to ask him whatever the hell I want." She cleared her throat, looking pained. "Did you drive him here? He brought the pot with him?"

I set my jaw, willing my lips not to tremble. "Yes. To both."

"So you drove with drugs in the car, then," she said, letting out a long breath. "And you're sixteen, so you're not supposed to be driving anyone in the first place! What if you'd gotten pulled over?" She was shaking her head, looking at me like I had spontaneously grown a tail. "And exactly what was the plan for him to get home, dare I ask? You were going to drive him back, the both of you high?"

"I didn't really think—"

"Clearly!" I hunched in on myself, wishing I could shrink small enough to slip between the couch cushions and disappear. "Lanie, I told Ryan this already, and now it's your turn. I will *not* have my daughter hanging out with a pothead. Just not happening. So whatever this relationship—friendship—*whatever*—is, consider it over. God, you know I worry about you not having close friends. But this? Hon, you can do better."

All the daydreaming I'd done about the spaghetti and meatballs dinner with my parents—and maybe a few months later, the doorbell ringing, Ryan standing on the doorstep in a suit, watching me descend the stairs in some floofy, glittering prom dress—all those visions evaporated away, as weightless and ephemeral as my ghosts. That door had decidedly closed; I had never seen my mom so furious.

I could feel the ache of impending tears, but I pushed my tongue to the roof of my mouth, trying to dam them up. "Mom, I'm sorry, okay? And you're right, and… Yeah, that's all. I'm sorry, and I won't do it again." A guilty pang shot through me as I lied. I still needed the third point to make my circle. And the bit about never seeing Ryan again? What was she going to do—follow me around at school? It meant more lying and sneaking, sure, but the two of us were on this roller coaster together, and there was no getting off now that the ride had begun.

I could tell from her eyes that she'd bought it. "Thanks for the apology. I'll hold you to that. Now what's going on in math? You said you were stressed about homework. Are you just not doing it?"

"I hate it. Math, I mean. Yeah, I've been slacking."

She shook her head. "You're sixteen, Lanie. I shouldn't have to tell you that there are lots of things people dread doing, but they have to do them anyway."

"I'll try harder."

"Yes," she said, "you will. I got the name of a tutor from

Mrs. Morrie. Consider raising your grade in math to be your number one priority right now. I've already hired the tutor to meet you at the gallery every day after school."

"At the gal—?"

She silenced me with a look. "You heard me. He's going to meet you daily for at least the next month. And I'm sorry about this next part, but it has to be done; you also won't be allowed to drive the car for the next month."

I collapsed further into the couch. Fucking fantastic. "How will I get to school? And to the gallery?"

"You'll take the school bus," she replied. "Hopefully spending your mornings with a busload of freshmen will help you not take your driving privileges for granted. And I'll pick you up after school and bring you over to the gallery."

Why couldn't she have just grounded me? But she and I both knew that would be no punishment; I was too much of a homebody. This way I would be at the gallery every day, under her vigilant watch.

More importantly, how was I to get away and find the third point?

"Is all this clear?" she asked.

"Got it." I did my best to keep my tone light and even. Yes, this was bad, but it could be much worse. I had an almost tangible feeling that I was close to discovering the source of my ghosts. There was no way I was waiting a full month to finish mapping their territory. I didn't have a plan yet—but I'd figure one out.

"Good," she said, then leaned forward and drew me into

a hug. "Lanie, you know I love you, right? Even if I have to be a hard-ass about this?"

"I know, Mom. I love you too." And I did, of course, even if this torturous conversation was liable to kill me if it went on much longer.

She released me from the hug. "Oh, one last thing. Why the baseball bat?"

I winced and looked down at my hands. "That's... Umm..."

She surveyed me coolly, the growing silence hanging between us.

"You're not smashing the neighbors' pumpkins or something, are you?" she asked at last, when it had become painfully obvious I couldn't answer her.

"No," I muttered. Didn't she know me better than that?

But I guess she didn't—not anymore.

My dad, just like I'd suspected, took the news of the weed and all the rest much better than my mom had. He'd already heard about the math test, but everything else I shared with him when he got home a few hours later, after my mom prompted me with another one of those looks that brooked no disagreement.

He was stony-faced as I talked, letting me plod through my crime and punishment. At last I finished speaking, and he remained quiet for a while before taking a long breath. His face stayed neutral, his tone light. "Well, it sounds like you'll be doing a lot of thinking over the next month. And a lot of math. But it will be nice to see more of you around the gallery." His eyes drifted away in thought. "We can always find a bit of grunt work for you to do, too, if you have the time."

And that was that. It was the best outcome I could have hoped for.

The next morning I awoke, bleary-eyed, to the blaring of my alarm. Six AM—an unholy time of day, one full hour earlier than my usual habit so that I could catch the bus in time. I stayed glued to my phone at the bus stop, ignoring the few curious looks cast my way. It had been the better part of a year since I'd taken the bus.

I was equal parts nerves and anticipation as I walked from study hall to the library a few hours later. What should I say to Ryan? Would he even show up? He wasn't there when I handed my pass in to the librarian. My gaze kept being pulled to the door like it was a magnet.

But there he was at last, eyes brightening as he caught sight of me. He straddled the seat next to mine, and the both of us started apologizing at the same time, our whispers loud enough to garner a disapproving "Shh!" from the librarian.

"I'm sorry about—you know—on your carpet..."

"I'm sorry my mom grilled you in the car!"

"No problem," he said, echoed by my own "Don't worry about it," and as easily as that, all was magically in the past.

We spent the rest of the period zooming in and out of satellite maps until we'd plotted the drop-off boundary and the one crossing Ferngrove. We were so close—yet however I was going to sneak away to plot the third point, that had to wait. If the tutoring and the loss of my car keys were my high school version of prison, I was determined to get early probation.

The bell rang to end the period, and Ryan smacked his hand on the desk. "Hey, we were going to call Rufner! What happened to that?"

He was right; I'd forgotten all about Rufner, what with worrying about Holt and trying to map the demoness's territory. But I had to play the part of the perfect daughter for the next few days.

"I can't," I said. "My mom will murder me if she catches me doing anything else secretive." *With you* was the part I left out.

He gave me a small smile and jerked his head at the librarian, then towards the door. I grabbed my bag and followed him outside into the hallway.

"What is it?"

"I told you I sneak off campus at lunch, yeah? So come with me. We'll do it then."

"But we have different lunch periods, right?"

"Yup, mine's sixth period. Tell your teacher you need to go to the nurse, then meet me over by the door at the back of the band room. You know the one I mean?"

I gave him a look. "Yeah, but listen—I'm the one whose parents are on high alert right now. How about *you* fake sick and come to *my* lunch period?"

He shook his head. "Won't work. The band director

always takes his lunch at the beginning of sixth period, so it has to happen then."

A vision of my mom floated through my mind, disappointment etched deep in her face. I ran a hand through my hair, tugging on a tangle. "I trust you. I'm sure it will be fine. But I just need to wait a little bit before we do it—next week, let's say. Just in case we get caught."

"Sure," he said with a nod. "Rufner won't be going anywhere, I'm sure." He pulled me into a hug as the warning bell rang. I walked to lunch with the warmth of his arms around me still lingering.

After classes ended I met my mom outside the school, weaving my way through hordes of yammering freshmen. I was in a mild state of dread on the ride over to the gallery, faced with my first tutoring session. Anyone recommended by Mrs. Morrie had to be some form of horrible. Yet the tutor seemed nice enough; he was an older man who sported a pair of glasses unsuitably large for his head, so that he was forever pushing them up his bony nose. Something about his reedy voice and the way he tapped his finger on the page as we worked through each question was relaxing. Math was still math, and I didn't think I'd ever grow to like it, but I could have had it way worse.

And so I waited out the days, stuck in the jail-like limbo of constant supervision of teachers and parents and my tutor. At least my fear of Edgar Holt had faded away—a combination of being around other people twenty-four seven and the fact that he hadn't already turned up. Ryan was right; something would have happened by now if Holt were involved.

I still kept the baseball bat stashed by my bed, though.

Chapter 14

I WATCHED THE clock, giving class a couple minutes to get started before raising my hand.

"Señora, I feel sick. Can I go to the nurse?"

It was Wednesday, a full week since we'd set our plan to call Rufner during Ryan's lunch period. A full week spent being a dedicated student and devoted daughter. A full week with no new leads. I'd tried not to think about my ghosts, lest I drive myself crazy with untestable theories. This was easier said than done, but I'd stayed decently distracted thanks to my new favorite online hang-out: Uncle Ed's Forum. The reptilian board, in particular, was its own mesmerizing strain of weird.

My teacher gave me a nod and scribbled out a pass. "Do you need anyone to go with you?"

"No, *gracias*."

Two minutes later I turned down the hallway toward the music classes and cautiously pushed open the band room door. The spacious room was deserted, just like Ryan had said it would be—save for Ryan himself, already waiting for me by the door at the back by the drums. I threaded my way around chairs and music stands, giving the cymbals a flick as I passed.

"Nice solo," Ryan said as the tinny note died. "Ready to go?"

I gave him a quick kiss on the cheek, and he grinned. "Yeah."

It was a brisk day, the sky a gray-white wash of clouds, but I was so alight with nerves that I couldn't feel the chill. It was stupid to be this nervous about a paltry forty-five minutes of stolen time—yet even so, I couldn't help looking back at the school, half-expecting a squadron of teachers to come pouring out the door after us, waving their hands in the air as they hollered about detention.

We'd emerged out the side of the building that faced the soccer fields, adjacent to a quiet residential street. "There's a trail this way that runs right along the Enville River," Ryan said, starting across the grass toward the neighborhood. "No one's ever there."

"How often do you do this?"

He laughed. "Like every day."

I gave him an incredulous look. "You smoke *every day*?"

"No, only a couple times a week. I just like to get away from all that." He gestured behind him at the school.

"Why?" I asked. "I mean, I get it. But why for you?"

He made a face as he took a second to answer. "Hard to say. I guess…" His mouth twisted. "I guess it's the bells."

"Bells?"

"Yeah, for the passing periods. I don't know, they annoy me. Like… like if I'm actually interested in something in class—or investigating the ghosts, or just being with you in the library—I only have fifty minutes to focus on that. Not even an hour! It's artificial."

I gave his shoulder a playful push. "What a rebel."

Ryan didn't respond for a while, his gaze fixed ahead as we crossed the field. Finally, he said, "You know, we read this dystopian short story in English last year, about this guy with a long, silly name. I can't remember what it was… But anyway, the essence of the story is that the guy's a bit more intelligent than the norm, so he has to wear head-phones that emit loud noises to scatter his thoughts. Point being that society's fairer that way. Smarts aren't an ad-vantage to anyone." He paused again, taking the lead as we reached the sidewalk. "Sometimes I think school is like those headphones, with the bells, and the worst thing is that's where we're supposed to go to learn. So I like to leave and take a break. Even if I go back every time—at least I have a choice to go back."

We'd entered the neighborhood by now—an older one from the looks of it. Tall trees on both sides of the street stretched high and wide enough to form a canopy of au-tumn leaves overhead. Ryan gestured at a narrow dirt path, easy to miss, running alongside the lawn of one of the houses into the forest beyond.

"There it is."

I followed him along the path, feeling my muscles relax

as rustling leaves and gurgling water supplanted the low rumble of cars. Maybe Ryan had a point about ditching school after all.

We went around a bend, and the Enville River came into view. The banks were high, courtesy of all the rain recently, but even so it was still more stream than river. Ryan led me to a bench, the wood worn soft from time, and we sat down.

"Ready?" he asked.

"Yeah." I took out my phone, our notes, and a pen, and started up the app to hide my phone number. Then, with one last look at Ryan, I dialed Rufner's number, my heart a thundering beat in my chest.

It rang four times, and I was just hoping to get sent to voicemail when Rufner answered. "Hello, who's this?"

Even from these three words, he sounded genuine, the timbre of his voice deep and warm, and I struggled to match his voice with his aloof-looking faculty photograph. Ryan scooted closer to me on the bench to listen in.

"Hello. My name is Amelia Britt." We'd picked the pseudonym purposefully, so as to be easier to remember; Amelia was my middle name and Britt my mom's maiden name. "I'm calling for Professor August Rufner?"

"That's me," he replied. "What can I do for you, Amelia?"

Ryan tapped a finger on one of our prepared lines. *I'm a fan of your early work, especially the series you showed at your first exhibition at the Teutsch Gallery in 1985. But I've recently seen some photographs online in a very similar style, with no photographer listed, and I've been wondering...*

I shook my head and hunched forward, looking up from the notes to the river, watching the currents and eddies, how the water streamed like liquid glass over the riverbed rocks.

"Amelia?" Rufner prompted.

"Sorry," I said. "Honestly it's a bit of a strange question. I... I was just wondering if you ever dated a girl called Melissa White in 1985."

There was a long, long silence. I could almost hear the impending beep of him ending the call.

But Rufner didn't end it.

"That is a strange question," he said, taking his time with every word. "Why would you think that?"

I sighed and leaned back on the bench. "It's a long story."

Another pregnant pause. Then, "Amelia, you sound young. Are you in some kind of trouble?"

"In a way. I can't talk about that. It's related to Melissa, though. Umm, Professor, I want to be as honest with you as I can. My name's not actually Amelia, but I can't tell you my real name. I'm sorry about that. Amelia will have to do." Ryan was looking at me like I'd lost my mind, but I ignored him, staring up through the trees toward the clouded sky. "And I'm also sorry to bother you like this. Talking about Melissa probably brings up bad memories. But I would really, really appreciate it if you could give me any information about her disappearance."

The line was silent. Then, "The answer to your question is... no. We weren't dating—but we were acquainted. A bit more than that, really. Amelia, I-let me just close the door. It's my office hours, and usually nobody comes by, but you never know."

As he went to shut the door, Ryan shot me a mystified look. "What are you doing?" he breathed. I pointed at the phone and gave him a thumbs up, but he shook his head in confusion.

"Amelia, are you there?"

"Yes, Professor."

"S-sorry, but you've really caught me off guard. I hope… I hope whatever I can tell you proves helpful in some way."

"I hope so too," I said. "Can you please start at the beginning?"

"All right. I met Melissa in early June of 1985 at Dunn College. We met in a bar."

"A bar?"

"Yes, just off campus. They were lazy checking IDs, and the cops didn't seem to mind much. So… you probably know that I was twenty-four and Melissa was sixteen. She didn't seem it. And this wasn't a case of not *wanting* to be able to tell she was so young—please don't think that. Please don't think that," he repeated.

"I believe you," I said—and I did.

"Thank you. She struck up a conversation with me in the bar. I bought her a drink—a vodka soda. She had this electric aura about her, like she was letting off light. I had to photograph her; it felt like a…" He hunted for words. "…like an imperative. I invited her back to my apartment to take some shots."

"I've seen three," I told him.

"What they published in the town newspaper when she disappeared. The photos found in her bedroom."

"Yes."

"The one on the spiral staircase was taken that night. There were others, but they didn't turn out as I'd hoped. That night, w-we did kiss. Nothing more. And then she left."

I nodded. "When did you take the other photos?"

"The next day," he said. I could hear his voice shaking. "Sh-she came back to my place around one. We shot for around two hours. That's when we took the picture in the alleyway and th-the one of her reading in the sunlight. She brought the dress with her, new with tags on. She was so beautiful. And afterwards we—she wanted to—she never told me she was sixt—" His voice broke. "God. S-sorry, Amelia."

"It's all right. Please, can you tell me what happened next?"

"Okay. Afterwards sh-she was interested in seeing the pictures, but she said she had to get going. I told her I'd develop the photos that night, that she could pick them up tomorrow.

"She came by the next day, early, around eight, and told me it was her last day on campus. I gave her the prints and we exchanged phone numbers. I asked her if I could put the photos in an exhibition I was preparing. She told me yes, that she was so excited about it, that she'd come to see it. That was the last time I ever saw her. We did talk on the phone, though, on and off. Mostly me calling her to save her the long-distance costs, at the times she'd told me she was free to talk."

"She didn't let on she was in high school?" I asked.

"Never. She steered clear of talking about the specifics of her life in Lanster, but she was always telling me how boring it was, how she'd get out of town in a few years. I could tell something had her tied down, but I figured it was family, something like that. She said she was counting down the days until the exhibition.

"But she was worried about how she was going to manage the trip. I thought it was just a money thing, so I told her she could stay with me to save some cash. And I told her I loved those photos we'd taken, that we'd take more when she visited, that I thought of her as a bit of a muse. Imagine hearing that, at sixteen.

"The day of the exhibition came, and she never turned up. I couldn't believe it. Well, I could, but I didn't want to. I'd been so looking forward to seeing her again."

I watched a brown, dried-out leaf fall into the river and get swept downstream. "When did you find out she was missing? How did you figure out she didn't just get cold feet?"

Rufner sighed. "The last bit was simple trust, I think. She was keeping secrets, but I could tell that whatever she did tell me was true. I just *knew* she'd wanted to come.

"So I called her house. An older woman picked up—her grandmother, I think. I didn't even get in a hello before she told me that if I was calling to get gossip or give condolences that I could get off the line. They were leaving it open for tips or, God forbid, someone calling with ransom demands."

"And you never told anybody she was planning a trip?"

"No," Rufner said. His voice had become a soft, trembling wreck. "No, I never did. And I have lived with that every day. Some days more and some days less, but it's always there. It haunts me. Tell me, Amelia, please," he said in earnest, almost pleading tones. "Do you know what happened to her? It won't help to know more, but—"

"She died in Connecticut," I blurted. Was it a good idea to tell him? I didn't know, but it felt like the kind thing to say. "I can't tell you how or why, but that I know for certain."

I held the phone to my ear, frozen, as his breathing grew ragged. I had never heard a grown man cry.

He composed himself after a moment. "So she did die, then," he said. "She's not… being held somewhere."

"Yes."

"Amelia, is there anything I can help you with? Are you in danger? You see, she died coming to see me. A senseless waste of a life, and all because of those stupid things I told her, what we… did, the photos, the allure of it all. But if I can help you… That balance can't be righted, but—"

"You can't help me," I interrupted, a cold gust of air setting me shivering. "I'm sorry, Professor. But thank you for speaking with me. It sounds dumb, but I really mean this: whatever you say that helps me—it also helps her."

And I hung up the phone.

Chapter 15

"HOW DID YOU know he didn't do it?" Ryan asked as we hustled back across the soccer field. "How did you know to talk to him like that?"

"I could hear it, just like you said before. Remember? You said he'd sound cagey if he did it."

He shook his head at me, jaw slack. "But all you'd done was say hello."

I shrugged. "I don't know. I could just hear it."

At last we reached the band room. The blare of the warning bell filtered through the door: two minutes until the next class. No way was I making it to art on time.

"All right," Ryan said. "Let's hope the director's not here. I've never come back so late before." He eased the door open, and I cringed as I heard the shrill tones of a flute moving up and down a scale. Yet it was just a freshman girl practicing in the corner; she eyed us confusedly as we dashed inside, around the bass drum and the timpani, and out into the hall, thronged with students. They flowed past us, chattering about class, sports, life. I felt a sharp stab of envy.

"Listen, are you okay?" Ryan said, turning to facing me, his eyebrows knit into a frown. "That can't have been easy."

"Yeah," I said as I finger-combed my hair to look less like I'd just power-walked across a field. "Yeah, I'm fine."

"All right, then." He pulled me into a tight hug. "Well, see you later."

"Bye."

But the truth was that I didn't know if I was fine. Had it been right to call Rufner? To ask him to recount painful events more than thirty years in the past, while offering him only a few vague statements as thanks? I didn't even think he'd told us anything useful; thanks to D_plexippus we had suspected the basic story already. The phone call had only filled in the sad details.

Then again, maybe I shouldn't care so much. Rufner's own actions were selfish—some might even say indefensible. He had obstructed law enforcement, denied Melissa's parents access to important, if heartbreaking, knowledge about their daughter. Maybe that information could have been the key linking Melissa's disappearance with all the other teenagers listed on Uncle Ed's Forum. Maybe their killer could have been found.

Every thought tugged me this way and that, drawing and quartering my mind. And the one thing I knew, the *only* thing I could say for certain, was that I could waste no more time finding the third point of the circle.

"Lanie?"

I blinked, realizing the math tutor had asked me a question. "Wh-what?" We were sitting at the table in La Belle et la Bête's back office, and I was struggling to keep my eyes on the thick packet of math problems in front of me instead of the clock on the wall. Twenty-three minutes left. "Sorry, say that again?"

"How are you doing with changing the bases of logarithms?" the tutor asked, pushing his glasses once again up his nose. "Can we move on, or do you need more practice?"

"I think I get it." In actuality I could still barely tell a logarithm from a polynomial—or were those both the same thing?

"Well then, let's take a look at—"

"Hey, Bob." My dad poked his head through the door, making the both of us start. "Would you mind knocking off early today? We'll still pay for the full session, of course."

"Well, sure," the tutor said, and he began to gather up his things. "Until tomorrow, then."

"Actually," my dad said, "how about Friday? And making it three days a week from now on instead of five?"

"It's all good to me," said the tutor to my dad. "I'm just happy to get out of the house. Don't retire! It's a death sentence."

I watched with delight as he left the room. Three days a week of tutoring couldn't count as early probation—but it was *something*, and I'd take crumbs of freedom right now. Anything that got me closer to that third point.

"Thanks, Dad."

He got up and closed the office door, shutting out the sound of my mom giving some details about a painting to a newlywed couple.

"Lanie," he said, sighing as he settled down in the seat across from me, "I'm not happy about the pot and the math and the boy." He scratched his head, squinting. "And the disregard for how driving fits into this. God, you really struck out all around, didn't you?"

Leave it to my dad to use baseball to discuss my failings. "Dad, I am really, *really* sor—"

"Yeah, I get it." He gave me a wry smile. "Even so, your mom's gone a bit overboard with the whole punishment thing. You know how she was brought up—not a toe out of line."

This was true; my mom's parents had been the strict disciplinarian type, expecting nothing but the highest accomplishments from their daughter. And she'd risen to their expectations, her eyes fixed on a career in law—then fallen head over heels in college for a boy majoring in art history. He'd had a mellowing effect on my mom—little had she known she'd been stressed out of her mind for the past decade and a half—and the future law career began to look like crushing pressure and seventy-hour work weeks.

So she'd discarded the dream, married the art history major, had me—but it was still always my mom freaking out about my grades and my dad doing his best to calm her down.

"We've both noticed," my dad said, continuing on, "that you've been really trying this week. Not that I'm expecting you to take multivariable calculus next year, but I see you working hard. So I have managed to convince your mom that we should give you a bit of slack."

"The car...?" I could stomach the three days a week of tutoring much better if I didn't also have to suffer the humiliation of taking the bus.

He shook his head. "Still off limits, I'm afraid. And your mom and I are not divided on this! A minivan's a multi-ton hunk of metal. You can't be cavalier about these things. But we'll give you back your afternoons on Tuesdays and Thursdays. Of course, there will be no boys, no pot, no nothing of that sort."

I felt giddy with joy. Tomorrow — *tomorrow!* — I could go find the third spot.

"Promise you'll be good, Lanie?" my dad asked, looking me in the eyes.

"I promise," I lied.

My morning classes the next day stretched to eternity. Ryan hadn't been on Facebook, and I hadn't been texting him for fear my mom would check my phone.

He saw my excitement as soon as he arrived in the library. "What is it?"

"No tutoring today," I said, lowering my voice when I caught the librarian giving us the side-eye. "Can you come home on the bus today with me to find the third point? I still can't drive the car."

"Sure," he said, "as long as it's okay if I'm there until five-thirty. My brother can't pick me up until then."

Heat bloomed within me, and I flashed back to when we'd hung out in his room, thinking my ghosts were a one-off. No Melissa, no Claw Hands—just me and him. "Of course it's okay," I said. "Stay as long as you want." My parents wouldn't get home until way later; they had yet another meeting with an artist tonight.

He slid his hand over to mine. "I was hoping you'd say that."

We spent the rest of the period browsing the reptilian board on Uncle Ed's Forum. Neither of us could tell whether the posters thought lizard people actually existed or if it was all some sprawling in-joke. I was driving on a road in northern North Dakota, someone wrote, when I saw a toddler all alone on the side of the road. I was about to pull over and call the police when the toddler morphed into a three-foot tall reptilian, then an owl, then back into a reptilian!! Then disappeared. So I'm wondering if maybe the reptilians are actually some sort of evolved dinosaur, because aren't birds and dinosaurs related? Maybe we also need to stay vigilant about birds, ESPECIALLY owls. Could be another mechanism in their surveillance system.

Everyone in the thread seemed to be taking this new hypothesis very seriously.

"Let me ask you something," I said to Ryan, once he'd stopped laughing. "These people are clearly insane."

"Clearly."

"But…" I picked at a hangnail. "Believing in ghosts and believing that lizard people secretly rule the world aren't that far apart on the crazy totem pole. What made you believe me?"

He sank back in his chair and didn't say anything for a long moment. *I don't* believe you! *I* almost expected him to say. *I've just been going along with all this for a laugh!*

But he didn't say that. "I guess it's because you didn't want to tell me—not at first, at least. You were all shy about it."

"Shy people can still be crazy."

He tilted his head, thinking. "I just sort of wanted it to be real. Because… well, if they're real, then something comes after our lives here, probably. Some sort of weird ghost limbo. Maybe heaven…" He gulped. "Or hell. Or something way stranger than anything anyone's ever considered. So I just figured I'd give it a go with the Ouija board and everything else and see what happened."

I ran a hand through my hair, blew out a breath. He was right, of course, but that train of thought was too much right now. I'd make it through the rest of classes, find the third point, put my ghosts to rest… Then I could switch my focus to the metaphysical implications of the paranormal.

But as soon as I walked into English, my eyes zeroed in on the yellow pass in the center of my desk. I frowned as I picked up the little slip of paper.

Lanie Adams to Mr. Battison, Main Office, printed clearly in black sharpie.

Mr. Battison—was that the vice-principal? That couldn't be right…

"You can go there now," my English teacher called to me as the rest of the class was getting settled. Clearly she'd been waiting for me to come in. Was it just my imagination, or was she giving me a weird look?

I slunk out the door, feeling like the entire class was watching me go.

When I got to the main office, I handed my pass over to the secretary. Looking down her nose at the paper, she nodded briskly, then waved me past the desk. "First door on your right."

The door was closed; a shining plaque in the middle read *Chuck Battison, Vice-Principal*. What the hell was going on? I'd never even come *close* to needing to step into his office.

I hovered outside the door, clasping my fingers nervously, then heard the secretary's voice from behind me. "Delaying won't help, dear."

So I knocked, and a man's resonant voice said, "Come in."

Opening the door with sweating palms, the first two faces I saw were Ryan and my mom.

<h1 style="text-align:center">Chapter 16</h1>

Shit, shit, shit, shit, shit.

They were both seated before Battison's desk. Battison was a big man with a barrel chest, and he motioned for me to sit in a chair beside them. Ryan looked pale but collected; my mom was looking at me with a pinched expression.

"All right, then, you two," Battison said, steepling his fingers and leaning far enough back in his leather chair for it to creak. "It seems like you've struck up quite the friendship lately."

He looked at us expectantly, and I realized after a few seconds that he was expecting an answer. "Y-yes," I stammered, hoping that was enough.

"Well, there's a lot to talk about here," Battison said, his eyes swinging over to Ryan. "Let's start with your English class. Anything you'd like to tell us about a certain *Dracula* paper? Your teacher noticed a distinct change in voice from your previous papers this semester." I felt a plummeting sensation in my stomach. So that's what this was about.

"I asked her to," Ryan blurted out, before I could recover

my breath. "It was my idea. I hated the book, and Lanie had read it a bunch of times already, so I asked her to write the paper for me."

"Is that true?" Battison asked me. In my peripheral vision I saw Ryan give me an almost imperceptible nod. Shame coursed through me. This was all my fault. I'd offered to write the paper, and here he was getting all chivalrous, trying to take the brunt of the blame.

I frowned and looked away. "That's right. But… I mean… He didn't force me to write it or anything. I wanted to." I risked a glance over at my mom. Her eyes were cast downward, her hands folded in her lap, like she was the one getting in trouble instead of me.

"That doesn't excuse either of your actions, though," Battison said. "Ryan, you should know I called your home and left a voicemail for your parents to call me back. I'd tell them about this yourself as soon as possible, though, if I were you."

"Yes, sir," he replied, his face a blank mask.

Battison rocked forward in his chair. "It's the first instance of academic dishonesty for the both of you. But on the other hand, both of you are juniors. Not impressive — you should know better. I'm sorry to say that further cases of cheating, plagiarism, et cetera will have to be reported to colleges on your transcripts when you apply next year. Let this paper be your one and only warning. Ryan, you may redo the essay for fifty percent credit. Lanie, this won't affect any of your own grades, obviously, but you'll get two Saturday detentions."

My face grew hot. Multiple detentions, let alone on Saturday? It had been wrong to write the paper for Ryan, sure, but wasn't that too much?

Battison wasn't done, however. "Let's move on to the second order of business." He grabbed two papers from the side of his desk and laid them side by side. Even upside down I could see that they were two school schedules—one for Ryan, one for me. "Lanie, Mrs. Gutierrez talked with me this morning. She told me you asked to go to the nurse yesterday at the beginning of class and never came back. She checked with the nurse to make sure you'd made it there safe and sound, but the nurse told her you never showed up. Now, I've heard from your mom that you and Ryan here have gotten quite close recently, for better or for worse." He flipped the school schedules around. "It doesn't escape me," he said, tapping one sheet, then the other, "that you have Spanish with Mrs. Gutierrez during the exact same period Ryan has lunch."

I stared at the two school schedules for a few seconds, then looked up to meet Battison's gaze. "Yeah, I really wish we had the same lunch period. But actually I was in the bathroom all of sixth period throwing up. I think it was something I ate at lunch the period before. Maybe the macaroni salad. I figured the nurse didn't need to see that."

Battison knew I was lying. My mom did, too; I could hear her blow out a long breath, could see her shift in her seat. But no one could force me to say anything, and I was happier to bear the uncomfortable silence than drag Ryan into even more trouble.

"Naturally," Battison said, crossing his arms, "it is of crucial importance that your teachers know where you are at all times, for your own safety."

"Naturally," I echoed. "I'll try to make it to the nurse next time."

Predictably, my mom bumped tutoring up from the mythical three times per week back to five, effective immediately. She also took my phone. That night I must have caught her staring at me ten times, like some stranger had taken my place. Everything she said to me was short and stiff, disappointment lacing every syllable.

Dinner was a solemn affair. The halting conversation, all a failed effort on the part of my dad, said all it needed to. *How was school today?* was off the table, as was *What are you thinking of doing this weekend?* I knew precisely what I was going to be doing over the next two Saturdays, from eight to eleven AM to be exact.

"What time are the tickets for *Psycho* with the orchestra?" I asked after a while, remembering that the showing fell on a Saturday, the day before Halloween. "It's not a matinee show, is it?"

"It's not," my mom said, "but consider it canceled."

My dad set down his fork. "Michelle, let's wait a bit bef—"

"Our daughter's been assigned two Saturday detentions," my mom said, her tone biting, "and if she so much as blinks the wrong way the school will report it to colleges. Don't tell me not to take this seriously."

"I got a couple of Saturdays in high school, and I turned out all right," he protested. "Got into my top school, actually! I think they saw it as a bit of spice on the application."

"Yes, but that was more than twenty years ago," she said. "Competition's tougher now. She can't have that on her transcript."

"Stop talking like I'm not here," I blurted. I needed this almost-argument to stop.

Yet when my mom turned her attention on me, I knew instantly it would have been better to stay silent. Fire seemed to burn behind her pupils. "Find some responsibility," she snapped, "and maybe then you can join the conversation."

We spent the rest of dinner in silence.

Afterwards I tried to lose myself in a video by one of my favorite vloggers. I made sure to leave my bedroom door open. God only knew what fresh trouble my mom could imagine me getting into behind a closed door.

I watched on dully as the vlogger pranced around a palatial Maldives resort. The sun was beaming, the sky a brilliant azure, the background music almost inanely happy: a picture-perfect life, everything accounted for, everything in its place. But I felt too sad and tired and heavy for the fantasy to sweep me away.

My parents' muffled voices, filtering up from the first floor, broke whatever spell the vlogger was failing to weave on me. I paused the video and crept down the stairs, skipping the creaky fourth step, then tread silently down the hallway toward the living room. Hovering just around the corner, I listened in on their conversation.

My dad was speaking. "Can't you see these restrictions aren't helping? Lanie's a good kid —"

My mom gave a sputtering sigh, and a wave of guilt washed over me. "Not lately," she murmured.

"No, not lately. But she's *sixteen*. Think back to all the stupid shit you did when you were sixteen. Well, maybe not you, Miss Valedictorian, but the stuff I'm thinking about for myself..."

Neither one of them said anything for nearly a minute, and I was just about to sneak away lest I get discovered when my mom spoke again.

"I've been thinking about St. Brigid's Prep down by the coast."

My dad swore as the world began to cave in around me. "It's the middle of the school year! You mean for her senior year?"

"No, I mean now. Remember that young couple we got in the other day? The newlyweds? They both teach at St. Brigid's, and they were telling me they take in a lot of girls mid-semester. They're not a therapeutic boarding school per se, but they offer a lot of support for their students. Counseling every day if needed, mindfulness integrated into the curriculum, daily check-ins with an adviser, things like that."

My dad snorted. "I don't know. You have to buy into that stuff. If she doesn't see the need for any of that, what's it going to help her?"

"I think it's worth a try, if this continues. She's stuck on that boy—Ryan. What can we do about that during the day, when she's at school? Nothing. But at a different school… And St. Brigid's is all girls. She'd be able to concentrate on her studies, without getting hung up on some stoner."

"Yes, it's Lanie's junior year, so her studies are important," my dad replied. "But on the other hand, it's also her junior year."

"What do you mean?"

"What I mean is that she's becoming her own person—there are going to be some inevitable growing pains. Think: these past few weeks have really been the first time we've ever seen *anything* like this from her. I vote to give her the benefit of the doubt and not act prematurely. It's October, for crying out loud. She's in the middle of the semester."

"But if we have her make the transition now—"

"Then we'll have a seriously resentful kid on our hands. No Ryan, but a different daughter, perhaps. Besides, St. Brigid's is a boarding school, right? You can send her away, just like that?"

My mom's reply came quietly. "If it's for her own good then I'll—we'll—manage."

"No," my dad said. His voice, too, was quiet, but his conviction snapped like a whip. "She deserves more than this. It's only been a few different things. She's figuring it all out."

"You know that? She really will?" My mom's voice

was watery.

"I'm going to trust that she will. I suggest you do, too. Oh, come here. It'll be all right." I bowed my head at the sound of my mom's soft crying, then stole back upstairs before they could catch me eavesdropping.

Chapter 17

I PASSED THROUGH Friday in a sad haze, heading to school, then to the gallery, then back home again in a cycle I hardly noticed. In study hall I discovered that my daily library dates with Ryan were to be no more; my study hall proctor had been informed, by Battison no doubt, that my time would be better spent in actual study hall, not "doing research" in the library. I only saw Ryan once that day — or the back of his head, really, walking ahead of me in the hallway. He entered a classroom, and I thought about going in to say hello, but then the warning bell rang. I gritted my teeth as I forced my feet to walk on towards my next class.

I spent the course of the next period lost in daydreams about the bench by the river. Someday soon, I resolved to find myself back there with Ryan. And I daydreamed that this time we would spend our time in that forgotten corner of nature wastefully, with abandon. No ticking clock in the back of our heads, no schedule, no third point. Maybe huddling close together because it was getting on toward winter.

The next day brought a first: detention. Yet what had sounded imposing in the meeting with Battison turned out to be almost trivial—three hours of quiet work, as a bored teacher at the front of the room slashed up papers with a red pen. The ride there and back with my mom was the worst part by far. She forced a normal conversation as she drove. "Would you look at those leaves? Oh, by the way, Grandma Ruth is coming over for dinner tonight. How does salmon and asparagus sound?" It was like she was dragging me into some game of make-believe, like she was pretending we were going to the school to pick up a textbook instead of to drop me at detention. Maybe I could get my dad to take me the next week.

But at dinner I learned that neither of my parents would be taking me to detention next Saturday. We had all just taken our seats around the table when my dad cleared his throat.

"I have a bit of an announcement to make." He looked around the table at us all, a glimmer in his eyes. "It's not set in stone yet, so this may be a bit premature, but Michelle and I figured why not share the potential good news? Nico Emerson is considering a one-year contract with the gallery."

My grandma let out a delighted trill. "*The* Nico Emerson? The whale picture guy?"

He nodded. "That's the one. When we reached out to him it seemed like a long shot, but he's actually very interested. There's a gallery in Providence that's been representing him for a while, but he says he's not overly satisfied with the relationship. Michelle and I are going to drive down to Virginia Beach next Friday to meet with him. We'll get back late Sunday night."

My mom's eyes slid from me to my grandma. "Ruth, do you mind if Lanie stays with you over the weekend while we're gone?"

She let out a huff. "Well, Lanie's sixteen! I'm happy to have her over, but surely she can look after herself for a few days. Can't you, hon?" She patted me on the hand.

"Just for our peace of mind," my mom interjected, a bit too quickly. Clearly she hadn't divulged any of my recent mishaps to my grandma.

"I'll talk to you about it later, Mom," my dad said, and I flushed, wondering what he'd tell her.

My grandma raised her eyebrows at the both of them, then turned to me and smiled. "Well, it all sounds fine to me! We'll have a girls' weekend, just the two of us. Shopping, nails, a restaurant." She snapped her fingers. "Oh, that's the same weekend we're seeing *Psycho*, right? Shame your parents will miss it, but we'll have fun getting spooked without them. What do you say, Lanie?"

"Sounds great!" I said, fighting back a swell of laughter when I saw my mom pinch the bridge of her nose; in all of ten seconds my grandma had steamrolled my mom's best parental intentions.

My mind, meanwhile, was churning out the murky beginnings of a plan. Not anything that would make me proud—more than a bit underhanded, honestly—but a plan all the same.

Another week passed in a blur of school and tutoring and pretending I was still the girl I'd been pre-haunting. Whenever I had a bit of free time online, I headed not to the more absurd corners of Uncle Ed's Forum, but instead to the sleek web page of St. Brigid's Preparatory School.

The girls in the pictures wore smart outfits and big smiles, and they all seemed to excel at lacrosse or crew or dance. Drone footage flaunted a sunshine-drenched campus of rolling fields and brick-faced dormitories. I tried to envision myself in those girls' ranks, sitting amongst them in class, frolicking with them on the green. Tried—and failed. Even though it was only an hour south of Enville, St. Brigid's felt about as real a place as Narnia. And just as I didn't feel any particular pull to travel to Narnia, nor did I want to escape Enville for St. Brigid's.

The week did bring one minor victory—scraping a B on my logarithms quiz, enough to garner a proud smile from my mom. I almost smiled back, then remembered my plans for that weekend. Even if I didn't have much of a choice, I was still leading her on. What was there to smile about?

Friday arrived at last. After school my mom drove straight home instead of to the gallery; my parents wanted to leave soon to get a head start on traffic. My grandma arrived to pick me up only fifteen minutes late—a minor miracle, just when my mom was starting to fret getting on the road. I didn't know what details my dad had shared with her, but aside from her near-punctuality my grandma was her same self, all chatter and smiles. I shouldered my duffel bag, gave my dad a hug, then turned to my mom.

"Be good," she said to me with a pointed look.

"I will." I forced my eyes up to meet her own, hoping she couldn't read my intentions within.

That night in my grandma's spare bedroom, cozy under a few hand-knitted blankets, I had no problems falling asleep. It felt like some long-clenched muscle deep inside me had relaxed; I could rest easy knowing that Claw Hands wasn't by my side, playing the part of demonic guard dog. And as I drifted towards dreams, I settled into that comforting feeling and found myself again trying to picture myself in the beautiful setting of St. Brigid's. If my plan didn't work, then perhaps... perhaps...

The next morning Grandma Ruth nearly talked my ear off on the way to detention, but unlike my mom's forced chit-chat, hers was genuine. She truly didn't seem to care that I'd gotten myself into "a spot of mischief," as she put it. It made sense, since her own son had gotten a couple Saturdays, and he'd come out okay. Better than okay, really, for he was my dad—loving, thoughtful, kind. I could still be that kind of person, even if I'd landed myself on the wrong side of the vice-principal.

Three hours later, I grinned when I walked out of school and my grandma greeted me with a beep of the horn.

"All right, you troublemaker, time to get the weekend started!" she said as I got into the car. We putt-putted off at grandma speeds to the mall.

That night, in one of the worn velvet seats of the Old Town Theater, I started when the lights dimmed and the violins began driving their way forward. How many times had I watched *Psycho* before—five? And the legendary soundtrack could still make me jump.

Beside me, Grandma Ruth chuckled and reached into the popcorn with delicate fingers; we'd just managed to squeeze in a visit to the nail salon before coming to the theater. I'd picked a deep, witchy purple in honor of Halloween tomorrow, and she'd gone for metallic fuchsia. "We'll see if it catches the eye of old Jerry Dahlman down the street," she'd told the nail tech with a wink. "I think there might be something there."

The opening credits came to a close, the strings settling as the camera languidly panned over the city of Phoenix before eventually zooming in on an open window—Hitchcock making the audience a peeping Tom to the doomed Marion's noontime tryst. My grandma heaved a dramatic sigh and fanned herself as Marion, breasts resplendent in their sixties-style brassiere, and her shirtless, hunky boyfriend Sam came into the shot. "That John Gavin," she whispered and gave me a nudge. "Not bad at all, eh, Lanie?" I giggled, and someone in the row behind us gave us a shush.

The community college orchestra represented them-selves admirably. As the film ended with the chilling shot of Marion's car being lugged out of the swamp and a final burst of strings, the audience gave a resounding ovation.

"How about Qing's?" my grandma asked as we strolled toward the exit.

"Sure," I said, and I placed an order for spring rolls, fried rice, and General Tso's as she drove back home.

An hour later, we sat at her dining room table in a grease-induced daze, empty carry-out boxes serving as the table centerpiece.

"So," Grandma Ruth said as I attempted to pick up my fortune cookie paper with my chopsticks, "tell me about this boy."

My fingers slipped as I lifted my chopsticks, and the for-tune fluttered back down to the table. *Lucky Numbers: 3, 7, 8, 16, 25, 41. Looking is halfway to seeing.*

"What?" I stammered.

"The boy your dad told me about," she said matter-of-factly. "Something about you and him and this detention of yours."

"I… uhh…"

My grandma laughed and waved her hands when she saw my reddening face. "All right, all right, no need to elab-orate! I get it. *Fast* romance," she added, eyes twinkling. "Must have been… oh… last Saturday that I asked if you had a new beau. And then later that same night I hear some-thing different from your dad! Well, have fun with your so-called bad boy, Lanie. You only live once." She took a sip of water, regarding me with an amused expression as I did my best not to self-combust from embarrassment.

I couldn't have asked for a better setup, though. I took a few deep breaths to steady myself as Grandma Ruth hurried off to make some tea.

"Ice cream?" she called from the kitchen.

"Sure," I said absentmindedly, running through what I wanted to say in my mind as she bustled about pouring the tea and scooping two heaping servings of vanilla ice cream into matching glass bowls. My grandma was nothing if not a good hostess.

I took a couple bites, then broached the subject at last. "Grandma, I was wondering if… Well, tomorrow's Halloween, and I was hoping that… I don't have a costume, but Ryan asked me to go trick-or-treating with him." I kept my words wobbly, my tone a crafted combination of hopeful and sad.

Grandma Ruth regarded me, unblinking, as she took a bite of her ice cream, like we had just entered an impromptu staring contest, the victor to prescribe my Halloween plans. I felt the moment stretch to an eon; whole species could arise, evolve, struggle, and perish in this silence, pulled long like taffy. My mouth had gone dry, but I didn't dare swallow.

Eventually she huffed out a sigh. "Well, how can I stand in the way of young love? But we'll have to get you a costume. I'll not have my granddaughter be one of those insufferable teens demanding half the candy bowl when they're only wearing jeans, a T-shirt, and cat ears."

My pulse quickened. "Really? I can go?"

"Conditionally," she said, thrusting a finger into the air. "Be back by eight. Not a word to your parents. And no funny business! Nothing that will make me regret letting you do this. Nothing beyond a hug and a couple tender smooches."

Oh good lord.

"I promise," I said.

Chapter 18

I WAS UPSTAIRS in my bedroom zipping up my costume when the chime of the doorbell sent my heart flying into my throat. It was five o'clock already? I'd been waiting to find the third point for weeks, but now that the time was finally here… And Ryan seeing me in this silly costume wasn't doing much for my nerves, either.

I heard my grandma open the door a second later, quick enough that I could tell she'd been waiting for Ryan to arrive. "Ryan Spina, I'm presuming?" she said.

"Yes, ma'am," came his reply, and I couldn't help a little smile to myself. Last night I'd sent him a message on Facebook telling him to be on his best behavior. It seemed he'd taken that to heart.

"Ruth's just fine, dear," I heard her say as I started down the stairs. "'Ma'am' adds ten years to my age, and that just might put me in the grave."

"Wow," Ryan said as I met them in the foyer. He was dressed as the Grim Reaper, complete with a long plastic scythe, but though his face was shrouded by the hood, I could still see his eyes widen. I fidgeted as his gaze wandered from my costume's own plush black hood, complete with two giant googly eyes, down to the black bodycon dress with its white middle panel. The bottom hem of the dress was trimmed with more ebony faux fur. "That's... really something."

My grandma and I had arrived at Enville's sole Halloween store right as the doors opened this morning, yet our hopes of finding the perfect costume had been summarily dashed when we'd caught sight of the picked-over merchandise. It was a Goldilocks and the Three Bears scenario: the vampire costumes were too big and the ghost costumes too small—something I hadn't realized was even possible for a glorified sheet with eye holes. In glum spirits, I had eyed the special effects makeup, weighing the likelihood I could use spirit gum and cotton balls to make myself into a passable zombie—then I'd heard my grandma's "Yoo-hoo!" from across the store.

"It's your size!" she'd said, waving a black and white costume in the air. "A bit short, but I think it'd be cute!"

So I tried it on, and when I opened the changing room curtain and heard her squeal of delight, it was clear the decision had already been made.

Ryan's eyes drifted further down to my black tights and boots, then back up to the googly eyes.

"Are you a... killer whale?"

"Sexy penguin," I said with a wince, dangling the dinky, orange felt beak with its elastic string from my index finger—the penguin version of a clown nose. "Selection at Phantom Halloween was pretty limited."

"But doesn't she look darling?" my grandma asked, hovering nearby. One look at her face told me she was loving every second of this.

"*Real* darling," Ryan answered, casting a bright smile at my grandma. Boy, was he turning it on. "We'll be back by eight. My brother's going to pick me up here."

"Eight sharp," my grandma repeated, "and not a minute later. Take these for candy…" She handed us each an empty pillowcase, and I tossed the penguin beak in. Trick-or-treating wasn't on the agenda tonight, so no need for the costume's pièce de résistance. Plus it itched my nose. "And… Well… Have a good time! Get out of here, you two!" She shooed us out onto the front step and closed the door.

"Your grandma's a real character," Ryan said with a chuckle.

"Yeah, she's the best," I said distractedly, tugging down my dress hem. Damn thing kept riding up. The plush material would have done a fine job keeping me warm in the cool October evening, were the hem not barely grazing the tops of my thighs.

"I didn't know sexy penguins wore combat boots," he said, deadpan, though I could see his lips twitching with a concealed smile.

"Good for a hike," I said. I wasn't in the right mood for jokes, not with the prize of the third point dangling right in front of me. "Are you ready to go?"

"Yeah."

"Okay." I cast a glance at the side window just to make sure my grandma wasn't spying on us; I wouldn't put it past her. But she wasn't there, so I thrust my arm into the dense bush beside the door and rooted around until my hand knocked against the plastic bag I knew to be stashed within. I drew out the heavy, lumpy bag, its top tied tight, then folded it up in my empty pillowcase.

"Let's go."

"What's that?" Ryan asked as we walked, nodding his head at the concealed bag.

"Wait just a second," I said, casting a wary look over my shoulder. The house was still visible behind us—which meant my grandma could still be watching us.

We rounded the bend, and I came to a halt. Bringing out the plastic bag, I undid the top and opened it. It was brimming with candy—candy I'd bought last week from the school lunch lady at outrageous single-piece prices with my fifty dollars of leftover birthday money.

"Our alibi," I said to Ryan, shaking half the candy into his pillowcase, then dumping the rest into my own. "We were out from five to eight trick-or-treating, not hiking."

Ryan looked impressed. "Sexy *and* smart. You're one unusual killer whale!"

I wrinkled my nose at him as I turned to face the woods. "Let's get off the road. We'll start losing daylight soon." I knew the area well enough that I could *probably* navigate with just the flashlight on Ryan's phone—but there was no reason to test that theory.

It took me a few steps before I realized Ryan wasn't following.

"What's up?" I asked, turning back around.

"Put on the beak so we can take a selfie. You're cute, and it's Halloween." He stood tall, chest puffed out, feet planted firmly on the pavement. I had no idea how he was doing it, but even in his baggy Grim Reaper robes he was looking handsome.

Still I wavered. The penguin beak? Really? This was the hill he was going to die on? Plus the costume was all-around embarrassing, and I didn't want an electronic record of it haunting me till I was ninety…

"You'd *really* be helping me out," he said, staunch yet cheerful. "I think I have hiking PTSD or something from almost throwing up on your mom last time, and I need to replace those memories stat with something better. And I can tell you're all nervous about what we're going to find, so, like… let's live a little."

I shifted on my feet. He could tell that? I mean, it wasn't *not* true, but I hadn't known he could read me so well.

"Come on, Lanie," he said, seeing me hesitate. "However tonight turns out, let's start it off good."

"All right, all right, I'm convinced." I slipped the beak on, then walked back to him. Little shivers raced up and down my skin when he put his arm around me and drew me in close for the picture. His hold around me was firm but gentle, and he was warm, so welcome in the crisp near-twilight.

If only we could stay like this all night, instead of tramping through the woods with a demoness nipping at my heels.

"I'd ask if you want to do a duck face," he muttered in between photo takes, "but I think the whole bird thing you have going on already covers that..." I couldn't help a laugh, and he snapped one last picture. "That's the one. The one and only sexy, laughing penguin. Very, very rare." He let go of me, and I felt a stab of sadness as chill air caressed my shoulders. Soon this would all be over—I would *make* this be over—and then I could focus on the things I needed to matter more.

My gaze swiveled to the woods lining the road. "Okay, you ready *now*?"

He thrust his scythe into the air like a warrior about to ride forth to battle. "Lead on, fair penguin. And by the way, you made a good decision back there."

"Oh yeah? Why's that?"

"I was prepared to permanently nickname you Shamu."

Thirty or so paces into the woods I came to a halt by a downed tree trunk and took a seat. "Let's smoke. Wait, you did bring the weed, right?" I felt a wave of panic.

But he was giving me another one of his big, patent smiles. "The reaper has many secrets," he said with a wink, pulling up his voluminous robes to reveal his regular jeans underneath and—

"A fanny pack? Seriously?"

He frowned at me. "Listen, don't trash talk my fanny pack. This shit is vintage. My dad used to wear it all the time, and it comes in handy in situations like… Well, really only this."

We smoked in silence on the log, the whispering leaves and twittering birds the only sounds. I leaned into Ryan as I felt the now-familiar high start to take hold, bracing myself for the inevitable. She was here, I knew, my personal demoness, just waiting to be revealed.

Sure enough, my eyes soon locked onto a daub of inky blue wrongness a few feet in front of us. It ballooned from thin air, bloating and swelling, here a gaunt arm shooting out, there a mass of knotted hair taking shape.

"I wish I could see her," Ryan murmured as my breath stuttered.

"You don't," I whispered back, then got to my feet and gave a full-body shiver. We had only left the house ten minutes ago, but it felt like the temperature had dropped twenty degrees. Some combination of my dress and my nerves and the demoness in front of me radiating evil, no doubt.

Hopefully some hiking would warm me up—and let me bid Claw Hands a final farewell.

I took us on a northward path toward Avanic's fenced-off campus. Claw Hands stalked along beside us, ever her guard dog self. *Did demons need to eat?* I wondered as I steered us left around a thicket of bushes. And if so, *what* did they eat—their spirit brethren? Was there a phantom food chain? I grimaced at a vision of Claw Hands ripping ghostly flesh from bone.

What about sleep? Had she had *any* occasion to stray from my side these past few weeks, ever since Melissa's visit in the bathroom? Or had she doggedly—ha ha—shadowed me every second I was within her domain?

Somehow I suspected it was the latter, and the thought quickened my pace, like an insistent wind pushing me onward. Soon enough I caught sight of the tall chain-link fence through the trees—Avanic.

The problem was that Claw Hands was still here.

"Is she—?" Ryan began.

"Yeah," I said, throwing her a glare. "She's right next to me." She was close enough to smell—a rank, rotting odor.

We crept closer to the fence. Even just looking in from the outside felt like trespassing. The pharmaceutical company's headquarters were expansive. A wide lawn of grass trimmed short lay between us and the buildings, and lamp posts tall as stadium lights studded the campus at regular intervals. The buildings' mirrored windows reflected a wavy image of the lawn and the woods back at us.

"Quite an operation they have here, huh?" Ryan said. "I wonder what drugs they manufacture."

"I think they do a bunch," I said, shuddering when Claw Hands growled behind me. "Medication for joint pain or something…" I looked both ways along the fence. Heading left would lead us to Avanic's gated entryway—and quite possibly a nosy security guard. "Let's head that way"—I jerked my head to the right—"and circle around."

We slowly skirted the fence, Ryan taking the lead. Every

few steps I checked to see if Claw Hands had fallen behind, but she never did. By this point the sunlight had dimmed to deep honey, the trees casting long, skeletal shadows. I jumped when the lamp posts on the other side of the fence flicked on all at once, flooding Avanic's campus in brilliant, artificial light and illuminating every blade of grass.

We reached the corner of the fence after a few minutes. I knew from the satellite map and all my time spent scampering through the woods as a kid that following the fence around the bend would take us north toward Carnarvon Avenue, one of Enville's main thoroughfares. Theoretically, there was no way to get lost.

So we left Avanic and the fence behind, plunging back into the forest. The ground here was at a sharp incline, the underbrush a thick tangle eager to snag our ankles, so we had to wend our way this way and that to keep pressing north. It was almost past sunset now, the fiery sky fading to dusky blue evening.

And still Claw Hands did not falter. She was in her element in the nighttime, near indistinguishable from the shadows of the forest but for her blue murkiness — like a demoness-shaped porthole into uncharted ocean depths.

We paused at the top of a hill, both of us breathing hard. It was hard to tell in the ever-dimming light, but Claw Hands seemed wholly unaffected by the climb.

"I haven't been this way in a bit," I said, bouncing my gaze away from her. I sucked in a deep breath and pushed off my penguin hood. The cool air drying the sweat on the back of my neck felt divine, and I suddenly didn't mind the costume's short skirt. "Guess it's an easier hike when you're a kid."

We sat down on a large rock to smoke again. The last thing I wanted was to have gone to all this trouble, only to discover that the high had worn off and Claw Hands had melted away somewhere behind us.

"How far past Avanic do you think we are?" Ryan asked, ripping open a Kit Kat.

Good idea—I opened my pillowcase and rooted around for a Milky Way. "Must be about… a quarter of a mile?" I didn't add what I was really thinking—that a quarter of a mile was just the roughest of guesses on my part. The past stretch had been such hard going that it was difficult to tell—and *that* was making me worry about being able to accurately plot the demoness's territory. Even if we did find a third point of the circle, we had to locate that area on the map, otherwise this whole exercise in subterfuge would be for naught.

Another worry was also slinking through the back of my mind: that somehow we'd gotten turned around despite trying to maintain a northward path. Trees in one direction looked much like trees in another.

I squared my shoulders and faced forward—at least, the direction I *thought* was forward. "We'd better keep going." My doubt I batted away to check on later, like kicking a ball under a bed where a monster may be leering in the shadows.

There's nothing like stumbling through the woods in the

dark on Halloween with a demonic stalker. The moon over-head was fat and luminous, but it did little to light our sur-roundings. In the gloom, the trees, naked from their autumn shedding, morphed into creeping, deformed figures, and the rustling of squirrels became the prowling of wolves.

Ryan and I maintained a mutual silence, some tacit un-derstanding that we were in an ill-advised situation on the very night when ghouls and spirits purportedly walk the earth. And it could have been paranoia from the weed, but the feeling felt deeper than that—almost primal, the same breed of fear that makes you take the basement stairs two at a time.

So we walked without talking, and every so often Ryan would turn to me, his eyebrows raised in an unspoken question, and I'd look back toward the demoness—still there, always still there—and nod to him.

It wasn't Ryan or I who broke the silence, but a growing rumble: cars speeding down a road. A few minutes later we crested a hill, and civilization spread out before us in the form of Carnarvon Avenue. The neon lights of the nail sa-lons, restaurants, and convenience stores had never looked so beautiful. Claw Hands was still with us—her territory must be far, far larger than I'd supposed—but that didn't matter so much right now. At least we were out of the woods.

I could tell Ryan felt my same elation, his relieved smile and Grim Reaper robes an ill-matched combination. To-gether we half-ran, half-fell down the hill, heading for the back of a CVS. Halfway down I realized we had an audience: one of the employees, a pudgy twenty-something girl out on a cigarette break, done up with face paint to look like a tiger. She watched us descend the hill with an astonished expression; apparently it wasn't a common occurrence for Grim Reapers and sexy penguins to erupt out of the forest and bolt towards her store.

She approached us cautiously as we reached the pavement and ground to a halt.

"Are you okay...?"

But I spun away from her, looking back up the hill. Ryan's eyes widened as I turned around, realizing what—who—I was searching for.

Claw Hands stood near the top of the hill, about forty feet away, her shadowed silhouette clear against the grass. She loped this way and that along an invisible line, but could clearly go no further, so she threw her arms back and roared— another one of those bellows that built to a banshee-like wail. I clapped my hands to my ears and leaned into Ryan.

"What is it? What's going on?" he asked, bewildered.

"She's not happy. She's screeching. It's... it's horrible."

"I'm so sorry." He hugged me tight. "But at least it'll be over soon, right? That's it—the third point."

The CVS girl cleared her throat. "Do you two need help? Because you're sort of not supposed to be back h—"

But my sudden gasp cut her off. "Oh my God." I drew away from Ryan, my mouth working up and down like a fish as I went back over it all in my mind. The point out by the drop-off, the one crossing Ferngrove, and now this one, far to the north of my house. I'd spent enough time looking at satellite maps in the last few weeks to pinpoint exactly what lay at the center of my three points.

"It's Avanic," I breathed.

Chapter 19

ALL MY VISIONS of finding the last point had always culmi-
nated in some wild third-act finale: the two of us lugging
shovels and my trusty baseball bat to the X marking the
spot, an entire string section poised to play a *Psycho*-style
melody as we dug down to find… what? A killer's concealed bunker? An unmarked mass grave? Yet my X had
been there all along in plain sight, and bats and shovels
couldn't do a damn thing about it.

"Can't be," Ryan said, falling back a step as he scrunched
up his face, visualizing the map. "No, no, we've missed
something. Right?"

But I shook my head. "I've looked at that map a million
times. It's Avanic, and… God, the explosion." Here I'd
been wondering why just *me*, why not Ryan, why not my
parents or my grandma, and the answer had been staring
me in the face.

"It's your fingers, isn't it?" he said. "Whatever you
touched—that chemical."

I shook my head, uncomprehending. It couldn't be… but

it *had* to be. "What do we do? I mean, they're a huge company. What can we even…?" I looked to Ryan, dazed, but I knew he had no answer for me.

The CVS girl/tiger had been looking at us through this whole exchange like we were high on something a lot stronger than weed. She took our stunned silence as an opportunity to butt in again. "Listen, you guys need to move along. My manager calls the cops on kids who loiter around back here."

Ryan nodded and glanced at his phone. "Oh shit, it's seven-thirty."

My inner doom deepened—no way were we taking the direct route home, back through the woods. That meant we needed to head towards Maple, which would circle us all the way back to Ferngrove. Just half an hour to cover what had to be two miles. Was that even possible?

Time to find out.

As we half-jogged, half-power walked back to my house I pored through my memory for everything I knew about Avanic. There had been the whole fiasco of the explosion when I was nine, obviously. I resisted the urge to beat myself about the head when I realized that was the same approximate time I'd suffered those nightmares. How had I not put this together earlier?

I winced as I caught sight of the Enville Inn's cheery sign on the other side of the street and more pieces fell into place. That was the hotel my family had stayed at for several weeks after the explosion—on Avanic's generous dime—

while the company swept the land around our house for dangerous chemicals. And that train of thought led me to the handsome payouts the company had made to so many Enville families in the wake of the explosion. Or perhaps better to say *payoffs*—enough money to keep the company in the townspeople's good favors. But of course Avanic would have been more than willing to take the necessary steps to keep whatever dark research they were conducting under wraps.

And what about that guy from Avanic who had visited us at the hotel to see how I was doing, bearing copious amounts of merch? I probably still had those stickers he'd given me stashed in my closet somewhere.

He'd been checking on me, trying to feel out if I was still a normal little kid or if I'd been affected.

Of course.

Of course.

But did their research necessarily have to be of the nefarious variety? For a moment I entertained the notion that Avanic wasn't knowingly up to no good. Maybe whatever chemical I'd touched was part of the manufacturing process for one of their medicines, coupled with a rare side effect. I could see the TV ad now: cheerful scenes of spry, silver-haired sixty-year-olds laughing, here strolling through a park, there pushing their grandkid on a swing. *Side effects may vary, including dizziness, nausea, and seeing dead people when you drink or get high.*

The ghosts, in the end, sealed Avanic's iniquity, for they

were proof that kids had died—at least five of them, if Uncle Ed's Forum was to be believed. Their spirits' territory radiated out from Avanic, and nothing about that looked innocent. And that was a whole other issue that I was only willing to look at from arm's length right now. If a research project at Avanic had ended in death, then what might happen if someone in the company realized I had some inkling of that?

As we turned onto Maple Street, another realization stole my breath. Hadn't Edgar Holt, too, mentioned some stray detail about Avanic? The kitchen renovation a few years before the death of his daughter… Hadn't he said construction was delayed because officials feared the digging might cause an electrical outage? I screwed up my eyes, trying to remember his exact wording.

Way I always heard it, their labs draw a fair bit of power.

What did Avanic need all that electricity for anyway? Whatever they were up to, I was starting to have serious doubts that it was just manufacturing medication to ease joint pain.

My lungs were burning and I'd developed a painful stitch in my side by the time we neared my house. Why did my street have to be so damn long? If only my parents hadn't wanted a house out in the middle of the woods, I wouldn't have inadvertently touched the rubble from the explosion, and then I wouldn't be in this predicament in the first place…

Two bright beams of light from behind us interrupted my

thoughts: car headlights.

"That'll be my brother," Ryan said, turning to me. "Chat online tomorrow?"

"Yeah, su—" My voice died as Ryan glanced behind us back toward the car. His face had gone slack.

What was I expecting? The bellow of one of Avanic's security guards, ordering us at gunpoint to get in the car?

The reality was hardly better. As I turned around, the headlights weren't brilliant enough that I couldn't recognize the car as my dad's SUV. It rolled to a halt fifteen feet from us. I could see my parents staring at us through the windshield. Sadness was painted all over my mom's face, but I couldn't read my dad's shuttered expression.

Then he rolled down his window and called out to us. Even from here I could sense the anger sparking under his calm words.

"Lanie, get in the house. I'll talk to you in your room, after I speak with Ryan."

I couldn't even remember the last time my dad had been mad at me—maybe that time in middle school my mom had gotten adventurous and tried her hand at making poutine. I'd secreted the french fries with cheese curds and gravy monstrosity to the bathroom in my napkin and flushed the whole mess. One expensive visit from the plumber later, my dad had sat me down for a scarring lecture about what was and was not supposed to go in the toilet.

Yet even then he'd been more annoyed than mad —not comparable to tonight, his anger an almost tangible, red-hot force that hit me as he soon as entered the room. This was a side of my dad wholly strange and terrible to me.

I sat huddled on the bed as he stood before me, regarding me silently as painful seconds ticked by.

At last he spoke. "I thought we'd be *celebrating* when we got back home, you know. We signed a one-year contract with Nico Emerson. Traffic was smooth, made record time, and then your mother and I find you…" He waved a hand at me, his jaw ticking. "You lied to us. Manipulated my mother—*your* grandmother. To hang out with a boy against both your mother's and my express wishes, a boy who I think we can all agree is a bad influence on you. And you smoked pot again—*God*, Lanie, you stink of it." He shook his head at me, and his gaze said it all; there wasn't just disappointment there, but a lack of trust. I'd become a problem to be handled and solved.

"I stuck up for you," he continued. "I believed in you. Told your mom not to worry so much. But even so, your mom's been talking about a boarding school down by the coast called St. Brigid's Preparatory School. I told her she was overreacting, that everyone makes mistakes. I'm a firm believer in that, so I vouched for you—and *this* is what you do?"

I bowed my head, curling even further in on myself. "I'm sorry, Dad."

"Sorry doesn't cut it anymore. I don't want to take you out of Enville High any more than you want that, but I need to see some serious changes from you. Actions, not just words."

I closed my eyes, allowing myself to live in the few seconds before I said my next sentence, like someone stuck in a flooding chamber taking one long, last breath of oxygen.

"Send me to St. Brigid's."

My dad didn't respond for a long time, so long that I wondered if I'd said anything at all. Finally he sighed and ran a hand through his hair. I could see his roiling anger cooling to a simmer.

"Lanie, what's going on with you? This isn't normal. Please, just talk to me. Something with the boy? Or math, or your other classes? Or your mom? What is it?"

But all I could do was shake my head and close my eyes to hide my rising tears. I couldn't stomach living in my house for the rest of high school, knowing I might see the dead any time I got sick or went to sleep. I was one girl against a shadowy pharmaceutical company. There would be no happy ending to my personal horror movie, so best to walk out of the theater.

"Dad, I want to go to St. Brigid's. Please. Mom's right."

He looked out the window, his spine sagging, his expression unreadable once more.

"I need to talk with your mother," he said at last, voice soft, and he left the room, shutting the door with a quiet click.

Only then did I let my tears fall fast but silent down my cheeks.

Chapter 20

I LET RYAN know the next day, after my parents had discussed whatever they needed to discuss and the final decision to enroll me at St. Brigid's had been made. I was at the kitchen table with my laptop doing homework, doing my best to pretend I was invisible as I waited for my mom to let down her guard. She kept glancing up at me as she prepped dinner, making sure I was writing my history essay and not sneaking messages to Ryan—but composing a note to Ryan looked much like writing the essay, and that was what I'd been doing for the past half hour, laboring over the words, rewriting, deleting, and starting again.

I'm really sorry about everything, ~~and I wish I'd never dragged you into this~~ though I'm happy you were there with me through it. I hope my dad didn't yell at you too much. I promise my parents are nice people. Maybe if things had turned out differently you could have seen that side of them. ~~I think they would have liked you too. I wish I could have been a normal girl who becomes your~~

~~normal girlfriend and we could have done normal dating~~
~~things together like go to the movies and homecoming.~~

~~My parents have decided to enroll me~~ I asked my parents if I can transfer to a boarding school called St. Brigid's, and they're going to call and find out if that's possible tomorrow. I feel ~~happy sad~~ sort of relieved about it. I don't know, I'm a mess right now. I can't wait until college to leave this house, and I'm ~~fucking terrified~~ scared of Avanic. ~~And honestly if I stay I'm probably going to do something else that will disappoint my parents, and then I don't even know what.~~ So hopefully I can transfer to St. Brigid's and get away from Claw Hands and Avanic and everything.

I think you should try to forget that any of this happened. Again, I'm really sorry. <3

I watched my mom sweep the vegetables for the stir-fry into the wok and braced myself as plumes of smoke shot up from the pan. Seconds later, right on cue, our smoke alarm began to blare. My mom let out a curse as she hurried away for a stool so she could reach the alarm. I quickly opened up a chat with Ryan and copied and pasted him the letter.

It took no more than twenty seconds for my computer to ping with a response. I hastily muted the volume.

Wow, I didn't expect that. Okay. :(Can we at least text when you're at boarding school? Your mom will let you have your phone when you're there, right?

I drummed my fingers on the keyboard, watching the

chat cursor blink as my mom silenced the alarm at last. I knew how I wanted to—*needed* to—respond, even though it felt wrong. Sneaking another glance under my lashes into the kitchen, I saw my mom was turned away from me, busy with dinner once more. No time for second-guessing; I typed the words in, something within me tightening as I hit send.

Yeah, but I think I need a clean start. Just for a little while. I'll text you when I'm ready.

He sent me back another sad face, then dropped a file into the message box. The image loaded a second later, and I quickly saved it to my computer before closing the chat window, this time for good.

It was the selfie we'd taken yesterday in our costumes. Ryan was looking his handsome self, one of his brown curls escaping his hood in a decidedly un-Grim Reaper-like fashion. As for me? The penguin beak and googly-eyed hood looked much cuter than I'd anticipated. My face itself was blurred, caught in the middle of the laugh that Ryan had so painstakingly dragged out of me.

He'd been right, I realized. *However tonight turns out, let's start it off good.* I'd been envious of my pre-fever self this past month, but more now than ever my heart blazed with jealousy for the ignorance I'd had and squandered just yesterday.

If leaving would let me pretend to be that girl again, then fine, off to St. Brigid's, because I couldn't fathom staying here, scared and helpless, clutching my worthless knowledge to my chest—knowledge hard-earned by spitting on my parents' trust.

Things happened fast over the next few weeks. Private schools, especially ones like St. Brigid's where the yearly tuition totaled more than sixty thousand dollars, can be quite willing to accommodate mid-semester transfers of troubled students, especially when said student's parents are paying full sticker price. A whirlwind of paperwork and admissions interviews and placement tests descended on our household, and I hunkered down, numb, in the center of the storm.

The horror books and movies that had once been my refuge now held no allure, like how a once-favorite food becomes suddenly repulsive if it makes you sick. Homework, to my surprise, took their place. If I were struggling through *Hamlet* for English or wrestling with the subjunctive for Spanish, it meant I couldn't think about anything else.

And at last the email arrived, sent to my parents but addressed to me.

> Dear Melanie Adams,
> On behalf of the admissions team at St. Brigid's Preparatory School, I am happy to congratulate you on your acceptance into our school! During the admissions process, we were very impressed with both your intelligence as well as your enthusiastic interview, and we are confident that you will make a great addition to our community. St. Brigid's provides a safe and nurturing environment for our students to learn and

grow. As discussed previously with both yourself and your parents in our meeting on November 5th, this is a conditional acceptance dependent upon your participation in mandatory counseling with one of our trained therapists on a biweekly basis.

Due to this being a mid-semester transfer, we ask that you fill out and return the attached forms as soon as possible so that we can swiftly facilitate your enrollment. I have also attached our school handbook and your class schedule.

Your move-in date is scheduled for this coming Wednesday, November 17th. Please be at the Admissions Office with your parents at 9:00 AM on that day to complete the admissions process. Should you have any questions, feel free to contact me; no question is too small!

Congratulations on commencing a new stage in your education. We happily welcome you to St. Brigid's!

Kind regards,
Jada Harris, Director of Admissions

Right now I was only nominally a St. Brigid's student, but I was still one step closer to joining the ranks of those girls from the website. Would I fit in? Would sitting in the same classes as them in my newly purchased, dress code-appropriate clothing be enough? Or would I stick out like a drop of oil in a cup of water, present but entirely different?

Well, I'd see soon enough—and besides, none of that really mattered anyway. What *did* matter was that I was out of Enville next week.

The seventeenth couldn't come soon enough.

Jada Harris was a commandingly tall woman with the biggest smile I'd ever seen. That smile, I thought as she strode towards my parents and me in the Admissions Office lobby, was brilliant enough to use as a solar energy source. For a woman who ran all of Admissions, this meeting had to be the barest blip on her schedule, but I couldn't help but feel that she actually cared. St. Brigid's was off to a good start.

"Lanie! Welcome to St. Brigid's. We are so glad you're joining our community."

"And thanks to St. Brigid's for being so accommodating and understanding!" my mom cut in. I suppressed a grimace at how over-the-top happy she sounded. My dad, on the other hand, hadn't cracked one smile yet today, his uncharacteristic quietness a statement all its own.

As for me? I was living so minute-to-minute that I couldn't separate out my feelings; introspection could wait for later. The important thing right now was to concentrate on not making an embarrassment of myself at my new school.

"Of course, of course," Mrs. Harris said. "Was it an easy ride down?"

"Couldn't ask for better!" my mom replied. "No traffic at all."

"Wonderful. Well," Mrs. Harris said, gesturing down the hall, "if you want to just step into my office then we can — oh, perfect, right on schedule!" Her eyes had flicked behind me. I turned around and saw an Asian girl with delicate features coming through the glass front doors of the Admissions Office. Her glossy black hair was swept up into a side ponytail, her outfit a flawless combination of preppy and casual that could have passed for a pet project by a J. Crew designer. The girl saw me talking with Mrs. Harris and came towards us, giving me a small, tentative smile.

"This is Naomi Guo," said Mrs. Harris. "She'll be Lanie's roommate."

"Hi," Naomi said to me. Her voice was high and singsong. "I'm excited to finally meet you. I've been living alone this semester, and that's been nice enough, but I'm really happy to be getting a roommate, honestly." Her attention flipped back to Mrs. Harris. "Should I take her over to Pendry?"

"That would be great," she replied. "Lanie, Naomi's going to show you over to your dormitory, Pendry House, while your parents and I finalize paperwork over here. Your parents can meet you over there in twenty minutes or so to help you get settled in."

I followed Naomi out of Admissions, my head spinning. Everything was so much more real now that I had a roommate and a new place to call home — Pendry. And the reality settling over me wasn't grounding, but freeing. As Naomi led me towards the dormitory, everywhere I looked could have been a movie set — architecture more reminiscent of a castle than a school; a fitness center big enough to satisfy an Olympic athlete; a rose garden, diminished now in late autumn, that would surely burst into bloom come springtime. Even the sunlight here seemed brighter, the sky more blue, the crisp, salt-tinged air energy-giving.

And this was a place with no ghosts—or maybe only the campus-legend variety used to spook freshmen. I felt light as a dandelion seed, liable to get caught on a breeze and float away toward the clouds.

"So here's Pendry House," Naomi said as we rounded a bend and a building of light brick and climbing ivy came into view. A second-floor balcony with a wrought iron balustrade overlooked the flagstone courtyard; I imagined a queen stepping forth from the room within to make some pronouncement to her adoring subjects.

"It's gorgeous," I said as Naomi pulled open one of the double doors and beckoned for me to follow her.

"Yeah," she said, eyes sparkling. "Actually, in the summer sometimes people get married in the courtyard outside. Isn't that romantic?"

Pendry's interior was just as elegant, with an open, echoey foyer, antique-looking wall sconces, and a wide staircase leading up to the second floor. Our footsteps were the only sound in the building; all the students were probably in class. I trailed Naomi upstairs, craning my neck this way and that to take it all in.

"And here we are!" she trilled, coming to an abrupt halt in front of Room 205. She dug a key from her pocket, then looked to me. "Oh, you'll need one of these, huh? I guess when you meet Felicity she'll give you a key."

"Who's that?"

"Our dorm mom." She crooked a finger down the hall. "She's in the room at the end on the right. And she's also a counselor. Basically, she's the best. You'll meet her later today, I'm sure." Saying this, she slipped the key in the lock and ushered me into Room 205.

The room was airy, with a high ceiling, drawers built into one wall for storage, and two bunked beds. Most college students didn't have it so good.

"That'll be your alarm clock," Naomi said with a laugh, pointing towards the window. Bright sunlight streamed through the panes, lighting the room. "This side of Pendry faces east, so we don't get nice sunsets, unfortunately." If a lack of sunsets were her only complaint, then I didn't have much to worry about.

"It's… really nice," I said lamely, walking to the center of the room and taking a slow spin around. *Really nice* was an insult to a room this beautiful. Naomi had decorated in tasteful, matching shades, from the cream bed comforter to the thick, apricot shag carpet on the floor, and she'd filled a good portion of the walls with posters, most of them the inspirational quote variety.

Be a voice, not an echo.

Draw near to God and He will draw near to you. James 4:8

When it rains, look for rainbows. When it's dark, look for stars.

It was like I'd taken a tumble down a rabbit hole and

landed in a Pinterest wonderland. The room even smelled good, maybe some lingering trace of floral perfume.

"So," she said, pulling a chair over to the bed for me, then taking a seat on the bottom bunk. "Welcome to St. Brigid's! What do you think so far?"

"I… I love it." How could I not? "It's so different from my school back home." *Duh.* I could have facepalmed, but Naomi was nodding at me with rapt attention. *Elaborate,* I told myself firmly. *Be friendly. Your parents and Ryan won't be here with you, so you need somebody.* "Umm, the school I transferred from is a public school in Enville. Co-ed, so girls-only will take some getting used to. And there were, like, nine hundred kids in my grade alone." Total enrollment at St. Brigid's was less than four hundred students.

"That *is* really different," Naomi said. "I've been at St. Brigid's since my freshman year, so I can't really relate. But a lot of girls here do transfer from public schools. I can introduce you to some if you want. They might be able to give you some good advice, help you make the transition, you know?"

"S-sure. Thanks."

Naomi shifted on the bed, the comforter crinkling beneath her. "Okay, so you totally don't have to answer this question. The answer's personal, I'm sure."

"Okay…" I thought I saw where this was heading. "Is it why I transferred?"

Naomi pressed her hands to her cheeks, which had bloomed a lovely pink. "I'm sorry! You don't need to say why!"

"No, it's all right. The reason is that… I was being haunted by some ghosts in my house, and I couldn't take living there anymore." I almost burst out laughing when Naomi's eyes went wide, her mouth forming a round O. "Kidding, kidding! I started dating this boy that was basically my parents' worst nightmare. And I was skipping classes and not doing my homework so I could have more time to hang out with him, stuff like that. Plus we smoked weed together sometimes, and my parents found out about that, which was pretty bad. So… here I am." I hadn't meant to divulge so much, but somehow as I faced this girl who I couldn't help but like, the words longed to spill out of me, like I was in confessional. Maybe being at a Catholic school was rubbing off on me already.

"Oh my," she said. "Do you miss him?" Her voice was soft, almost tender. Coming from anyone else I would have bristled at the tone, but Naomi seemed as sincere as they come, more perfect paper doll come to life than real human being.

My gaze dropped away. Ryan was pretty much all I'd thought about on the drive down. Had it been right to ask for a break? And when I did text him again, would it be the same as ever, without ghost hunting to be the glue sticking us together?

"Yeah. Yeah, I do. But it's not like I don't want to be here. I sort of feel like…" I frowned down at my hands. Sometime during the course of this conversation I'd clasped them together tight in my lap, my knuckles white. "I miss him, but that's okay. I know in my head that being here's a good thing, but the rest of me hasn't caught up yet. That makes no sense, I know."

"No, it does," Naomi said. "It's really good you feel that way. Change starts with just one spark."

I jerked my head toward the wall. "Sounds like one of your posters."

"It should be!" she said sunnily. "But actually it's just something Felicity always says. I think you'll really like her."

A knock at the door broke the sharing-with-strangers mood, like kicking a pebble into a still puddle of water. I could hear my parents' muffled voices out in the hall. Naomi darted off the bed and opened the door.

My parents came in and goggled at the room just as I had a few minutes ago. "Sorry I'll messy it up with moving boxes," I said to Naomi, but she put up her hands.

"I don't mind a little mess. After all, that makes getting things back to clean more meaningful, right?" My mom nodded along to that, clearly impressed, as my dad, standing behind Naomi, shot me a look — something along the lines of *Is this crap a girl thing?* mixed with *You can still back out of this.*

I gave him the tiniest shake of my head. *I want this. Please, just let me be here.* He nodded back, then spoke, his voice some approximation of a cheery tone. "Well, should we move you in?"

My parents had grabbed a parking spot at the back of Pendry; between the four of us (Naomi graciously helped out) Room 205 was cluttered with cardboard boxes in short order.

Then came the moment the day had been ticking down

to. Naomi left the room in a lissome glide that I hardly registered — until it was just the three of us in the room, standing in a semicircle together on the shag carpet as we all gazed out the window over St. Brigid's stunning campus grounds.

"We love you so much, honey," my mom started.

"And I'm happy — we're *both* happy — you're here, as long as it's what you really want," my dad added.

"It is," I said, and I hoped at least a fraction of Naomi-like sincerity seeped through those two teeny words. Enough for them not to worry. Enough for them to know how much I needed this.

"Be good," my mom said to me, and I flashed back to the last time she had said those words to me, when I had lied to her face.

"I will." This time I meant it wholeheartedly, and when she brought me into a hug I squeezed her tight. She felt thin, her shoulder bones poking into my arms. Had she lost weight, the product of me causing her stress this past month and a half? Or had she always been this small, the pillar of her staunch mom-ness keeping me from noticing?

My dad wrapped me up in a big bear hug next. "Make sure to call," he grumbled in my ear.

"Of course, Dad."

With promises and goodbyes shimmering unseen in the air between us, I could feel the moment coming to a close, like how you can hear a chord's resolution before it happens. The conductor might keep his baton raised, stretching the last note for drama or beauty, but there's always some rich, quivering point where any more delay will break the magic.

So I told my parents goodbye and to have a safe trip home, acting the part of the conductor myself, though the words felt awkward and unwieldy in my mouth. Quicker than I could have believed the door closed behind them — just me in the room now, our strange song and dance concluded. No audience claps, no bouquets flung onstage or cries for an encore.

Just a humming silence.

Chapter 21

I LET A few minutes lapse, standing in front of the window looking out across the campus. From there I could spy the front gatehouse that checked all visitors to the school in and out, and I kept my eyes fixed on its forest-green roof, waiting until I saw my parents' car pull past the gatehouse and around the bend.

Gone at last. My skin prickled. An end and a beginning, a new place to harbor me for the next year and a half until graduation. I'd have to do something about breaks and the summer vacation—either bear a few weeks back at home or let school trips or an internship be my excuse to not go back—but I could worry about that later. What mattered was that I'd made it here unscathed, no one the wiser of my discoveries save for Ryan. Hopefully he would drop the Avanic stuff, like I'd asked him to.

I heard a knock on the door, quiet enough that I could almost have imagined it. It was so strange, I thought as I went to the door, for someone to be knocking, presumably looking for me, when I'd only been able to rightfully call

Room 205 home for less than an hour. Stranger still for the person on the other side of the door to be my new roommate, knocking on her own door.

"How are you doing?" Naomi asked, her brow creased. I could see her searching my face for watery eyes or red, puffy skin. No doubt she had a full box of the world's most velvety tissues stashed away for the occasional crying jag.

"I'm okay, actually. At least right now."

"Do you mind if I come in, then?"

"Yeah, sure," I said, falling back from the door. "I mean, it's your room."

"*Our* room," she said, waggling a finger at me as she slipped inside. "I don't want you to feel like you're intruding." She picked her backpack up off her bed and unzipped it, checking the books and notebooks inside, then looked back up at me. "You're really feeling all right? You're sure?"

"Yeah, I'm fine."

"Then we should head out. Mrs. Harris asked me to bring you to class as long as you were feeling up to it." She glanced at her phone, checking the time. "That should be Spanish 3 Honors with Señora Delacruz. It starts in about ten minutes. I'm in the same class."

My throat tightened. "I bought the book, but it's packed up somewhere…" I nudged the closest cardboard box with my foot.

"I guarantee she won't care on the first day," Naomi said. "You can look on with me if we need the textbook, but probably we won't. Mostly it's a discussion class. I hope you're ready to give a self-introduction in Spanish!"

Uh oh. I always did pretty well in Spanish class, aided by all the time I'd spent over the years chatting with Josefa, but I still didn't relish making my grand entrance *en Español.*

Nevertheless, ten minutes later I found myself standing at the front of a classroom, cheeks hot as I plowed through a shaky introduction. Yet even when I messed up a verb tense and shot the teacher a sheepish glance, she just gave me a nod and an encouraging smile. The girls in class, too, all seemed friendly; we spent the class doing our best to analyze some song lyrics. Before I knew it, Señora Delacruz was calling out the homework as we packed up to leave.

I swiftly got my intro speech down pat. *Hi, I'm Lanie Adams, and I'm in form five.* (Private school lingo for eleventh grade.) *I'm from Enville, about an hour north of here. I'm really happy to be at St. Brigid's, but I was going to a big co-ed public school before, so it's going to be a big adjustment.* I even had my random token facts ready, for those teachers who thought such commonalities as favorite ice cream flavors or TV shows could help forge friendships. (Salted caramel pretzel and *The Twilight Zone,* by the way.)

The last class of the day, theology, was the one I'd most worried about; I hadn't the slightest hope of pretending to have any solid background knowledge about Catholicism. Yet the class turned out to be more along the lines of a philosophy class. The teacher, an older man with a wealth of wrinkles, lectured at us for a while about Plato's Allegory of the Cave before making us respond to a prompt.

As we funneled toward the door at the end of class, I heard a woman's voice call my name.

"Lanie!" There was Mrs. Harris from Admissions, standing right outside the classroom, presumably waiting for me. Another woman stood by her side; she looked to be in her mid-thirties, with olive skin, a cloud of chestnut corkscrew curls, and startlingly green eyes. She was dressed in a style that could best be described as "professional hippie" — a floral tunic in rich earth tones over loose cotton slacks and mixed metal bangles on her wrists.

"How was your first day?" Mrs. Harris asked.

What was she expecting me to say? *This school hardly feels like reality it's so nice?* "Great. Everyone's been really friendly. And lunch was good, too." This was true; I had feasted on a buffalo chicken wrap, baked acorn squash, and a lemon bar as Naomi and a few of her friends chattered away beside me. St. Brigid's even got cafeteria food right.

"I'm so glad," Mrs. Harris said, treating me to another one of those blinding smiles. She gestured to the woman at her side. "Allow me to introduce Felicity. She's Pendry's dorm mom, and she's also one of our school therapists."

Felicity's eyes crinkled as she gave me a little wave. "If you're up for it," she said, "I thought it might be nice for us to sit down for a chat." Her voice was warm and resonant; just listening to it felt like slipping into a warm bubble bath.

A silent beat passed before I realized she was waiting for my answer. I had mandatory counseling twice per week — but it seemed I at least had a say on whether that should commence today or later.

Well, what was the harm? "Okay," I said, and her green eyes twinkled.

"Fantastic."

"I'll leave you to it, then," Mrs. Harris said. "I'm sure I'll see you around soon, Lanie."

"So," Felicity said when it was just the two of us, "how are you at getting around campus? Can you get us back to Pendry Dorm?"

"Uh, sure." I didn't have St. Brigid's campus memorized yet, but I was close. I took off down the sidewalk, Felicity following my lead. A turn here and a straight shot there and soon we came around the bend to the welcome sight of Pendry's rosy brick and ivy.

"Nicely done," Felicity said. Inside she took the lead, climbing the steps to the second floor and bringing me to the very end of the hall. The dorm, so still a few hours before, had roused itself from slumber. I heard eager conversation, punctuated by bursts of laughter. From somewhere down the hall came the faint strains of a guitar.

Felicity's door was papered with motivational quotes and countless photos of St. Brigid's students: girls frowning in concentration as they bent heads over chem lab workstations, posing for group photos at Niagara Falls and the Great Wall, mid-yell as they dove for a volleyball. The key clicked in the lock, and Felicity opened the door to reveal a cozy apartment made charming with area rugs and yet more photos tacked to the walls.

"Welcome to my home!" she said, leading me to a little room past the kitchen, just big enough for two facing armchairs, a cluttered side table, and a crammed bookshelf. Felicity sank into one of the armchairs and motioned for me to sit in the other. "All right, first question, and this is very important: bergamot, angelica, jasmine, ginger, or citronella?"

What was this—botany class? "Uhh… ginger?"

"You got it." She grabbed a small blue glass bottle from the side table, twisted it open, and dripped a few drops of golden oil into a diffuser. Seconds later, spicy warmth enveloped the room.

"Smells good," I said, offering her a weak smile. All this—the tiny room, the armchairs, the essential oils— wasn't an accident. Every element here had been picked, all playing a role in getting students comfortable and ready to open up. It didn't feel crafty, exactly—but I couldn't forget that I'd met this woman not fifteen minutes ago.

Yet it seemed Felicity knew that, too. "So," she started, "we've just met, which means introductions are in order. You're probably sick of introducing yourself at this point, so I'll go first. I'm Felicity Ortega—Miss Ortega if that makes you comfortable, but most kids call me Felicity. This is my tenth year at St. Brigid's, and I can't predict the future, but I don't see myself ever leaving. It's a wonderful school, and I'm proud to help students here achieve a healthy headspace. Last things last, I feel like you always need some sort of random factoid in these introductions. I bet you've been telling people your favorite ice cream flavor all day."

I couldn't help a smile, this one genuine.

"Yeah, I thought so," she said. "I'll give you two. St. Brigid's has allowed me to become a bit of a world traveler, because I volunteer all the time to chaperone on school trips. We've gone to China, France, Spain, Paraguay, Vietnam… And I'm sure I'm forgetting a few places. Second thing…" She tapped a finger on her lips, thinking. "Yeah, I'll be boring. I like vanilla ice cream—no toppings necessary, nothing fancy, just plain vanilla. So that's me, in the tiniest of nutshells."

She leaned forward, her armchair creaking slightly. My turn now.

"O-okay. I'm Lanie Adams. I'm a junior. My last school was a big public school in Enville. My two facts…" I groped for something I hadn't said today already. "My family has a golden retriever called Mustard. He's a bit of a dope, but really cute. And my second fact…" I made a split-second decision—no joking around this time like I had with Naomi. "The second fact is that I believe in ghosts."

"Really!" Felicity said, sitting up straight. "That's one I haven't heard before. I have to say, I remain to be convinced on the ghost front. Any personal stories?"

"No, i-it's just what I believe."

"Well," she said, proffering her hand to me, "it's nice to meet you, Lanie."

I took her hand, and we shook. Her palm was cool, her grip firm. "Nice to meet you."

"All right," she said. "I'm going to give you the same

spiel I give every student. And I say spiel, but it's important, truly. In our sessions, I aim to be someone you can trust to give you professional and caring advice. I'm a firm believer in student privacy and dignity, and everything said between us remains confidential, with three important caveats." She held up three fingers. "One, if you indicate abuse. Two, if you indicate potential for harm to yourself or others. Three, if I deem it necessary to speak with other professionals to support you. Everything else remains between you and me. Is that clear?"

I nodded.

"Great. Mrs. Harris told me we're going to be meeting twice a week. I took a peek at your schedule, and it looks like Tuesdays and Fridays at two-thirty will be good for you. As for our chat today, I'm okay calling it here. I'm sure you're exhausted from your first day. How's all that sound?"

"It sounds good," I said, and I wasn't lying. I was still leery about opening my inner thoughts to someone else—almost two months of constant secret-keeping will do that to you—but Felicity's attempts to win me over were working. And if therapy was a prerequisite to remain at the paradise that was this school, I might as well try to get something out of it.

"Perfect. Our goal for this Friday's session will be to debrief on your first few days here. Initial impressions of the school and your classmates, worries, goal setting—any of that works. And looking ahead to next week we'll start discussing why you transferred to St. Brigid's. Sound like a plan?"

"Yeah, okay. Thanks."

"It's my pleasure." She rose from the armchair with a cat-like stretch and led me back to the apartment front door. I was almost sad to leave the snug armchair nook behind. Not quite—but almost. This part of my new life was too unfamiliar for me to say for certain that I liked it… but I could see the misty potential there, waiting to crystallize.

Back at the door I remembered something. "Felicity?" It was so strange to call an adult by their first name, but "Miss Ortega" felt far too rigid for whatever this was to be between us.

"What's that?"

"Naomi said you could give me my room key…?"

She smacked her forehead, then fished a brass key from her pocket. "That's right, that's right. Some dorm mom I am, huh? I did forget to mention that bit. If you need help with anything—getting locked out, dispute with your roommate, things like that—I'm always here, right down the hall."

"Thanks."

"Of course. And Lanie, I know you'll have heard this a million times today already… But welcome to St. Brigid's."

Chapter 22

FIRST DAYS BECAME first weeks, and Naomi and I came to know each other not quite as friends yet, but as something inching towards that. Room 205 became *our* room, just as she'd declared it would, pictures of Mustard and my family interspersed with my roommate's own. I'd thought about printing out the selfie Ryan and I had taken on Halloween, but decided against it. It might invite questions that I'd rather not answer, and I didn't want a visual reminder of the stress of October.

I did think about texting Ryan. First in a *don't do that* kind of way, next in a *yeah I should, but maybe tomorrow* kind of way, then in a *why haven't I texted him and I've been here for weeks and it's too late now* kind of way. What would we even talk about, now that he was in his world and I in mine, with sixty miles of highway stretched between us?

Then one day it finally felt right, like some invisible door in my mind that I hadn't even known existed had just swung open. I didn't spend much time laboring over writing the perfect text; I just hoped he'd respond at all.

Hey. How have you been?

I eyed my phone for thirty seconds, waiting for a response. When none came, I pulled out my English homework with a sigh. My teacher had thought it would be fun to do a quick study on Dickens's *A Christmas Carol*—and I'd just reached the part with the Ghost of Christmas Past.

I jumped when my phone buzzed.

Good. Where have you been?

A minimal reply—and he knew I was at St. Brigid's, of course, which meant his real meaning was, *How come it took you so long?*

I'm sorry. I meant to text you earlier. I just… didn't, even though I missed you. That's my bad. It's really nice here. My roommate's so perfect it hurts, like Barbie-level perfect. I have to do therapy here, but that's been ok too.

It took another long while before he responded. I felt a heavy aching in my chest as the minutes stretched on, and I realized I'd been reading the same lines over and over again: *"Spirit!" said Scrooge, "show me no more! Conduct me home. Why do you delight to torture me?"*

My phone vibrated again.

So he forgave me—or at least he said he did. It was a first step. Suddenly it felt like it wouldn't be quite so bad to print out the Halloween selfie.

As I skimmed *A Christmas Carol*, we continued to chat back and forth about St. Brigid's, Naomi, Felicity, my teachers. Through silent agreement, we let the dangerous topics lie—Melissa, Claw Hands, Avanic. At five Naomi came back from basketball practice; this was when we always went to dinner. I told Ryan I'd text him tomorrow.

I wished I could hear his voice behind the word. Was that a happy "okay?" Was it encouraging? Indifferent? Maybe next time he'd be up for an actual phone call.

I settled into my now-familiar armchair and watched as Felicity riffled through her blue bottles, like a sorceress rummaging through her ingredient cabinet for eye of newt. Our six or so therapy sessions thus far hadn't just been an exercise in learning about mindfulness, but also given me strong opinions about essential oil aromas. Forming any sort of clear thoughts two sessions ago had been near-impossible with the screeching stink of angelica torturing my nostrils.

"So how're things?" she began, finally finding the right bottle. A dropperful of oil later and the room filled with the thick, heady smell of jasmine.

I drew in a deep inhale, shaking off the stress of the day. "Pretty good. I got my math quiz back today—B plus."

"That's great! How'd the history essay go, do you think?"

"I'm not sure. Miss Brown said she'd get them back to us before Christmas break."

"Ah, Christmas break." Felicity underlined something on her notepad. "That's something I wanted to touch on today."

"Because I volunteered to help out buildings and grounds over the break?" I tugged on a damp, frizzing lock of hair; we were doing swimming in PE.

"Ding, ding, ding. Call it simple curiosity. Most students, let alone new students, are raring to get home. This campus is going to be a ghost town come next Friday afternoon. You know that, right?"

I pressed my lips together. If only she knew how much of a ghost town Enville itself was. "I get that. But I'm still going to be spending Christmas with my parents. I have train tickets to head back on the twenty-fourth. It's just that my hometown can be kind of boring, and I thought it would look good for colleges to do some volunteering."

"Which is great," Felicity said. "You're right—that does look good to colleges. I'm just bringing up the possibility that you might also be avoiding something. Tell me if I'm way off-base! But that's something I did wonder when I heard you planned to spend the break here."

I swallowed. You couldn't say she didn't have good instincts.

"I... Uhh... There's someone in town I don't want to run into."

"Ryan?"

I focused on the space between her eyes, hoping she wouldn't spot my lie. "Yeah."

She blew out a breath. "All right. I am not going to try to dissuade you from this volunteer work. But I do want to spend today discussing proactive strategies for handling stressful situations. We talked before about how you've used marijuana and alcohol to de-stress. I've never met Ryan, and from what you've said about him he sounds like a nice kid overall, but he definitely hasn't helped with those temptations. Is that an accurate assessment?"

This part required no falsehoods. "Yes... But I *really* don't feel any need to smoke or drink, I promise. I just... don't want to go back. I-I love it here. And I'm a total introvert—I won't mind there hardly being anyone around."

Her green eyes glittered. "And didn't I tell you I'm not trying to convince you to do anything otherwise? Goodness gracious, most of the time it's *me* trying to convince kids to volunteer, not the other way around! So don't worry on that front. Okay?"

"Okay."

"Let's start this way: can you list some stressors for me?

Anything that makes you anxious, worried, fears that hang around in the back of your mind."

I ticked them off on my fingers. "Uh, running into Ryan over the break. Math—though that's gotten way better. Disappointing my parents." *Melissa. Claw Hands. Two-faced pharmaceutical companies.*

"Great," she said. "All I'm saying is wouldn't it be nice to look at those stressors from a proactive angle? Sometimes we get so bogged down in worry that we forget the world isn't just happening to us. We can happen to the world, so to speak." She chuckled. "Hmm, that sounds a little dastardly, but I'm sure you catch my drift."

And I felt a sudden sliding sensation in my gut, time around me slowing to a crawl as my thoughts began to race.

Felicity, watching me closely, cracked a smile. "Light bulb moment?"

Less like a light bulb and more like a thousand-watt spotlight, with me blinded and cringing in the center. I nodded my head, dazed, and spent the rest of the session doing my best to seem with it. Afterwards I went straight back to my room and lay in bed, staring up at the ceiling.

How much energy had I devoted to puzzling out the ghosts' rules and boundaries? Enough to figure out it took an altered mental state to see them. Enough to find the third point and land myself in a boarding school.

Always I had thought about what *they* could do—what rules governed *them*. Yet if my ghosts and demoness had paranormal laws that held true for them—were there different laws that governed me?

And as I stared at the ceiling, wondering, another idea smacked me with a sudden, pummeling force. In the butterfly dream, hadn't Melissa talked to me like a regular, living being, rather than the watery, strained screaming I'd heard from her and Claw Hands?

Lanie, can you hear me? she'd whispered.

I hadn't made much of the fact that I'd felt glimmers of Melissa hanging around in that dream.

What can I do? I thought to myself.

They talk normally in dreams…

I hardly breathed as those two thoughts prowled around each other, scenting each other, sometimes slinking closer with cautious steps, sometimes pulling away with a snarl. At last they twined together, and I let out a soft exhale, then sat up and went to get my computer.

It was time to pay another visit to Uncle Ed's Forum of the Weird, Secret, and Inexplicable.

The Beyond the Veil sub-forum, dedicated to out-of-body and psychedelic experiences, had never really caught my attention. When I hadn't been combing through D_plexippus's post about Melissa or the other post about the suspected Connecticut serial killer, I'd spent the rest of my time laughing at the nutjobs who believed in shape-shifting lizards.

But now Beyond the Veil had my full attention, since I had a new goal in mind: learning how to lucid dream. If I could become aware in my dreams, could do as I pleased in them with a conscious mind, perhaps I stood a chance of having an actual conversation with Melissa—and of figuring out how to get her and Claw Hands and the rest to leave me alone for good.

And even if my plan didn't work, well, what was the harm in trying? At the end of it at least I'd still be able to fly and visit alien realms and have wild dream sex with smirking, horny vampires.

The lucid dreaming sticky post at the top of the forum was a sprawling block of text, peppered with users' personal anecdotes. I'd clicked into the forum with a good-sized dose of wincing skepticism, but nobody was calling bullshit. Everyone was swapping tips, and most people said it only took them a few nights to achieve lucidity.

According to the thread, there wasn't one perfect method to do this. Techniques were hit-or-miss, and everybody said it took them a few tries to develop their own personalized induction routine. But the overarching themes were to keep a dream journal, set an alarm to interrupt REM sleep, and use a familiar mantra to wake yourself up in the dream.

Shushing the protesting of my internal sleepyhead, I set my alarm for five AM, six hours after I aimed to fall asleep, and laid a notebook and pen at the ready by my pillow to serve as my dream journal. As I got into bed that night, I felt giddy, almost nauseous.

Breathe, I told myself, drawing on Felicity's constant advice about meditation and mindfulness. *Relax. It's literally just dreaming—nothing more.* In any case, there wasn't any rush to try to contact Melissa the first time I achieved lucidity. I could spend the first few nights riding a dragon or visiting Mars—or being courted by an insatiable vampire. Then I'd decide whether or not to dip my toes back into the mystery of Melissa White's disappearance.

Breathe. In and out. In. And. Out. At last my heartbeat slowed, and sleep, soft and creeping, caught me and spirited me away.

I jolted awake as soon as the five AM alarm sounded. I'd set my phone to just a hair above silent, but it felt like I'd been waiting for it to go off for hours. The room was dark, not a hint of dawn outside, and the only other sound in the room was Naomi's soft, even breaths as she slumbered in the bed below me.

Okay, no time to waste. I could feel my dreams trying to flee my mind, like water cupped in someone's hands finding the inevitable gaps. I let out a moan as I grabbed the pen and notebook and switched on my phone's flashlight.

I remember walking over a dusty plain towards a silver lake. The ground is all cracked, like dried mud. I look down and see an orange glow between the cracks. I run towards the lake, but end up in Felicity's apartment instead. But she has way more aromatherapy bottles than normal, like a thousand bottles, and they're all stacked on top of each other on that little table. I'm looking for the bottle of jasmine, but it's at the bottom of the pile. If I pull it out I know the whole pile will topple down like Jenga. But I grab the bottle and start tugging it a little bit this way and that, and just as I'm about to pull it out someone comes in the room and says something and I don't remember anymore and then I woke up.

I threw down the pen and lowered my head back to the pillow with a sigh. One last step: the mantra. In a low murmur so as not to disturb Naomi, I began to repeat "I will have a lucid dream" to myself, feeling a bit like I was performing some sort of satanic ritual. The people on Beyond the Veil said two to three minutes of repetition worked best.

"I will have a lucid dream. I will have a lucid dream. I will have a lucid dream. I will have a lucid dream..."

"Hey, wake up."

I cracked one eye open, flinching at the bright sunlight filling the room. I couldn't recall a single thing I'd dreamed post-mantra.

"Come on, Lanie," Naomi said, shaking my shoulder. "It's almost seven forty-five. You slept through your alarm. I brought you a bagel from the cafeteria. You can eat on the way to class."

"Thanks." My eyelids felt heavy as boulders, my brain almost bruised, like someone had grabbed it out of my skull and kicked it around like a soccer ball.

I'd just have to try again tonight.

Chapter 23

Dreams on dreams on dreams, recorded by my tired hand in looping, clumsy letters, most of them forgettable nonsense. Riding up a mile-long escalator in a mall. Grandma Ruth telling me all about how she'd taken up water skiing. Opening my wallet to find a miniature family of frogs where my ten dollars should have been.

And then there were the ones that stuck with me. A baby Bactrian camel, giving me a lazy, whiskered smile as it bent its neck for me to pet it. One of those nightmares where you realize you came to class naked; this particularly horrifying variant featured the presentation I had to give the next day in theology. A bittersweet vision of holding a hand I knew to be Ryan's own, vivid enough that I could have sworn I felt the warm press of his palm.

Meanwhile, in real life, my interactions with Ryan weren't exactly lukewarm, but something felt off—like the tie between us had turned brittle, little pieces crumbling away each day. I couldn't tell whether it was the distance or because we were still shying away from any Avanic-related topics.

My quest to lucid dream, too, had grown frustrating. After nearly a week, despite my avid journaling and the mantra, I still hadn't induced lucidity. I was remembering my dreams easily at this point, which was the point of journal. The stupid mantra was the problem, and I was getting impatient.

So back to Beyond the Veil I went. The general consensus was that if mantras didn't work it was best to adopt reality checks as a real-life habit: looking at your hand and counting the fingers to check you actually had five; scrutinizing your mirror image for irregularities; pulling at your skin to test the tautness (dream skin stretched like a rubber band, apparently); looking at a clock, glancing away, then turning back quickly to see if it now displayed a totally different time. In theory, once the reality checks became automatic habits, your dream self would perform them too. Then, when the reality check inevitably fails, you realize you're dreaming, and bam: lucidity inducted.

The clock-checking wasn't going to work; exactly what percentage of my dreams featured clocks? The mirror method, too, was out of the question, if only because peering deeply into dream-mirrors was basically begging to get scared.

But I'd always have a hand to check, I realized, remembering my dreams of petting the camel and holding hands with Ryan. I became hand-obsessed, pulling out my hand upwards of fifteen times a day to pinch my skin, then deliberately count my fingers. I couldn't decide if I felt more like a madwoman or like someone held back in kindergarten innumerable years for failing to master how to count to five.

The rest of the school, teachers and students alike, were also in counting mode. There were just a few days till winter break, and if we didn't have an exam in class then we were putting final touches on semester-end essays and presentations.

That evening I was settling in for a long, romantic date with an Algebra 2 review packet when I decided to text Ryan—just a simple *Hi* and a smiley face. I hadn't been able to get the hand-holding dream out of my mind. I missed him—or missed whatever we'd once been. Who knew where we stood now?

I picked at my chipping purple polish as I waited for a text back. Naomi had given me a funny look when she'd caught me doing a hand check yesterday, and I'd told her I was trying to decide on a nail polish color. We'd made a night of doing each other's nails and watching *The Cabin in the Woods*, me anticipating the best jokes because I'd seen it three times before and Naomi peeking through her fingers at the scary bits. She claimed to be a scaredy-cat, but I'd win her over to the dark side in the end.

At last, my phone lit up.

Hi, how's it going?

Good. Exams suck. I'm actually trying to study for math, like, REALLY study, but somehow I feel like that's just making it worse. What's up with you?

I was so lame. *This* was the best conversation I could come up with?

His response came a few long minutes later.

Haha, yeah, exams are
the worst. You can do it!

He added a thumbs up emoji a second later, then that was it—radio silence. I felt a few more pieces of the line between us disintegrate into dust.

That night I brought my math textbook into bed for some more studying, snuggling under the sheets with it like *Integrated Intermediate Algebra and Trigonometry* was a beloved bedtime picture book. When the time climbed past eleven, I scooted the textbook under the dream journal beside my pillow, then checked my phone just in case I'd missed a text from Ryan.

I hadn't—and as I glanced at our conversation, I felt the ache of disappointment as I realized I'd asked him what he was up to.

He hadn't given me an answer.

I squinted at the thick math exam in front of me, willing the questions to make sense, then looked back up at the clock. Four minutes until time was up, but I'd had to leave most of the questions blank—and what I *had* managed to solve was suspect chicken scratch, more guesswork than anything else.

Was I the only one still working? I snuck a look around the room. Naomi, seated next to me, was doodling a unicorn on the back of her test good enough to take first place in an art competition, and all the other girls were staring bored into space or watching the clock.

"Eyes on your own paper, Miss Adams," the teacher said, shooting me a baleful glance.

Stupid, stupid, stupid. How could I have studied so hard, for it all to come to this? I knew there was no sense trying for any extra points. Less than a minute now to go… There would be no sudden breakthroughs to turn this disaster around.

How far would an F on the exam sink my grade in the class? I'd gotten my grade up to the low end of a B, but now all that work was for naught. I imagined my mom opening up my report card, her face stiffening, then later the inevitable talk. *We're paying this much for school, and THIS is the grade you get?* I let my pencil slide from my fingers to land in a clatter on the desk, then went through the motions of my hand check.

Thumb. Pointer. Middle finger. Ha, I wished I could flip off the entire idea of math as a whole.

Brrring! That was the bell to end the period. The teacher stalked over to my desk as the rest of the class stood up as one.

I pinched the skin on the back of my hand and pulled.

And my skin stretched long in one fleshy string. *Rubber bands.* I was dreaming.

I let the skin go and watched, entranced, as the peachy string slowly contracted back, deflating like a balloon until the back of my hand was smooth once more. It should have been disgusting, but a cool calm had taken hold of me. None of this was real—my actual math test was still two days away. I could do anything I wanted.

For kicks, I tried to count my fingers, but now that I was concentrating on the task they swam and blurred in front of my eyes, some fingers missing, some echoed like I had double vision. Three total? I started again and this time lost track at seven. And now as I looked back down at my test I saw that the test questions and my panicked answers had vanished, replaced by fuzzy, squirming letters.

DREAM DREAM DREAM DREAM DREAM DREAM

I glanced away and back again.

WHAT? TO? DO? SEXY? VAMPIRE? CAMEL? FLYING? MELISSA?

I carefully slipped out of the desk and looked around the room. The teacher and students were all frozen in place, like the entire room was a scene from a movie, paused by some god's holy remote. The scowling teacher, who I now realized looked nothing like the sweet, elderly Mrs. Johnston, was mid-reach towards my test. The students, too, were more my sleeping mind's equivalent of classmates than any reflection of reality. Naomi was the most fully formed, though her face and body were blurred—the overall *feeling* of Naomi rather than a perfect likeness. The rest of the students were merely human-like hunks of gray matter—though if I gazed at any one student for half a second they slowly took on clearer features.

"Go," I commanded, and the teacher and students all funneled toward the classroom door. Then I thought better of it. "Stop." Everyone ground to a halt, like we were playing an impromptu game of Simon Says.

This time I merely thought, *Go*, and I pictured a fading instead of a leaving. And fade they did, leaving me the sole person in the classroom.

But who needed a classroom? I'd have enough of that once I woke up; what a waste to spend both waking and sleeping at school. What I needed was air and sunlight, flowers and sky.

There it was around me in an instant: an open field of verdant grass and flowers bright as jewels. The sky above was blinding blue, with smatterings of merry cotton clouds. I eyed the clouds, their distance making my head spin. So far away. So tantalizing…

I leaped.

I could fly. *I could fly!*

I sped towards the clouds above, riding buffets of wind upward like I was surfing on air currents, the field below me shrinking until it was small as model train scenery. One blink and I saw a shining crimson train on the horizon, chugging onward to parts unknown.

Oh my God. I could go to Hogwarts and fulfill every fantasy of my middle school self. I was the queen of the universe. I was the queen of any universe that could ever be imagined. Oh my God, I *was* God.

My theology teacher would have a fit at the philosophical

implications.

But this thought was forgotten as I whooshed to a mid-air halt in front of the fluffiest, most picturesque cloud I'd ever seen. I trailed my three-to-seven fingers through it, feeling the cold kiss of vapor on my skin. On a whim I willed raw energy and power into the cloud; a tingle raced down my spine as I watched its downy mass darken, the shadowed center flashing with white-violet electricity. Then, wheeling away, I looked back down to earth and thrust out a hand.

Lightning raced down from my cloud and drove into the field below, leaving a crater in its wake.

I threw out my other hand. *Flash! Boom!* A second burst of lightning hewed out another crater half a mile off.

Enough. I bid the storm cloud goodbye, and it was gone as simply as that, the sky around me restored to blue and white harmony. I floated back down to my field, cushioned on a warm air current like a hammock, wending my way towards the first crater. As I drew nearer I saw that the earth inside was smoking; great hunks of dirt, large as boulders, lay scattered all around. I landed softly on the grass, then gave a little cry as I stepped to the very edge of the crater.

An earthworm lay at my feet, cleaved sharply in two. Both halves were wriggling madly side by side. Tears sparked behind my eyes. Could earthworms feel pain? Clearly they could at least feel distress at being chopped in two.

I could wish the earthworm into the void, I knew that, but instead I knelt down and gathered up both halves into my hands. "Shhh..." They slowed their writhing death dance, and I frowned, wondering how to proceed next. Trains I knew well enough to form an image of—the same with clouds and fields and the rest. But magic? I had no prior knowledge guidebook for that.

Yet there are no rules in dreams. (Save for dying. Everyone seems to agree that dying in a dream is the surest way to wake up, since the mind can't handle the confusion of not existing.) Which meant I could make my own breed of magic.

I drew in a breath, scenting the smoke, the summer air, the fresh, unearthed soil. And then I thought *life* and blew that concoction of air and thought back at the earthworm.

Its pink-brown body lit up with golden sparks, the severed wounds of each half glowing bright as a sword just plucked from a blacksmith's forge. I drew my cupped palms closer to my face, watching the lights blaze and dance. I had the wobbly sort of feeling that either I was growing smaller or the earthworm growing bigger.

Together.

Fine threads of light sprang from the glowing wounds and knit the two halves into one. The sparks faded, and the earthworm lay whole in my hands. It squirmed in a placid, earthwormey way, death throes forgotten.

I laid it gently beside the still-smoking crater, then waved a hand over the hole, gesturing for it to fill. The ground rocked under my feet, like the tectonic plates below were shifting. The inside of the crater roiled and cracked, revealing dark, loamy soil. And when the crater filled, blades of

grass nudged their way through the dirt, baby shoots ma-
turing in seconds into a thick carpet of grass.

The crater was gone and the earthworm whole again, no
doubt happy and burrowing into the dirt at my feet. All
was well.

What now? The earthworm felt like a warning from my
deep psyche; the danger of being able to do anything is that
you can do anything. What kind of person would you be if
your choices had no consequences? I wondered how many
people used lucid dreaming to act out their most sordid,
twisted fantasies.

I had uncountable nights ahead of me to get acquainted
with the reaches of my imagination. Better now, then, to use
tonight's lucidity to talk to Melissa.

I let the field around me go; it didn't blink out so much
as split and fade away, like how a firework bursts into a
fast-dying shimmer. The void it left behind was a murky
red-black that stretched on in every direction.

I twisted this way and that, feeling for… what? I wasn't sure
how to go about my task—wasn't even sure if it was possible.

Melissa? I tried, thinking her name as clearly as I could.
Where are you? Maybe she could meet me in this dreamless
space.

A misty blue shape of a girl blinked into existence in front
of me. I started, then drifted in closer to the motionless figure. It was Melissa—but not, just as dream-Naomi had only
been a blurred approximation of the real Naomi Guo. This
was my brain, then, trying to fulfill my request.

Go. The figure melted away like smoke.

Melissa? The silence around me was absolute. I tried once more, giving my thought-shouting everything I had. *MELISSA?*

Was that the faintest echo of a voice or just my imagination? I tried to speed towards it, though the zero space all around me made it impossible to tell if I was moving any closer.

MELISSA?

Here!

MELISSA?

Here!

MELISSA?

Here!

A blue dot was floating far off, one bright pixel in a sea of darkness. The dot grew to a blue cluster, then to the tiny shape of a girl in the distance. The world around me was changing as well: shadows still, but now they gave the dim suggestion of streets, trees, houses, mountains. I was flying through the ghost of a town.

Enville.

I had almost reached Melissa now. Her form was clear, not hazy; this was no dream likeness. I could see her watching my approach, could hear her waving and shouting at me.

Here! Here! Here!

And then there I was, and so was she, misty ghosts of trees towering around us.

We gazed at each other for a moment, me at her wide-set eyes and flaxen hair, all cast blue from her ghostly filter,

and her at—well, I had no idea what my dream-self looked
like.

"Hi, Lanie," she said.

Chapter 24

"Hi," I replied. "Is… is this real?"

A smile flickered on her lips before dying. "As real as anything." Her voice was light and breathy, each word clear, without any distortion. From where I was standing I could see the delicate hairs of her eyelashes, the flecks of her freckles. Something about her eyes, I noticed, belied her youth, like an older woman was staring out at me from within.

This had to be the real Melissa. My slumbering mind couldn't craft an image this detailed—could it? "I could be imagining you right now," I said, backing away. "This could be me imagining you talking to me in my dream, saying this is real. All this detail…" I waved an arm at her. "It could all be some brain trick."

She turned away and took a few ambling steps toward a towering, shadowy oak tree. "You need some proof," she said lightly.

"That would be nice."

"Hmm." She gazed up into the branches, then gave a half-hearted laugh, more somber than happy. "You know,

I've known you ever since you were a baby. I was there on every birthday, every Christmas… In some ways I feel like some long-lost aunt or big sister of yours. I could tell you so much. But none of that can serve as proof, can it?"

"You were there on my birthd—?"

"Ryan's on Avanic's radar," she interrupted, looking back over her shoulder at me. "When he got home Halloween night, he searched some things about Avanic online. Dangerous things." Her jaw was set, her eyes hard. Hard and sad, I realized as I stared at her—a lived-in sort of sadness.

"What do you mean?" I prompted her. "What dangerous things?"

Melissa left the oak tree and came back to me, though she was having trouble meeting my eyes. "It was stupid of me to set you on this path," she said. "I see that now. I don't know what I expected. Things are so different now from when I was… not like this. Everything gets tracked and monitored and filed away. The whole world's locked down tight. So Ryan typed the wrong words together in a search bar, and now they know he knows. I overheard them talking about it."

I shook my head; it made no sense. "How does Avanic know what Ryan typ—?"

She interrupted me. "So there's your proof—ask him what he did that night. As to what will happen to him—well, you're in a Catholic school now, right? Best pray he stays safe."

My mind was reeling. "Wh-what could happen to him?"

"Best-case scenario, they just keep an eye on him. If he's

unlucky… likely they'll disappear him." She peered around the dusky forest clearing. "This is really something. I can't believe you've done this. If Brixham found out…"

I gritted my teeth. I felt like I was understanding less than half of what she was saying. "Sorry, who's that?"

"Avanic's director," she said, turning back to me. A gentle wind kissed my cheek and set her feathery hair trembling. "The man who went to visit you, after the explosion."

"And when you say *disappear*… You mean they'll k-kill Ryan?" I could hardly say it. "Like they killed you? Like one of the other kids?"

"Yes, something like that. Likely they'll just kill him, nothing more. Our particular project has essentially been shuttered since the early nineties."

Nothing MORE? Project? Every answer she gave me was just seed for more questions, like two new heads sprouting from the bleeding stump of a hydra's neck.

I cleared my throat. "Avanic's performing illegal human experiments, right? What the hell kind of research are they doing? Testing some sort of risky cancer treatment or something?"

She looked at me with a mixture of pride and that fathomless melancholy. "Oh, Lanie, I really can't believe how close you came to figuring it all out." She chewed on her lip. "The thing is that Avanic as a company is not *just* Avanic. Yes, people work there making arthritis medication, things like that. Good, ordinary scientists and researchers." Her mouth twisted. "But there's another side of the company.

You see, Avanic was founded in 1958 by the CIA."

I stopped breathing. The image of Uncle Ed's cartoonish face popped into my head, then the memory of scrolling past one of the many ludicrous sub-forums. *CIA Programs: MKUltra, Project Monarch, front organizations, etc.*

"And," Melissa said, "what you said about human experimentation isn't wrong. The others and I—Pamela, Scott, Tina, Anna-Marie—we were all unwilling participants. Plucked off the streets. Brought back to Avanic. And then… this." She gestured at her body.

My voice was a bare thread. "What did they do to you?"

Her too-old eyes unfocused and floated away from mine—reliving some memory. "We were the human test subjects of Project SPECTR."

Another breeze set the trees around us swaying and creaking. "Specter?" I breathed.

"S-P-E-C-T-R," Melissa said. "Sensory Projection to Eliminate and Control Threats to the Republic." As she spoke she seemed to grow smaller, like a dense kernel of sadness was pulling her inward.

Threats to the republic? She'd said Avanic was founded in 1958… I could feel the presence of my history teachers breathing down my neck, willing me to make the connection.

"Did… SPECTR…?" I said the word slowly, tasting its sharp syllables. "Did it have something to do with the Cold War?"

"That's right," Melissa said. She was so visibly uncomfortable that it almost hurt to look at her. "During the Cold

War the CIA was bringing on droves of scientists. They basically had free reign—and unlimited funding. MKUltra and SPECTR were contemporary projects…"

Jesus Christ. You couldn't have a predilection for all things dark and not have heard a few nasty tidbits about Project MKUltra.

"That was the one where they tried to discover methods of mind control…?" I asked, just to make sure.

"Yes." Melissa's soft voice grew icy. "Truth serums, hypnosis… The CIA was running LSD experiments out of brothels, dosing the johns. Soon enough someone had the idea that astral projection was worth exploring. They were hoping for a foolproof way to spy on the Soviets."

I'd seen the term bandied about on Beyond the Veil. "That's when you have an out-of-body experience, right?"

"Astral projection is a *willing* OBE. Out-of-body experience," she explained. "Lots of acronyms with the CIA. Many people have an OBE due to something sudden and traumatic—a near-death experience, for example. Under those circumstance the OBE is uncontrollable. But with astral projection the whole experience is willing. You have more control. You can decide to leave the immediate area around your physical body and go somewhere else."

"Like the Soviet Union," I said.

"Right. Theoretically." She sank into silence, the only sound in the forest clearing the whoosh of the rising wind through the trees. The air was thick with words unsaid; I felt like I could reach out and touch the stories she wasn't sharing. Why was she so closed off?

"Melissa," I said gently, "I know you came to me for help. So you can be put to rest, I think." Was that the right terminology when dealing with the undead? *So you can die? Pass on?*

She dropped her head, the shining blue-gold of her hair swishing down like a curtain to separate us. "Just forget about it," she mumbled.

"Why?" I asked. And another louder "Why?" when the moment stretched on without an answer. How much time did we have left in this place? Too little to spend it only listening to the wind moan.

I tried a different tack, gesturing around us at the shadow-glade.

"Is this how you always see the world?"

That got an answer. "No, I see the real world much as you do. This is all you—some form of astral projection that I don't understand. I heard your voice, then this space sort of melted in around me. We're in your realm right now, as far as I can tell."

"So *I* made this place? How?" I asked when she nodded. "How can I do this? *Any* of this? I'm just a normal girl. I'm just… just Lanie!"

"No," she said, her expression pained. "You'll never be 'just Lanie.' You've figured out why all this is happening to you, I'm sure."

"The explosion. The chemical I touched."

"That's right. Of course you were special before then, as special as every other nine-year-old… But afterwards you became *very* special. Like I said, Dr. Brixham and his team would be over the moon if they knew." Her sadness sharpened, her eyes fiery. "You *can't let them find out.*"

Well, I certainly wasn't going to march on up to Avanic's gated campus and tell them I knew all about the blood on their hands, and by the way, I had some sort of unexplored ability to commune with the teenagers they'd murdered. But someone else could always tip Avanic off… Remembering the back-of-the-neck tingling of Claw Hands creeping through my dreams, I looked over my shoulder. "Do you think anyone else can come here?"

"I doubt it."

"That's good, then." I frowned. "Listen, I need more details. Can't you tell me anything more? I get that you were put into Project SPECTR, but how did you die? What was that chemical I touched? Who is Claw Hands?"

But her eyes were shuttered. "I'm sorry, but I won't tell you anything else. I was wrong to come to you, that day in the bathroom. Warn Ryan, and forget about all of this."

"Please," I begged, ignoring her words. "Give me *anything.*"

Another biting wind came gusting toward us, its doleful howl nearly human. The wind pushed at my torso, sucked the breath from my lungs and set me coughing, twined round my ankles like the world's most insistent cat. A few of the trees behind Melissa shook and groaned before melting away into darkness. This whole astral projection thing was new to me, but I could read the signs well enough. Our time in this desolate corner of the shadow-woods was coming to a close.

"I want to help you," I said to Melissa, raising my voice to be heard over the wind. "I don't know how, but I want to help you pass on."

She shook her head sadly at me. "Don't."

"But—" I broke off as a tress of Melissa's shining hair blew away. She didn't seem to notice.

She raised her voice to a shout. Her form was going blurry. "I mean it, Lanie! Don't try to be a hero! Just warn Ryan."

"I—"

But at last the wind climbed to a wail, rending away the shadow-trees, Melissa now just a faint blue haze.

"Please, Lanie!" Her voice cut through the tempest, hollow and echoing like she was miles away.

And then the wind was whisking my body away from the glade, my stomach dropping like when a roller coaster takes its inevitable first plunge. The last remaining trees grew small as I sped away, the muddy shadows around me lightening to pale yellow-gray. Someone was shaking my arm...

"Come *on*, Lanie," Naomi said as I gasped awake and launched into a coughing fit. I felt like someone near drowned. "You all right?" she asked.

"Y-yeah," I rasped, then raised my hand to my face. Five fingers, crystal clear. I pulled at the skin on the back of my hand; it snapped straight back to the bone.

"Oookay," Naomi said with an odd look as she observed my reality check. "Anyway, first period's in forty-five minutes. You overslept your alarm again."

School. Studying. Exams. Life rushed back to me in a breathtaking blur.

"Thanks." I wiped the sleep from my eyes, then put a hand to my forehead. My head was one giant ache.

"Maybe you should go to bed a little earlier tonight," Naomi said as I climbed down the bunk bed ladder. "I had to shake your arm pretty hard to wake you up, you know! Really spooked me, sleeping like the dead like that."

Chapter 25

I CALLED RYAN on the way to class, praying he'd answer. Best case scenario he'd just say I was suffering from overactive dreams.

But he didn't answer my call. At the voicemail beep, I left him a message, trying to keep the panic from my voice. "Hi, Ryan, sorry to call. Umm, I'm heading into my chemistry exam, so if you call me back I won't answer, but can we talk today? Or send me a text? Please?"

I didn't want to go into any more detail. My brain was refusing to believe that Avanic was a front company for the CIA, much less that Ryan had landed on their radar—but if that *were* true, I had to count on the possibility that they were monitoring his phone. And if it became apparent to them what *I* knew, then that would land me in a heap of trouble as well.

When he called me back, how could I ensure I didn't get pulled into this spiraling catastrophe? A catastrophe which definitely, certainly, one hundred percent was not happening, I reminded myself. Then again, I also hadn't believed in ghosts and demons until a few months ago…

I breathed a sigh of relief when the chemistry exam got out and I could at last check my phone. One text from Ryan.

> What's up? Everything ok? I can
> talk at 11:30 if you're free then.

Perfect—that was right after English let out and we headed to lunch. I texted him back a quick *Okay*, then fidgeted through the next interminable hour and a half of presentations on *The Crucible*. Incredible how literary analysis could make a play about the Salem witch trials drier than the Gobi Desert.

I scarfed a sandwich at lunch, then got out my phone, annoyed at the sweat my fingers were leaving on the screen. Why was I letting a stupid dream make me so anxious? There was no way that Avanic was a CIA front—

Ryan answered seconds after I hit dial. "Hey, Lanie, how's it going? You all right?"

"Yeah, I just, umm… It's been a stressful last couple days with exams and stuff. I've been really missing you. And wanted to hear your voice." Not untrue—though I failed to mention that I wanted to hear his voice first and foremost to check that he hadn't been "disappeared" by CIA agents.

"Aww, I missed you too!" he said, and tingles washed over me. "So how're exams? I just turned in my final English paper. Mrs. Naples gave me a bit of a dirty look when I handed it over. I don't think she's gotten over the whole you-writing-my-essay thing."

"Ha ha, yeah…" God, that felt like a lifetime ago. "Enville High's letting out for break tomorrow, too, right?"

"Yeah. I have Latin after lunch today, then math and history tomorrow, then I'm done, finally. How about you?" he asked.

"Math for me too, tomorrow morning, and Spanish after that."

"And then you're back in Enville for a bit, huh?" he said, voice brightening. I could picture his smile, happy as a balloon bobbing in the breeze. "We should do something when you get back! See a movie or something. There's that one about Santa's evil elves coming out, right? That's up your alley. The ads look… not atrocious."

A pang shot through me. "I'm actually not going to be home except for a few days around Christmas."

"Oh," he said—the kind of *Oh* where you know you've said just the right thing to make everything tip sideways. Funny how one sentence can form a needle just perfect for popping balloons.

So I blundered on, trying to patch up the conversation. "It's just that buildings and grounds at St. Brigid's were looking for some volunteers over break. I didn't want to be in town because… Well, I just didn't feel like it," I finished, bringing myself up short as I remembered all the things I couldn't say, just in case.

"Makes sense," he said. I waited for him to say more, but those were the only two syllables he gave me.

"So…" I said, trying to keep him on the line. "What are you doing over the break? Are you—?"

"Listen, Lanie," he interrupted, "I have to eat and do some cramming before Latin. I'll talk to you later." Clipped words. Low tone. This wasn't good.

"Wait!" I said, desperate to keep him on the phone. "That game you like to play…" What was it called again? "*Our Fate?*" Ugh, I sounded like someone's grandma.

"*Hour of Fate,*" he corrected me. "What about it?"

"Would you want to play sometime? Maybe tonight?" That had to be a safer way to communicate; surely the CIA had better things to do than spy on two teenagers' in-game chat.

Dead air on the line. "Maybe some other time," he said at last. "I don't think your Mac can even run the game."

"But—"

"And I've got exams, remember? You do, too. Plus I haven't been playing much lately."

Now it was my turn to give a dejected *Oh.* "Oh. Okay. Well, good luck on your exam."

"Yeah, you too," he said, then ended the call.

So that had gone terribly, and I wasn't even relieved. *Warn him,* my subconscious clamored. But what was I to do? I had to stay cautious, and Ryan didn't want to talk to me.

That night my sleep began fitfully, a slew of worries pressing at my brain. Ryan. My imminent math exam. Being tackled and chloroformed by a CIA agent on my way to said math exam. It didn't help that I'd spent so much time working on remembering my dreams lately that these were almost waking thoughts, not the regular dream nonsense delved up from some unconscious grotto, shown the light of day, then promptly forgotten.

Yet at last my worries sank away, and I found myself in some sort of medieval-ish town square, dusty flagstones beneath my feet and flower garlands overhead. A swarm of furry gnomes all sporting ginger beards were having a group argument off to the left, and to the right a hulking half-cobra half-centipede monstrosity was hissing and stamping its many legs. Ryan was at my side, looking out of place in his nondescript gray hoodie and jeans.

"How about a meat pie?" he said to me, his voice enthusiastic.

A tad *too* enthusiastic… I looked back at his hoodie, now a shifting greeny-gold. His face, too, was blurred, in that dream way that was becoming more and more familiar to me.

Just to be sure I went through my reality check. Uncountable fingers: check. Back-of-the-hand rubber bands: check.

Back in dreamland… and fantasyland, from the looks of it. I scanned the rest of the square. A cooing nymph was holding hands with her werewolf boyfriend over yonder, and in the distance pranced a herd of… pegasi? Pegasuses?

"Oh my God," I muttered. "Is this *Hour of Fate*?" Or at least what my imagination supposed *Hour of Fate* to look like.

"That's right!" piped up my chipper not-quite-Ryan companion. I noticed he'd materialized a steaming meat pie from dream hammerspace. "Welcome to the kingdom of Viningal! And what a stupendous kingdom it—"

Go, I ordered him, and heaved a sigh of relief when he and all the rest faded out, leaving me alone in the reddish-black void.

Much better—and now to business. *MELISSA?!* I thought-shouted. *WHERE ARE YOU?*

No reply. An awful thought popped into my head: what if she, too, didn't want to talk to me? I remembered her depthless sadness, her unwillingness to tell me any more than the bare minimum.

Well, maybe a bit more pestering could fix that. *MELISSA?!* I called again. My heart leaped when I heard a faint *Here!* waft from somewhere far off. I envisioned myself as an arrow shooting towards the voice.

Soon enough I spotted a blue speck, radiant against the inky nothingness. I sped closer, shivering as the shadows condensed into the umbral realm of my hometown. *My* realm, as Melissa had called it yesterday. I still had no idea what to make of that; if I were being honest, I was trying *not* to think about it. "Realm" was a word for games like *Hour of Fate*, not high school girls from Connecticut.

I waved a silent hello to the unmistakable, big box building of Enville High as I zoomed past. Half a breath later I sped across Carnarvon Avenue, the CVS with the girl/tiger employee a hazy blur in my peripheral vision as I headed towards the forest surrounding Avanic.

I hit the woods, slipping around trees like quicksilver. *I'm here*, I heard Melissa call again, but she hadn't needed to say anything at all; I could see her blue form shining through the shadow-trees. A moment later I alit in front of her, moving at blinding speed one second and at a standstill the next, like a gymnast rocketing through the air and sticking a perfect landing. *My realm.* The laws of aerodynamics weren't so hard and fast here, it seemed.

"You seem to be getting the hang of things," Melissa said, her expression pinched.

"Practice makes perfect," I said, surveying the woods around us. It was the same clearing as last time. "So how do you think this works?" I wondered aloud. "Do you hang out in this spot often? Is that why we're back here, specifically? Do you think I could call out to somebody else and visit them?"

Her eyes infused with that same sadness from yesterday. "You shouldn't *be* practicing, Lanie. Can't you just forget all about it? It's too dangerous."

She was dodging my questions again. "Knowledge is power," I said, trying to keep my tone even. "Plus life would be pretty boring if it were all padded walls and rounded edges."

"There's a difference between taking risks and hurling yourself headlong at a pit full of spikes."

Something snapped within me. "Listen to me," I hissed. I'd been through so much, come all this way, plus Ryan might be in danger—and she was going to keep wagging her finger at me and giving me safety lectures? "*I* am the one jetting around astral planes. *I* am the one still in the land of the living. *I am the one who has to warn Ryan about Avanic but he doesn't want to fucking talk to me.* I am. Me. *Not* you. So how about helping me out a bit here, okay?"

Her jaw had gone slack. "You didn't tell him?"

Not like I hadn't tried. "You heard what I said."

"Lanie, that's bad. You have to—"

"Yeah, I get it! But we have this time, right here, right now, so you better start talking."

Her gaze dropped. "Okay," she said haltingly. "Fine. So… what do you want to know?"

Chapter 26

What *didn't* I want to know?

"Tell me about SPECTR," I said. "How did you become a… well, a specter? A ghost?"

She opened her mouth, then closed it again, clearly trying to figure out where to start. "It's not a pleasant story," she said at last.

"Yeah, well, I already know the basic ending, so…" I could feel bad about being too harsh later. Already a gentle wind was caressing my cheek, making the forest around us rustle. Our time was slipping away like sand through an hourglass, and I needed all the answers I could get.

"Fine," Melissa said. She still wasn't meeting my eyes, instead opting for somewhere over my left shoulder. "The scientists working on SPECTR started off doing the standard ESP experiments. Asking supposed clairvoyants to guess the shapes on the backs of cards, that sort of thing.

"At the same time, the people in MKUltra were testing out a whole slew of new drugs, trying to find one that would work well for interrogation purposes. One of the experiments led to the development of a highly caustic substance that induced a catatonic state. People who came into contact with the substance reported a strong dissociative effect. This was all useless for MKUltra's purposes—but the scientists over in SPECTR were intrigued.

"So the SPECTR team started working with the substance. They refined it a little, began to run some preliminary experiments with live test subjects… And that's how CC gel came to be."

"CC gel…?" I repeated. "What's that stand for?"

"Consciousness capture. And the gel did live up to its name. It was great at capturing the human consciousness."

"But…?"

Her lip curled. "The ultimate aim of the program was to spy on the Russians, right? Suffice it to say that no one in SPECTR made it quite as far as the USSR."

"How far did you make it?" I hardly needed to ask.

"Less than a mile and a half from our… containment center." She spoke these last two words without bothering to stifle her revulsion. "It's not really possible to go further than that." She hadn't said it was *im*possible, I noted, but let that slide for now.

"Why pick you?" I asked. "Why teenagers specifically?"

"They found that the CC gel worked best on people who were immersed when they were still young. The consciousness of anyone much older than eighteen rapidly deteriorated in the gel. The scientists picked sixteen as the sweet spot."

I squinted at her. "Did you say 'immersed?'"

"That's right," she said. "CC gel requires total immersion for the transference. But that's not all. They discovered that—" She broke off as another, wilder wind set the trees bending and swaying around us. "They discovered that intense stress and sudden pain guaranteed the most successful results—just like those conditions can trigger an out-of-body experience."

I shivered and brushed my thumb over my blurred fingertips, remembering how they had smarted and burned. "This gel, it's… what, acidic?" I asked. "They get a big vat of the stuff and just chuck you in?"

Her eyes were steely, her voice low. "They locked me in a harness. Lowered me into a tank of CC gel. And then they held me down there. Held me down until I drowned in it."

Oh God. Now I understood her hesitation to divulge this "not so pleasant" story. "Melissa," I asked, swallowing back nausea, "w-what color is the CC gel?"

"Don't you already know?" she replied, her lips forming a cold, close-lipped smile. "It's blue."

Of course it was.

If that was what Avanic had done to Melissa, then what might they do to Ryan? Yet there was simply no time to grapple with past atrocities and future what-ifs. Our time here had a hard limit; I had to forge ahead. "You said the gel requires immersion—but I only brushed it. Why am I like this? How come I can see you when I dream or get a fever or smoke weed? How come I can be here, like *this*?" I spun around in a circle, the ghostly trees blurring together into muddy darkness.

"You still touched the gel," she said, at last looking at me square on. Her voice had softened slightly. "You were young—only nine—and CC gel works best with younger minds. And the explosion was a traumatic event, yes? Your adrenaline was pumping, and you were scared enough for your parents' safety that you went to go find them. All those things combined, I believe, have allowed the CC gel to affect you in this way."

"How do *you* know what I did after the explosion?"

"Because I was there," she said. "CC gel is quite a volatile substance, and it requires a lot of delicate machinery to maintain. An equipment malfunction that day caused Tina and Anna-Marie's tanks to explode. They died—their *souls* died—that day. The lab was on fire... I thought the fire might spread to my own section of the lab, to my tank—that it was the end at last. That finally I'd be allowed to die.

"So I went to go find you, to say goodbye in my own way. Like I said last time, Lanie, I've been hanging around you pretty regularly ever since you were born. When your home's a vat of toxic gel, you have less than a two-mile radius to explore, and you only have one friend to talk to— well, three at that time—visiting the family down the road with the cute little girl is pretty cathartic. Being in a normal house with a normal family, even though I was invisible— it made *me* feel almost normal."

"That's what you were doing the day I had a fever," I said, dazed. What had she said yesterday? *In some ways I feel like some long-lost aunt or big sister of yours.*

She nodded. "Scott and I were chatting together in your room. Then you saw me, and here we are."

Yes, here we are, I echoed in my mind, looking around the murky glade. What time was it in the real world? How much longer could I stay in this dream space? Shadow-leaves, stirred up by the wind, eddied around our feet.

"The nightmares when I was a kid," I remembered. "What about those?"

She sighed. "We—Scott and I—realized early on that you'd been affected by the CC gel, and not in a way any of us in SPECTR had known was possible. We could enter your dreamscapes, a bit like what you've done here. So I tried to talk with you. I was hopeful that we could form some sort of odd friendship."

I couldn't help a snort.

"Yes, I know," she said with a rueful look. "But it had been decades at that point since I'd been taken into SPECTR. That much time with so few people to talk to can make you entertain some strange possibilities—plus two of my friends had just *died*, for good this time. I wasn't thinking very clearly.

"But you were having none of my barging into your dreams, and who can blame you? When your mom took you to a psychologist I knew it was time to stop. Scott and I agreed to hide everything we knew about you from Avanic, of course. And that was that, for seven years.

"Then you got that fever back in October. Right place at

the right time—I discovered you could see us in altered mental states, though our speech was distorted. And I began to wonder if you could help us in some way. It was the longest of long shots—but you were my only hope."

"Your only hope to die. For your *soul* to die," I clarified.

"That's right. It's a half-state, this existence of ours. And even if you couldn't help us, I thought you might at least gain some understanding of what had happened to us. Even a crumb of the truth coming out felt like justice. So the day you came home high, I took a risk and told you my name."

"And then Claw Hands did her thing and dragged you away."

"Yes," Melissa said. She made air quotes with her fingers and gave me a sardonic smile. "'Claw Hands.'"

"She's Pamela, isn't she?" She'd mentioned Tina, Anna-Marie, Scott—only four of the five SPECTR test subjects.

She nodded. "Pamela Billings was the initial girl they brought into the project, back in '83." I remembered Pamela's story from Uncle Ed's Forum—how she'd disappeared after leaving a friend's house, theoretically kidnapped on the two-mile stretch of road between her out-of-gas car and the nearest service station.

"How did she get like that?" I asked.

Melissa pressed her lips together into a thin line. "Pamela had a rough time of it. She was the sole test subject of SPECTR for more than a year. Imagine being murdered, then waking up from death to find your soul tethered to a tank. But even worse was that Pamela was effectively in solitary. You see, the scientists have a special machine they use to sense us. They can see us, though the image is blurry, but they've never managed to work out auditory functionality. Pamela had no way to talk to anyone, besides crude sign language. And who wants to chat with their murderers, anyway?

"After that first year they brought in another test subject: Scott. He doesn't like to talk about those times much, but he told me once about those first few days after he was inducted. Said that Pamela was half-feral—muttering to herself, had a hard time approaching him, stuff like that.

"Still, she calmed down a lot eventually. Scott's a cute guy, likable, kind. And he needed her too, of course, after everything he'd just been through. So they fell into a strange kind of love. A necessary love."

"What happened next?" I whispered as the tree trunks around us creaked and moaned. It sounded like the forest was in pain.

"The first stage of SPECTR—perfecting the CC gel—had been successful beyond the scientists' wildest hopes and dreams. But now they wanted to move onto the second stage: crossing the boundary that hems us in."

This was new. "That's possible? What happens if you do that?"

"I tried going out one time on my own—twenty years ago, maybe." Her voice had taken on a detached edge. "Didn't tell the others, and Brixham's team has no idea either. I knew it would be awful, but..." I could see her gaze drifting away into memory. "I wondered if it might kill me. I was trying for that. And even if it didn't, I felt an obligation to understand what was fencing us in. Know thy enemy, so to speak."

She laughed bitterly. "I only made it a few steps before turning back. You get this terrible feeling when you hit the boundary, like all hope's left your body. Like doom's descending on you and you can't remember what happiness is. If you step past the boundary the air gets all hot and thick like honey, so thick it's hard to walk. And if you keep going, then there's this horrible, wrenching feeling like... like you're trying to force your body through a metal sieve."

I fought the urge to vomit.

"The SPECTR scientists hadn't anticipated such an obstacle, of course," she continued. "Their hypothesis was that the boundary was like a moat you could cross—that all you needed to do was force your way through it and sooner or later you'd come out on the other side."

"And Scott and Pamela were willing to help with the experiments?" I asked, frowning. "Why would anyone put themselves through that?"

"Exactly right," she said. "The scientists didn't have a way to make them do anything. Except they knew that Pamela and Scott were in love.

"So they played the two of them against each other—said, for example, that Scott had to try and cross the boundary or they'd shut Pamela's tank off. Once your tank powers down, you're gone for good, you know." She gave a quiet little sigh. "Peace at last. Must be nice.

"Scott wouldn't hear any of it; he knew they were bluffing. Here was the CIA investing millions of dollars into this project; they weren't just going to get rid of one of their precious test subjects.

"But Pamela thought they might go through with it. She'd already spent all that time alone. No one to talk to. No sleeping, no eating. Every day the same as the last. Scott begged her not to believe them, but she decided to try. She made it out five feet the first time before she had to turn back."

"The first time?" I echoed.

"She tried to cross the boundary four times. Each time they'd give her the same old threat, and each time Scott would plead with her not to go. And she'd tell him that this time she'd be strong, that she knew he was right, that the scientists were lying. But she always gave in to the fear in the end.

"The second time Pamela went out she made it twelve feet. When she came back she was a bit taller, sort of stretched. The third time she made it twenty feet, and when she came back the scientists saw her suddenly teleport four feet to the right. Venturing past the boundary was changing her for good, each step molding her into who she is now. The teleportation was especially exciting to the scientists; that alone secured them four more years of funding and the go-ahead to add more test subjects.

"But the scientists decided to wait on bringing anyone new into the project for a few months. They had the leverage they needed over Pamela; they didn't want to risk additional test subjects disrupting that. Just one more time, they told her. Just a few more feet."

I drew in a breath. "How far did she make it?"

"Forty-two feet. Scott watched her do it, and—" Her voice caught. "He told me he'd never heard anyone scream like that. H-her scream started out human, and then… Then it wasn't. And when she came back, Pamela was gone. She'd become what she is now. The scientists brought me into the project a few months later, then Tina and Anna-Marie, but they never pushed any of us to cross the boundaries.

"So I have never really known Pamela; all I've ever known is the state she's in now. Her monstrous self. She's stronger than the rest of us. Where we have to move around our territory on foot, she can teleport around. That's what happened that day in the bathroom: she didn't like me telling you my name, because she knew it could cascade into so much more."

I gasped with sudden realization. "Because she still loves Scott." I wheeled away as the last puzzle piece slid snugly into place. "She's been guarding me, keeping you away. She *wants* to keep SPECTR as it is."

Melissa bowed her head. "Yes."

"She's happy in her… state?"

"As happy as someone like her can be, I think," she said slowly. "Scott and I both want to pass on, though we didn't see eye-to-eye on talking with you. He thought it would only bring danger to you—and he was right about that. So he's stayed out of it. He's resigned to SPECTR continuing on."

"But didn't you say that the SPECTR project ended in the nineties?" I said with a swallow.

She sagged. "Project SPECTR may be shuttered, but Avanic won't let us die. Why would they? For all the CIA knows, some genius might figure out what to do with us one day. It's not like we're *going* anywhere. So we're just… here. Sometimes I sit in the woods and wait for my consciousness to fade out. A sort of meditation—I can lose a day or two that way. But I always come back in the end."

I'd been wondering why I'd found Melissa here in the exact same clearing. "You do that here?"

"Yes. Scott knows it's sort of my spot, so he doesn't come out here. Your house is, well, *your* house, not mine, and my tank and the lab are all bad memories, so I think of this place as my makeshift home." She crooked another gloomy smile at me. "Like what I've done with the place?"

"What about Scott? Where is he?"

"He has his own sort of place, in the lab… One of the scientists knows sign language and taught Scott. So they actually talk every day."

"You never learned?"

"Didn't want to," she said, her face hardening. "Scott can separate that scientist from his job, somehow—can ignore how he works for the company that murdered him. I could never do that. I think… Maybe that friendship is the reason he doesn't feel the need to pass on so urgently."

The wind was growing more insistent, slapping at my

cheek. "I'll have to go soon," I said. "Is there anything else I need to know?"

She shook her head. "Just warn Ryan. Don't know if it will help him, but still, he needs to know. And stay safe yourself."

"I still want to help you. There must be some way."

Her eyes were glassy with tears. "You can't. Please don't try. I… I've had the honor of watching you grow up. Watching you become such a…" Her voice was wobbling. "…Such a smart, beautiful, capable young woman. So you need to live, Lanie. Don't risk your own life for someone already dead."

"But—"

The tears spilled from her eyes now, carving shining blue streams down her forever-young cheeks. "Live," she repeated. "That's the best thing you can do for me."

My own lips were quivering, a lump rising in my throat. Give up? That was the only solution? But the wind continued to rise, and my thoughts were skittering first to the nebulous enormity of the CIA and then to the human points of happiness in my life. My parents. My grandma. Ryan. Naomi and Felicity. Perhaps even Melissa, now.

I nodded. "All right. Yes." And before I could second guess myself, I leaned forward and gave her a hug.

Have you ever taken a bath in a ghost? Suffice it to say that the experience is not *usually* pleasant. But this time… this time we weren't in the real world, but in my realm. And though Melissa was as incorporeal as ever, in my realm she wasn't smarting cold, but an effervescent warmth.

Sunshine drenching the earth. Sparks off a firecracker. The CC gel was the culprit behind the blue, but I wondered if my ghosts weren't pure gold on the inside.

And then I released her from the hug just before the wind swept me away toward consciousness.

Chapter 27

THE HEADACHE I'D had yesterday morning had been bad, but that was *nothing* compared to this. I yelped and slapped a hand to my eyes, the gray dawn light coming through the window assailing my vision. Then I cautiously raised my hand again, holding it a few inches from my face. The light lanced through my fingers like daggers.

I was seeing double—but the double was a blurry, darker version of my hand overlaying my own. It deepened, then faded to a light mist when I blinked, reality and shadows warring for my attention.

Five fingers, I noticed, so I wasn't dreaming—but something felt seriously wrong. I raised myself up on one elbow, looking around the room. It wasn't just my hand; the room itself had a ghostly twin fading in and out, like half my brain was mired in the shadow realm, the other half seeing the bright, solid matter of reality.

And God, how my head ached—no, *ache* wasn't a strong enough word. It felt like some enterprising insect had crawled into my brain through my ear and was worming its way out the other side. What was this, some sort of migraine?

I threw my blanket over my face, blinking hard and rubbing my eyes. Some of the throbbing in my head released, and I peeked out at the rest of the room. The dark had nearly all gone, just a few determined wisps of shadow clinging on here and there. A few more blinks and those bits were gone too, the spears of pain in my head evaporating with them.

I drew a juddering breath. "What the hell."

"You okay?" Naomi's voice was raspy with sleep. The alarm on my phone went off the next second; time to get up and confront my math exam. I'd put in the work studying for it, but I wasn't expecting much in the way of returns; math and I just had that sort of hate-hate relationship.

But even before I worried about that, there was another thing I needed to do. When Naomi slipped on her fuzzy pink bathrobe and trundled off to the bathroom, I dialed Ryan's number.

It went straight to voicemail. Well, what had I expected? Our last conversation hadn't exactly gone swimmingly. I left him a message pleading for him to call me back, then started getting ready for class.

A few minutes later Naomi and I set off for breakfast. I hissed when we stepped out of the dorm into the weak winter sunlight. My brain still felt tender, like the shifting shadows might reappear at any moment. Some residual side effect of spending time with Melissa, maybe?

My heart pattered a nervous beat. I was a clandestine test

subject of Project SPECTR, and even Melissa's conclusions about my abilities were just based on guesswork. Whatever was happening to me, I was alone in the journey.

I kept my phone on max up until I took my seat in math class and Mrs. Johnston ordered us to put everything away save for a pencil and calculator. With a sinking feeling, I silenced my phone and slipped it into my bag. I'd call Ryan again the second I got out of the test.

The exam, at least, was making sense to me. Quadratic equations, logarithms, polynomials, even imaginary numbers—my greatest nemesis—were all somehow coming together. Was it possible I was actually... getting it?

After what felt like the thousandth graph I flipped the page, only to smile. *You're done!* the last page of the exam proclaimed in Mrs. Johnston's tidy handwriting. *Don't forget to check over your work and HAVE A FABULOUS BREAK!*

I glanced at the clock—just ten or so minutes until the end of the period. Had Ryan called me back? My eyes slid down to my backpack. I'd call him just as soon as—

A knock at the door broke everyone's hushed concentration. Felicity poked her head into the classroom and bobbed her head in apology to Mrs. Johnston. The two of them had a brief, whispered conversation before Felicity scanned the room and found my face. She threaded her way over to me through the rows of desks.

"Hey," she murmured. "Are you done with the test?"

"Yeah, pretty much. I just need to check it over. What's going on?"

"Let me just talk to you outside for a sec." I followed her out of the classroom, nerves tickling the back of my neck.

"First of all," Felicity said once we were in the hallway, "don't worry about missing any exam time. Mrs. Johnston said she'll let you stay after for a few minutes if you need it."

"Okay…?"

"Lanie, I just got a call from your mom. She and Ryan Spina's mom both tried to call you earlier, but you were in taking your exam." The floor began to fall away. "Ryan's teacher marked him absent for his morning exam. The school called home, but his parents say he walked to school around seven-fifteen this morning. They're not sure where he is. So everyone's a bit worried about Ryan, even though he's been gone only a few hours. He has exams, so it's obviously a weird day for him to skip class."

"And his mom called me because…?" I asked, my voice high. The ground under my feet was still descending, but my head felt like it was rising higher and higher, like a balloon sailing up toward the stratosphere.

"His parents tried calling him, but it went to voicemail. So they logged onto their provider account to see if they could get his phone locator working, but it seems to be broken. Then they noticed you gave him a call earlier today. You don't happen to know where he is, do you? Hey, Lanie, you all right? You look pale, hon. Do you want to sit down?"

"Water," I croaked as I fell against the wall and slid down to take a seat on the floor. My chest was tightening, black dots crowding the edges of my vision.

"Sure," she said. Then, "I'm going to get the nurse. You don't look well." I watched her hustle away down the hall.

And when she rounded the bend and was out of sight, I got to my feet, knees wobbling, and headed back into the classroom.

The other students were all looking at me curiously. "Everything all right?" asked Mrs. Johnston.

"F-fine," I said, stumbling to my desk and sweeping my calculator and pencil into my backpack before heaving it onto my back. I grabbed my abandoned exam and brought it over to her. "Here you go. Have a good break."

"Err, you too, dear," she said, her expression mystified.

On my way out the building I scheduled an Uber to meet me in fifteen minutes on the road adjacent to the far side of campus.

Normal me would have balked at scaling the fence that ringed St. Brigid's campus, but adrenaline-soaked me found the fence to be no problem. I'd made a pit stop at Pendry to grab my wallet and dump my textbooks. Wallet, house key, phone—what else did you need to save your could-be-boyfriend from killer scientists? Whatever Mac-Gyver inventions might prove useful, I wouldn't find them in my dorm room.

And then over the fence I went, hardly thinking about it until I was on the other side. My PE teacher would have been so pleased.

The Uber driver pulled up a few minutes later, just when I was getting worried he wasn't going to show. He rolled down his window and gave me a squinty look. "You eighteen?"

"Uh, yeah?" I lied, doing my best impression of an eighteen-year-old. This turned out to be very much like staring back at him hoping he believed me.

A few interminable seconds crawled by. "Well, all right," he said at last. "Hop in."

I got in with some reservation; I'd never been in a taxi or Uber by myself before. It had been my dad's idea right before I moved to St. Brigid's to install the app and set it up with his credit card, just in case I ran into any sort of trouble. He was a smart guy, my dad, though I doubted he'd ever anticipated *this* sort of emergency.

Thankfully the Uber driver wasn't one for small talk. Even better, when he saw me pulling my earbuds from my pocket to listen to music, he offered me an aux cable instead. He raised his eyebrows a bit when he heard my music selection: the playlist I used with Felicity to practice meditation. The burble of a stream and the tinkle of wind chimes suffused the cabin, like this little Honda Civic were the world's tiniest yoga studio.

"Listen," I said, "I've got a bad migraine, and this helps me relax. If you just get me to Enville within an hour and don't laugh about the music, I'll give you a fifty dollar tip. My merry Christmas to you."

"No joke?" he said, shooting me a skeptical look in the rear-view mirror.

"No joke."

And when we got onto the highway and the trip back to Enville was truly underway, I settled back into my seat and braced for pain.

I was still fumbling around in the dark when it came to my newfound abilities; that much was obvious. But even in my blundering I was starting to form a clearer picture of what I was dealing with. Communicating with Melissa via dreams was by far the best, now that I'd cleared the hurdle of lucidity—no garbled speech, no need to be sick or high or tipsy.

But I found myself wondering if there wasn't one last way to talk to Melissa while I was awake—and I was betting the answer was yes. The giant, glaring problem was that I needed to figure it out in the next hour, because I didn't much relish the thought of getting buzzed and sneaking onto Avanic's campus.

I'd save *that* for Plan B.

So I closed my eyes, let the New Age music wash over me, and tried to focus on—nothing. Long breaths in, long breaths out, letting intruding thoughts drop away like pebbles falling into a ravine.

Until I wasn't Lanie speeding north on a highway but just breath and a heartbeat. Only then did I try to send out one word.

Melis—

The car swerved violently right, and my eyes jolted open.

"Sorry!" the driver called. "Scrap of tire in the road!"

I gritted my teeth, closed my eyes, and began tunneling down into myself once more. *Inhale. Exhale. Inhale. Exhale.*

Down, and down, and down.

And then I tried again, one tendril of thought, fine as a single hair.

Melissa?

I could tell it was working when my head started aching again. The daylight filtering through my eyelids grew bright as a spotlight.

Lanie… More an echo of a voice than anything audible.

I'm coming, I told her. *Meet me in the clearing.*

All right, came her answer from what sounded like thousands of miles away.

And the driver's GPS dinged; we were taking the next exit. I nearly cried out when I opened my eyes; the strange blurred shadows were back, my head pounding like a bass drum, the sunlight sharp as needles. It felt somewhat akin to an ophthalmologist dumping an entire bottle of dilating fluid into your eyes, then sucker-punching you in the head.

That was what I should have brought with me—sunglasses. Well, too late now.

"You okay back there?" the driver asked, hearing my swallowed gasp. "You carsick or something?"

"I'm f-fine," I said, blinking to make the shadows disappear. Worryingly, it didn't seem to be working.

"Well, just a few minutes more."

True to his word, within ten minutes we were turning onto Ferngrove. My dread began to crystallize as the insanity of my Plan A began to sink in. But turning back now simply wasn't an option.

Let Operation Become A Super Spy/Ghost Medium commence.

Chapter 28

"AND A VERY merry Christmas to you too!" the driver called as I slammed the door. I'd realized just as we'd passed 2 Ferngrove—likely visible from space with its flashing LED Christmas lights and ten-foot tall inflatable snowman— that if anyone were home I couldn't risk them seeing a car pull into the driveway. Which had then necessitated barking at the driver to stop the car and let me out on the side of the road, earning me even more side-eye. The promised fifty dollar tip, though, ended everything on a positive note.

The sunlight now that I'd left the shade of the car was dazzling, though the shadows in my eyes were finally subsiding. Thank goodness there was no snow on the ground. I waited until the Uber was gone, then scrambled off the road. Best to pick the rest of my way home through the woods, to ensure no one saw me.

More luck greeted me when the house at last came into view: no lights on, Josefa's car mercifully absent. The first bit of my plan, at least, was going off without a hitch. I let myself in and braced as Mustard rocketed toward me across the foyer, tail wagging at hyperspeed.

"Hey, buddy…" He showered me with dog kisses as I stood in the center of the foyer, feeling like an intruder in my own home—and in a sense, I was. This was an illicit trip home, after all; I was ditching my Spanish exam to be here, hadn't told a soul—well, no *living* soul—that I was coming.

If I got kicked out of St. Brigid's, I wondered, what then? Would I be off to some other, less crunchy private school, with teachers like prison wardens? I envisioned Felicity sadly shaking her head at my parents, my dad putting on a stoic face, a silent tear slipping down my mom's cheek. *We've unfortunately determined that St. Brigid's cannot provide a supportive learning environment for Lanie. Here's a list of juvenile detention centers that we think might be a good match for her, and best of luck with your incorrigible daughter.*

I shook myself out of the vision, remembering my unknown yet ticking deadline. Ryan might be in pain right now—or worse. No time for daydreams.

First I headed upstairs to my parents' bedroom, Mustard trotting along beside me. I gave a little whoop when I spotted a glasses case on my mom's dressing table. Bingo—sunglasses. I slid them on, and the world darkened and instantly grew ten times more bearable. Extra side benefit: now I looked more the part of a spy.

My phone vibrated—a text from Naomi.

Reading her text didn't even feel real—like I'd left real life and was acting in some play. How had it come to this, that I was standing in my parents' bedroom right now wearing sunglasses? The half-joke I'd told Naomi the first time we'd met flashed through my mind.

I transferred to St. Brigid's because I was being haunted by some ghosts in my house, and I couldn't take living there anymore.

As I turned to leave the bedroom, I wondered what would have happened if I'd told her I wasn't kidding. Would she have believed even half of the truth?

I heard the clatter of a key in the downstairs front door and stopped dead. Mustard's ears had perked up, and a second later he took off down the stairs. A few floorboards on the first floor creaked, then there was a thump and the muted strains of an untrained but pretty soprano voice.

Josefa.

I listened hard, trying to figure out what room she was in. It sounded like the kitchen, which meant she'd probably be there for a while. The door to my next destination—the basement—was on the opposite end of the house from the kitchen. If I stayed very, very, *very* quiet, I should be able to sneak downstairs without her noticing.

Or should I not risk being found out by her? I could stroll casually downstairs, say hello, hope she didn't notice anything was off. It would be easy to tell her a story — felt homesick, exam got out early, something like that. She probably didn't even know my school schedule. Probably.

Yet Josefa had known me since I was a little girl; she could read me like a master poker player. She might see through my lie—plus I'd have to forsake the sunglasses, and she'd notice my teary eyes straightaway.

Best not to involve her. I tiptoed down the stairs at a snail's pace, skipping over the creaky fourth step from the bottom. Then I made a creeping, roundabout passage through the house, keeping to the carpet wherever I could, freezing every time her singing paused, like I was playing some bizarre version of musical chairs.

At long last I reached the basement door. I shivered when the doorknob gave a slight *shick*. And then down into the basement I crept, slowly, slowly. The darkness, split by a lone shaft of sunlight from the far, high window, was like medicine to my hurting eyes.

First I headed past the air hockey table towards the bar. I grabbed a bottle of merlot with a screw top from the wine rack, then turned towards the unfinished part of the basement in the back, designated for storage.

Between a filing cabinet and a bin of craft supplies I found a hodgepodge of old camping equipment. I had no use for tents, sleeping bags, or coolers, but...

"Gotcha," I whispered, reaching for a silver canteen with a cross-body strap. It was a bit banged up, but what did that matter? I quickly filled the canteen with the wine, thus concluding my preparations for Plan B, and began padding back toward the stairs.

The chime of the doorbell and Mustard's accompanying howl made my heart hiccup in my chest. Josefa's singing stopped, and I heard her footsteps overhead moving towards the front door.

"Hello?" she said a moment later, sounding confused. Who could it be? We never got solicitors; they couldn't be bothered to drive down our long, bumpy road for only three houses.

"Hi there," replied a baritone voice I didn't recognize. "You the owner here?"

"No, no," she said. "They're working. You'll have to come back."

"Habla español?"

"Sí…?" Here I was, ditching my Spanish final so I could huddle in the basement and eavesdrop on a full-on Spanish conversation. My phone buzzed in my hands, and I nearly dropped it; someone I didn't know with a Connecticut number was calling me. I sent it to voicemail.

The man spoke again. "Usted y sus vecinos deben evacuar de esta calle. Soy de la compañia de gas natural. Hay una fuga en la tubería." I frowned; this was above my level. His tone sounded urgent, like there was some sort of emergency.

Josefa gasped, cementing my suspicions. "Una fuga de gas? En serio? Ay, Dios mío." My heart thumped a beat against my ribs. A gas leak? Did I really have that right?

"Sí, Señora. Hay alguien más en la casa?" *Is there anyone else in the house?* The back of my neck started crawling. What were the chances some worker would come by talking about a gas leak *right now*?

"No, no, sólo yo." *No, no, just me.*

"Por su propia seguridad debe salir. Escriba su número aquí. La llamaremos cuando todo esté seguro." Something about Josefa having to leave, for her safety.

"Déjeme agarrar mi bolso. Ah! Y el perro." *Let me grab my purse. Oh! And the dog.*

"Claro que sí… Pero hágalo de prisa, por favor." *Of course… But please be quick.*

I heard the tramp of Josefa's footsteps moving towards the interior of the house, then back to the front door. My phone buzzed two more times as the door slammed shut and the house fell silent.

You have 1 new voice message from Unknown, 860-555-3817.

Text from Unknown, 860-555-3817:

Lanie, this is Felicity.
Where are you??

And gazing down at my phone, my blood chilled with straight, icy fear. It was too coincidental for there to be some dire gas leak right now. I thought I'd been playing it safe, watching my language over the phone, keeping Avanic from connecting the dots.

But the dots were just too easy to connect. Avanic wouldn't have thought it *just a little bit odd* that Ryan was talking with the very same girl who'd come into contact with their precious CC gel? A girl whose family they'd paid a gigantic settlement?

And then what would Avanic do, aware that the both of us knew too much, perhaps even suspecting my newfound abilities? I could see the newspaper headline, the opening paragraph.

Two Teenagers Reported Missing

ENVILLE—The police and the FBI are conducting a search for sixteen-year-olds Lanie Adams and Ryan Spina. Both were reported missing on Friday. Sources say the two were romantically involved, though there was some parental disapproval of their relationship. Spina is a student at Enville High School, which Adams also attended until a mid-November school transfer to St. Brigid's Preparatory School in South Arland, Connecticut. Police believe the two teenagers are together; any information should be directed to the Enville Police or the FBI.

The story wrote itself.

And maybe I'd disrupted Avanic's plans a bit, sneaking away from St. Brigid's when I had. Maybe they'd planned to kidnap me today at school, only to find I'd unwittingly given them the slip. But here I was, reading texts on what essentially doubled as a tracking device; this was *the fucking CIA* I was dealing with, after all. Ryan had landed on their radar from just a few Google searches.

All this shot through my head in a few heartbeats as I looked at my phone.

And then I heard a familiar creak overhead; someone had just opened the front door to my house. Panic closed over me like a tsunami as I helplessly scanned the ceiling. I was a mouse caught in a trap down here.

My eyes snagged on the high basement window to my right. I knew it opened; my elementary school self had squirmed through it too many times to count. The question was whether my sixteen-year-old self could be just as agile—and if I could do it silently.

I darted over to the bar to fetch a stool, doing my best to keep my footsteps light as a ballerina's. Bringing the stool over to the window, I placed it down gently, then climbed up, my jaw clenching when the wooden legs wobbled. The click when the window latch released was like a cannon shot to my ears.

I pushed the window open, flinching as it squeaked. The chill December air wafting in was laced with the smell of pine trees; I could see the tree line from here, so close and yet so far. I readied myself, trying to picture myself pushing up through the window in one smooth, gymnast-like motion. Visualization was supposed to help with things like this, right?

I heard the light tread of a footstep, almost directly overhead.

Grabbing the window sill, I heaved myself up. Too late I

felt the jerk of the canteen strap snagging on a nailhead as I vaulted upwards and out. There was the unmistakable sound of threads snapping, then weight lifted from my shoulder as the strap gave way. Down the canteen went, hitting the basement floor with a bouncing, resounding clatter. I froze mid-clamber out the window, one leg in, one leg out.

Did I have time to climb back down and grab it? Heavy footsteps overhead were racing toward the stairs. Whoever was in the house was no longer bothering to stay quiet.

I hurled my phone back into the basement and heard it land with a shattering crunch. Then I scrambled out the window, got to my feet, and flew towards the woods, leaving Plan B behind me.

Chapter 29

NO TIME TO meet Melissa in the glade, no time to concoct the perfect plan, no time, no time, no time. I tore through the forest towards Avanic, dodging trees, weaving around bushes, twigs snapping under my combat boots. And as I went I opened myself to the pain, ripping off my sunglasses, widening my eyes at the blinding light, welcoming the pounding in my head and the crawling, deepening shadows. Hadn't Melissa said that CC gel could be activated in much the same way as an out-of-body experience, through fear and trauma and pain?

So let it be painful. I had no convenient cave to hide away in and meditate. This last, desperate hypothesis was the only hope I had left.

MELISSA, I cried, and the pain swelled. *MELISSA*. I tried to focus on the sound of the words, tried to ignore the grinding in my head. *NEW PLAN. I'M HEADING STRAIGHT TO AVANIC.*

The pain became everything. My mind was crying out for relief; I could hardly see the world around me anymore for the flickering light and shadows…

And then I lifted out of my body like an airplane peeling off the ground. I could see myself running below, could feel the pounding of my feet on the ground and the growing stitch in my side, yet somehow there I was, floating high above it all.

Well, this wasn't what I'd been expecting, but it suited my purposes well enough. I looked back the way I'd come, spotting a patch of bushes rustling a ways off: a shadowy male figure following at a run. I looked forward again: Avanic's complex of buildings loomed in the distance, growing closer by the second. Between the fence and the buildings lay a wide expanse of shorn lawn. I'd be clear as day to anyone who happened to look through the windows. It was the equivalent of a corporate, landscaped no man's land.

Yet I didn't fancy my chances at slipping past the guards at the front gate. Hopping the fence was still my best shot.

I called out to Melissa again, shouting through the pain.

HAVE TO HOP THE FENCE. TELL ME WHERE.

No, Lanie… It's too dangerous…

My fear, my pain, my rage—all of it exploded out of me in a scream. *TELL ME! HOW CAN I BREAK IN.* Not a question anymore, but a demand.

All right, came her far-off whisper. *Overhanging tree… Opposite the dumpsters… I'll meet you…*

That I could work with. I soared closer to Avanic, searching desperately for the dumpsters. A streak of blue to the north snagged my attention for half a second: Melissa racing away from the glade where she'd been waiting for me. Too bad she couldn't teleport, like Claw H—no, Pamela.

I spotted more movement about a quarter of a mile south of Melissa, this person fully corporeal. Had my CIA stalker run so far already?

No, wait, that person was me. I gasped, having almost forgotten that I, too, was down below. How was any of this possible, anyway? A paring away of my consciousness, my body on auto-pilot as I sprinted towards Avanic? I'd been able to feel the ground under my boots a minute ago… Now the sensation of my physical body was duller, faded.

Not good. Whatever out-of-body hocus-pocus this was, I needed to locate the dumpsters right stat now, then quit gliding around up here. The pain, the throbbing light and shadows—who knew what sort of snarling tiger I was poking? The last thing I wanted was to accidentally cleave my mind from my body for good, leaving my body below a soulless zombie.

I looked back to Avanic. Where the hell were the dumpst—?

A rock below my boot. My foot rolled inward. Somewhere far, far away there was a lurching sensation in my gut, then a dizzying feeling as I remembered I had a gut. The world spun below me as I felt my body down below pitch forward. *(Remember you have a body? Remember?)* Pain everywhere: mind, lungs *(remember what breathing feels like?)*, knees *(jeans ripped, blood gushing and sticky)*, palms slamming down hard onto the cold ground. *(Remember?*

All this as I careened downward, soul smashing back into the meat of my body, until all of me was together again, lying in a pathetic, panting heap on the forest floor.

I promptly rolled over and vomited. So that was it, then; I'd found my limit. Dream astral projection? Fine. Real world out-of-body experiences? Not even once.

And then, when I'd successfully emptied the entire contents of my stomach onto the ground, I forced myself to my feet (nothing broken, miracle of miracles) and took off running once more.

How far back was the CIA guy? Surely he was a swifter runner than me; surely he was armed. What was his intention? Probably to bring me in alive... But it didn't mean he wouldn't try to shoot me if I became too much of a hassle.

How did it feel to get shot? And what if I died? Would my soul float off into the ether or would the CC gel get the last laugh, anchoring me to earth like Melissa?

I ditched my coat as I ran; its plum fabric stuck out too much amongst the winter foliage. Thank God that when I'd gotten dressed this morning I'd decided on a dark brown sweater instead of the cheery red one Grandma Ruth had knitted me last year.

My heart leaped when I caught sight of the high chain-link fence through the trees. I slid to a halt and took cover behind a wide tree trunk.

There! I spotted the dumpsters at the side of one of the

larger buildings. Yet from my vantage point it was impossible to see if there was indeed a tree opposite them overhanging the fence. I'd have to get closer.

Leaves rustled somewhere behind me. Just a squirrel? Or the CIA guy, caught up to me at last? I waited a few breaths, pressing my back into the tree trunk as I listened hard.

Nothing, save for the usual sounds of the forest. Maybe he'd lost me. I pushed off the tree trunk and crept along the fence, doing my best to use the trees and foliage for cover.

A twig cracked, and I froze. Hadn't that been too loud for just a squirrel? My pulse pounded in my ears as I stooped down behind a bush, waiting.

And then I heard another twig snap and realized the birds had stopped chirping.

Still crouched behind my bush, I lowered myself all the way to the ground until my cheek brushed cold earth. There, about fifty feet off, I could see a burly man with close-cropped hair dressed in workman's clothes. He was looking right at me.

And then he looked away, just when my muscles were tensing to push off the ground and take off sprinting. As I did my best to keep still, I watched the man take a step forward. His eyes were trained on the ground—trying to mask the sound of his footsteps.

So he knew I was here—but from the look of it, he didn't know *exactly* where I was. Had I dripped any blood on the ground? Had I made any scuff marks in the dirt to give away my location? His gaze swiveled back in my direction; I

reigned in the urge to pull my head up, trying to remind myself that movement would attract his attention. I blinked, and
it felt like the equivalent of standing up and waving.

He turned away at last, and I snaked my hand out in
front of me before I could psych myself out of it, grabbing
hold of a good-sized rock, feeling the solid weight of it.

Easy… Easy… Wait for it…

And when he focused back on the ground again and took
another step, I hurled the stone up over the bush, aiming
for… Well, anywhere far from my pathetic hiding spot
would do.

I was already creeping onward when I heard the stone
land with a thump. The ground here was hard-packed
dirt—good for moving silently. I resisted looking back over
my shoulder; checking his location wouldn't help me now.

Time moved slow; what couldn't have been more than a
minute of crawling stretched into days. I kept expecting to
see movement in my peripheral vision, to glance to the side
and see a pair of scuffed black boots—and then to lift my
eyes and find myself staring down the barrel of a gun.

Yet the man seemed to have moved off, though I didn't
dare lift my head and check. What I *could* see from this position, though, was the dumpsters directly across from me,
with only the chain-link fence and the broad lawn to separate us. And just as Melissa had said, here was the tall tree,
a few boughs overhanging the barbed wire that lined the
top of the fence.

It would be a long drop down, more than fifteen feet from

the look of it. Yet I was way past the point of chickening out.

At a creakingly slow pace, I raised myself up to standing and stood there quivering behind the tree trunk for a moment. Then I grabbed hold of a branch and began to climb, wincing as the bark bit into my already raw palms.

Climbing trees is one of those activities that looks blindingly easy if you're the one on the ground—it's not. There are always aching arm muscles, branches just out of reach, tree limbs a tad too bendy for comfort. Then add hands shaking from adrenaline, a body bruised, bloodied, and sore from scrabbling around on the ground, and a man from the CIA into the mix, and you'll have concocted the worst possible scenario for tree climbing. As I crawled from branch to branch, at every moment I expected to hear a man's shout.

Yet finally I arrived at the limb overhanging the fence. It was a sturdy-looking branch, coming to a tapered point about ten feet past the barbed wire. If I scurried along its length like a squirrel, hopefully my weight would drag the branch down enough that the fall to the ground wouldn't be quite so far.

Perched here in my tree, I took the opportunity to scan the area around me. The man was nowhere in sight, though with all the trees and the underbrush I couldn't see that far in any direction.

And what about Melissa? Hadn't I seen her running through the forest in this direction when I'd floated out of my body? But I realized now that the pounding in my head had subsided, the pulsing light and shadows not gone but much diminished. Perhaps Melissa was here right now, unseen.

And I couldn't do the rest of this alone, I realized as I gazed at the open stretch of land between the fence and the buildings. Ryan was in Avanic—but in which building? The last thing I wanted to do was dabble with more of my abilities, but I needed Melissa's guidance.

So as I looked out at Avanic—at my enemy—I let my eyes glaze over. Cool air in, warm air out, just like back in the Uber, before everything had gone to complete shit. I was a being made of water, each inward breath cooling me down, stilling my ripples, turning me to ice. The light beamed bright as a lighthouse beacon through my eyelids…

I opened my eyes, and there she was down below, blue amongst a chiaroscuro nightmare. I pointed at my eyes, at her, gave a thumbs up. *I see you.*

As for how long I'd be able to see her, I'd cross that bridge when I got to it.

"Really?" Melissa called, and I drew in a sharp breath at her loud voice before I remembered that nobody else could hear her. I nodded, and her eyes widened. "All right. Wow."

I made a finger gun, then gave her a quizzical look. *Where is he?*

"Off that way," she called, pointing behind me and to the left. "I can see him from here. I'll tell you when. Umm… Don't break a leg when you jump down. And run like hell if you can. Ryan's in the building right across from you, and once you get in I can tell you where to go, where to hide.

The passcode to get in is 2-4-9-0-4." So at least I had a guide—and an invisible guide at that.

It should have been comforting, but all I could feel was my stomach clenching with nerves. No more delaying. I was really going to do this.

I squared my shoulders, then watched for her signal. I could see her eyes tracking the man in the woods as she waited for the perfect moment.

And then she waved her arms at me, calling me onward. "Go, go, go!"

Without letting myself think about it, I scampered forward on the branch. The ground spun alarmingly beneath me as the branch bowed and swung with my sudden weight. I could hear it creaking; would it fall? Just a foot more…

And then I'd passed the barbed wire and found myself dangling over Avanic's property. I gripped the branch tight with both hands and swung my legs down, clinging to the branch like it was the world's scariest set of monkey bars.

I'd never been great at the monkey bars—especially not after the CC gel had burned my fingertips. Already my sweating palms were slipping off. I looked down and wished I hadn't.

A splintering crack, and gravity took its course. This time it was both my body and spirit tumbling down as one, and once again I landed in a heap on the ground. I opened my eyes and found myself looking at Melissa's blue, sneakered feet.

Not exactly the super-spy landing I'd been hoping for. I pushed the tree branch off my body and hauled myself back to standing, swaying on my feet a bit. From behind me, I heard the sound of something—someone—moving swiftly through the forest brush.

We both took off running.

"Straight ahead!" Melissa called as we hurtled towards the building. All I could think of was the chain-link fence behind me. Hadn't some senator recently been shot at through a chain-link fence?

I tried to do the over-under of getting shot. Moving target—one point for me. Chain-link fence—not exactly bullet-proof material. Guy from the CIA—had to be a decent shot, right? Target in an open area—this whole exercise was going downhill.

So hundred-to-one odds, then? Good, good.

Eighty feet away from the building. I could see my reflection in the mirrored windows, absent Melissa. *So ghosts don't have reflections*, I thought. Funny the things your brain can choose to focus on in the moment. The world around me was a blur of light and shadow.

I heard a muffled crack. A clod of dirt just to my left exploded out of the ground. "Hurry!" Melissa cried.

Fifty feet away.

A few more muted gunshots—he must be using a silencer. Two shots? Three? What did it matter?

Ten feet away from the building's heavy, metal door. I could see the keypad to the right of it.

"What's the code?!" I screamed.

"Two-four-nine-oh-f—no!" Melissa's voice broke off.

A hulking, midnight blue form had just melted towards us through the door. *A trap, a trap.* Claw Hands swung her long, lanky arms toward Melissa, snared her with those wicked claws, dragged her through the door. She left a low, echoing cackle in her wake.

Alone again, oh God.

My hand shook in front of the keypad. What was the last digit of the code?

2-4-9-0-5.

Invalid, the screen blinked at me. It had to be a four, then. Hadn't it sounded like she'd been just about to say that?

"Hey there!" Another man was running towards me from the left, about fifty feet off. My trembling finger came down just above the four, entering a one.

Invalid.

"Fuck!" I screamed as I waited for the screen to clear. A bullet smashed into the door, just to the right of my thigh. There was a sudden sting in my cheek.

Once more. *2-4-9-0-4.*

The keypad flashed green, gave a long beep. I wrenched the door open and dove through, into Avanic at last.

Chapter 30

GRAY, TILED HALLWAY, fluorescent lights, no people—yet. Doors to the right, doors to the left.

I shot down the hall, my only aim to get away from the door behind me. How long until the other guy burst through? He'd know the codes, he'd have a gun. I was vying for mere seconds of time.

I skidded to a halt at the end of the corridor and peeked around the corner. The connecting hallway was also mercifully empty, though there were more doors, as well as observation windows into adjacent rooms. How much longer until some scientist inevitably emerged and caught sight of the sixteen-year-old girl panicking in the hall? I had to find some place to hide.

Let's see what's behind door number one! clamored a game show host in my head as I lurched toward the nearest door. A giggle burst from my lips, then another. This had to be shock, right? But knowing that didn't make me want to laugh less.

I brought my ear to the door: no sounds from within. I

jiggled the handle: locked. *Aww,* sighed the disappointed audience as I choked back another burble of laughter.

But what about door number two?! cried the game show host, amping up the crowd as I pivoted toward the opposite door, listened for voices, scrabbled at the handle.

Locked.

I can't believe it! shrieked the game show host over the exultant crowd. I plunged down the hallway toward the next door, ducking under a window. There were muffled voices from the room within. *Bit slow on her feet, isn't she?* said the host. *Will this really be the end of it all?*

"Shut up!" I snapped as I dashed to the next door, listened for voices, grasped the handle. I knew what was going to happen, was already looking onward down the corridor...

But the lock gave way and the door swung open, revealing a small room full of filing cabinets. More importantly, it was devoid of people and there were no security cameras.

Also no place else to go other than back out into the hallway, I noted, and no real place to hide. Yet it was better than standing in plain sight, just waiting for someone to spot me. I darted inside and closed the door.

There was no interior lock. In vain I tried to push one of the filing cabinets in front of the door, but it was too heavy to budge. I leaned against the door, cradled my head in my hands, considered my options.

There weren't many. I could venture back out and try my luck at another door—*Oooh,* exclaimed the sadistic audience—or I could stay here, maybe giving the man the slip. I pressed my back to the door, ran my hands through my sweat-dampened hair, surveyed the room for anything that could serve as a weapon. There was nothing that could even remotely count.

Stay or go? Think, Lanie, think.

But it was so hard to weigh my options with my heart racing and the man maybe right outside the door and my headache pounding, pounding, pounding. What were the odds he'd find me in the next minute?

Headache... My heart sank as I made a decision. Not twenty minutes ago I'd vowed to never fool around with out-of-body projection again. But what were promises in the end of times? If I could float out of my body, see my surroundings from outside myself, then perhaps I could navigate this place after all.

Provided I didn't forget I had a physical body again.

Against every instinct I welcomed the pain once more, looking straight up at the dusty fluorescent light fixture above, daring on the incoming shadows. I could see them wriggling in the corners of my vision. My brain felt like it was being mashed to a pulp by a mortar and pestle.

Yet I was still earthbound. What was I missing?

Oh, right—I'd called out to Melissa last time. There was no telling where she was now, but it didn't mean I couldn't do a bit of yelling.

I loosed a blood-curdling psychic scream and felt a strange rush of pride when the pain swelled and deepened. There it was... I leaned into the pain, drinking it in. Just a bit more… My stomach swooped as I surged upward toward the fluorescent light…

"Stop! Stop! Oh my God, what are you doing?!"

I let go of it all and plunged back into my body, once more collapsing to the ground. I couldn't see anything for the agony in my head and the freakish light show clouding my eyes.

"Don't shoot…" I gasped, then heaved and spat a mouthful of bile onto the tile floor.

"I'm not him," said the voice again. Male. Young. I blinked my eyes, trying to see around the rave in full swing in my head, and spotted a blotch of my favorite, familiar blue. *Oh boy.*

"Scott?" I croaked.

"That's right," said the voice again. "Now breathe. Don't speak. I'll tell you what to do."

"Where's Ry—?"

"Stop talking!" he barked. "He's close by, checking each room."

Oh.

I began rapid-fire blinking as my heart beat its way up into my throat. Two armed men on my tail, and now I could barely make out anything more than six inches in front of me.

Good going, Lanie.

"Okay," Scott said. "I'm leaving for a moment. Just a few seconds!" he said when I opened my mouth to protest. The blue dissolved into the wall, leaving me alone with the thrashing shadows.

He hadn't been kidding; not three seconds later he was back as promised.

"Time to go. *Be quiet.*"

"But I can't *see* anything," I whispered. "My eyes are all messed up."

He paused for a too-long beat. "I'll, err… I'll guide you then."

I scrambled to my feet and squinted at the door, trying to make out where the handle was.

"There you go," Scott said when I found it after a few bumbling seconds. I cracked the door and frowned as my hands came away from the smooth metal; it felt like there was something sticky coating my fingers.

Shivering, I crept from my filing room cubbyhole back into the hall. I was beginning to recognize this feeling of entering no man's land—like jumping into a swimming pool, anticipating the first chill shock, thinking you'll get used to it… But then the water just gets colder and colder and colder.

"Turn right," Scott commanded me, his voice steady—though it sounded like a forced steadiness. "Good. Go forward." His voice moved to somewhere behind me; he must be checking on the man's position. "Keep going… Oh, he's moving this way again. Stop there, door on your left! Go in—now, Lanie, *now!*" My heartbeat, already in overdrive, accelerated to warp speed when I caught the new thread of panic in his voice. As I felt for the handle, I wasn't praying, but cursing internally. Cursing out-of-body experiences. Cursing these goddamned shadows. Cursing the world in general.

I found the handle and tried to open it, only to discover that the door was a pull, not a push. Of course it was. One curse to that, too.

And then I was through into... whatever this fresh hell was. I had no clue; my eyesight was still a blurry, pulsing disaster. I resumed my frenetic blinking.

"All right," Scott said, his voice all low and scary. When the ghost guiding you around starts whispering, that's how you know things are real bad. "Couple steps forward." I followed his instruction, and my thigh brushed something hard and brown: a desk. "Grab the paperweight up and to the right." I ran my hands over the desk surface, my fingers colliding with pens, papers, a foggy stack of books... And then there it was, a hefty bronze object. I hoisted it up and heard what sounded like a thousand sheets of paper cascade in a fluttering whoosh to the floor.

"Good," Scott said. "Back to the door behind you."

"Wait, what's the plan?" I whispered.

"Move. Back. To. The. Door."

"Okay, okay." I shuffled backwards.

"I'm leaving for a second," he said, and the blue melted away again. The shadows had calmed some, more squirming than writhing now, but the light was still piercing, my surroundings one big blur. I ran my hands over the paperweight, feeling that same gumminess on my fingers. What was that?

Scott shifted back through the door. "Still only him, so far. He's checking rooms—probably about forty-five seconds until he gets to this one. You're going to stand right there—"

"Wait, what?" I sputtered.

"Stand there! Don't move an inch from that spot! And bring the paperweight down on his head when I say 'now.' Once he's knocked out you can grab his gun."

"*That's* the plan?"

"You have anything better?" he growled. "I can't exactly teach you kung fu or anything. And there are security cameras all over the damn place, so you can't hide out anywhere."

"What if I miss?"

"Then you die. It's a big paperweight. Probably you won't miss."

"*Probably?!*" I hissed. But I found myself addressing no one; he'd shifted through the door again to check on the man's progress. This time, though, he didn't come back.

I stood there, stunned, until Scott's voice through the door jolted me back into action. "Get ready!" I raised the paperweight up over my head, tried to think fierce thoughts.

"NOW!" yelled Scott, just as I heard the rattle of the door handle and felt air sweep by me as the door opened. I smashed the paperweight down toward the hazy silhouette of a man in front of me and felt it connect *hard*, like a baseball player smashing the ball out of the park. He crumpled forward into the room, and I heard the thump as he hit the ground. I'd just bashed in a man's skull.

"The gun!" Scott was shouting. It was hard to hear him over the rushing pulse in my head. "Get the gun!"

I dropped down to the ground, my knees hitting not the

hard coolness of tile but the man's body. I yelped, then fumbled around for the gun, feeling the fabric weave of his coat, then something thin, light, plastic— "Take that, too," Scott said. "It's his key card."

I slipped the card into the pocket of my jeans, then continued my search, finding the man's hand. He was still cradling the gun. I eased it out of his grasp.

Scott yelped. "Christ, don't hold it that way!"

"In case you've forgotten, I'm *kind of blind right now!*" I snapped at him, setting the gun down as gently as I could. My palms itched with nerves. "I'm going to need a minute."

"But—"

"Non-negotiable! Sixty seconds! Go out in the hallway and yell if anyone's coming."

Once he was gone I pressed the heels of my palms into my eyes, the back of my neck crawling as I anticipated Scott's shout. Slowly more of the shadows ebbed away, the light dimming to a few hairs below blinding, the pounding in my head fading to an acceptable throbbing.

Intentionally not letting myself look down, I glanced around to find myself in someone's plush office—a gleaming mahogany desk with expensive leather chair to match, an entire wall of bookcases filled with scholarly tomes, a long line of official plaques tacked to the wall, all of them detailing various achievements and degrees. The room could have been ripped straight from the pages of a furniture magazine for CEOs and Nobel Prize winners were it not for the disarray on the desk (my doing) and the papers strewn all over the floor. (Also me.)

And now came the time to look down. I steeled myself, then lost my nerve and dropped my eyes instead to the paperweight. This turned out not to be a proper paperweight at all, but really some sort of fancy metal trophy; perhaps my instinct about Nobel Prize winners had been correct. My vision was still too poor to make out the words engraved on the base, but the blood on the corner was obvious enough.

I forced my gaze downward. More blood — the top right of the man's head was a mess of it. *I* had done that. I watched his chest, waiting for an inhale that didn't come. Something in my gut coiled tight, and my chin began to quiver.

Stop that — it was either him or you.

I set my jaw tight and reached for the gun, then started. My hand was covered in drying blood; it was all over my fingers, caked under my nails. That couldn't be from the CIA guy, could it? All I'd done was hit him once over the head.

Then I felt a deep ache in my cheek and remembered the sting I'd felt just before I'd punched in the security code — grazed by shrapnel from the bullet hitting the door, most likely. And then in the room with the filing cabinets I'd been looking for pain... What had Scott said when he'd caught me just about to lift out of my body?

Oh my God, what are you doing?!

I brought my hand to my cheek and gasped when my fingers brushed ribbons of torn flesh. Had *I* done that?

I picked up the gun (from the proper end this time) and

called out to Scott.

He didn't answer—but another man did.

Chapter 31

"WHAT TH—?" The timber was low and gravelly—an old man's voice. A moment later he appeared in the doorway, the man's body slumped between us. We gaped at each other—him at me crouched on the floor, clutching a gun, my cheek a shredded wreck, and me at him. Clad in a lab coat, he was white-haired, stooped, and thin as a shriveled-up weed.

The old man cleared his throat. "Last time I saw you," he said lightly, "it was to give you a bunch of stickers."

"You're Dr. Brixham," I answered.

He bent his head toward me slightly in a nod. "Things have really come to a head, haven't they, Lanie?" His gray eyes were boring their way into my own. They were clear and sharp as ice chips—clear enough that I almost felt like I could see straight through him to a pulsing well of greed within. He had to have heard my call to Scott; if he hadn't known what I was capable of before, he'd surely worked out a good portion of it by now.

As for where Scott had disappeared to, that was my own stupid, careless error, I realized—for of course, when my shadows had gone, he'd gone, too.

I scrambled to my feet and pointed the gun at him. "Back up." When Brixham hesitated, I raised my voice. *"Now."*

I moved forward slowly as he did an old man shuffle backwards. I kept a good few yards between us, just in case he lunged at me.

"Now take me to Ryan," I said.

He nodded. "Fine, fine. I'll have to grab my key card from my desk drawer." He indicated the desk behind me. "It's a high security area."

Alarm bells went off in my mind. What were the chances he didn't have the key card on him? And besides, I had the CIA guy's key card in my pocket; surely that could gain us entrance wherever we needed to go, right?

But what if it couldn't?

"I'll get it for you," I said, watching him closely. Had his eyes just narrowed? "Stay where I can see you," I ordered him. I opened first the top left drawer to find—

"Bottle of scotch, huh?"

"Perks of being the boss," he said, lips twitching into a cold smile.

I moved over to the right-hand drawer and tugged. Nothing happened—yet one more thing in this facility that was locked. There was a small gray pad beside the handle, I saw now. A fingerprint lock?

I crooked a finger at Dr. Brixham. "Get in he—"

That was when everything happened. Dr. Brixham was there and then he was not, the second CIA guy in workman's clothes shoving him aside as he charged into the room, gun in hand.

I didn't think about it, my finger tensing on the trigger automatically. The force of the gunshots set the bones in my arms humming, turned everything in my ears to high white noise. And then he, too, was on the ground, not dead, but God oh God oh God oh God. Blood everywhere: floor, walls, down his front.

The man gave a watery cough as he lay on the floor where he'd fallen. "Bitch," he sputtered. "You fucking bitch."

"S-sorry," I said—the reflexive kind of sorry you say when someone reveals some sadness that's befallen them—dog died, mom has cancer—and you know you need to say something but you've never been in this situation before and what—?

He raised his hand weakly. There was still a gun in it.

Time moved fast-slow, the world contracting to this here, this now. "No!" Not me shouting. Confusion lanced across the man's face, and his gaze jittered away from me toward the doctor. I brought up my own gun, pulled the trigger.

One light click, and that was all. I was out of bullets.

A polished leather shoe kicked at the CIA guy's hand: Dr. Brixham. The gun skittered down to the ground just in front of him. We both dove for it, our hands touching…

The man gave a wrenching half-scream half-gasp. There'd been blood before, but now it leaked out of him onto the floor like an internal dam had burst. He went still.

And the gun was in my hands. I dropped the other

useless one to the floor, held the new one aloft, pointed at Dr. Brixham who was looking at me, horrified, through the doorway. Nobody had ever looked at me like that before.

As for me? I was oddly calm—had reached some new state beyond panic. I gazed blankly at the doctor for a second before my eyes alit on a familiar red panel behind him.

"Pull that fire alarm," I said, "then get in here and close the door behind you." The skin around the doctor's eyes tightened. *"Pull it!"* I commanded, and I felt a trickle of relief when he reached for the panel. The alarm began to blare, echoing up and down the hallway. The less people around, the easier this next bit would be.

He picked his way over the two men's bodies into the room. I shuddered when he had to nudge the second CIA guy's foot back to properly shut the door. Outside the room, a man's cry joined the fire alarm, followed by someone else's blue curse. They'd seen the bodies.

Then I heard the unmistakable crackle of a radio, muffled through the doctor's lab coat pocket.

"Orders for the kid?" Brixham visibly stiffened as tingles raced over my skin.

"He means Ryan?" I asked.

"Yes."

"Tell him to evacuate and keep Ryan there."

He pulled out the radio. "Leave him there. Harry, you take care of yourself and Ian."

The radio hissed. "Copy that."

Harry and Ian—not Vlad or Damien or Adolf. Such

ordinary names for employees at a facility in the business of experimenting on teenagers. These people lived in my town?

I pushed the thought away and met Dr. Brixham's flinty gaze. "You have your key card already. I have one too, by the way. And there's a gun in the other desk drawer." The doctor nodded mutely as I stated these facts. He knew. I knew.

"Open the drawer," I said, motioning towards it with the gun. "Carefully. Slowly. I don't want anything to happen to you, and I *know* you don't want anything to happen to me. And then you are going to take me to Ryan."

Chapter 32

I FOLLOWED DR. Brixham down the now deserted corridor, each of my hands gripping a pistol. As the fire alarm wailed, my thoughts were a slide show of still images, each one drenched in blood.

There are some things you can't ever really get over, some things that claw their way into the marrow of your bones and bind themselves to your soul, until you are them and they are you and going back is a foolish, worthless dream. The crunch of the paperweight meeting bone… My finger pulling the trigger… The man's final, wretched cry, his blood pooling on the tile… These things were all part of me now, and it made me want to tear my skin off. I'd start at my cheek, finish the job I'd started there, then keep going, until I'd finally laid bare the monster within.

Because surely I couldn't have done all that.

"So you can see Scott, somehow," Dr. Brixham said, raising his voice to be heard over the alarm. He came to a halt in front of a door and swiped his key card. "What about Melissa and Pamela?"

"Them too," I said bluntly. The bare minimum of information would do, just enough to keep this hostage situation civil. The doctor's life's work was overseeing Avanic and SPECTR; he must think of the program as something like a child. And what did that make me? Some prodigy daughter he'd never known he had? Whatever he thought, it had been enough for him to save me getting shot.

We entered a giant laboratory that put any school science classroom I'd ever been in to shame. The center of the room was full of cluttered work stations, many abandoned mid-experiment. Shelves of neatly labeled beakers lined one wall, beneath them what had to be twenty cages all in a row, each with their requisite mouse resident. A few gleaming silver machines nearly tall enough to scrape the ceiling hummed away in one corner, and the far wall featured an array of panels, with various readouts and gauges and blinking lights. The room looked like mission control for All of Science.

Dr. Brixham led me to a door at the back of the room labeled AUTHORIZED PERSONNEL ONLY. Opening the door revealed another corridor, this one carpeted. When the door shut behind us, the electric purr of the machinery in the other room died, like someone had hit the mute button. The alarm was still sounding, but it was flattened. Soundproofing?

A crimson door loomed at the end of the corridor, emblazoned with more bold text forbidding interlopers. My feet felt heavy, as if I were wearing leaden shoes.

This was the one.

The doctor swiped his card, and the lock clicked; we were through, entering another huge room. Lights on the ceiling were flashing in time with the fire alarm, and the air still felt deadened—more soundproofing, no doubt to mask cries from Avanic's non-rodent test subjects. The room was filled with all sorts of blinking, high-tech equipment; I spotted one machine off to the side that looked like a more complicated version of the device they use at the eye doctor's to check your prescription, complete with countless knobs and levers. This must be the machine that Melissa had mentioned, the one the scientists used to see the ghosts.

And there were the tanks, three in total. They were bigger than I'd imagined, taking up one entire half of the room, crafted from thick glass like the kind they use in aquariums. The blue liquid inside emitted a radioactive glow. It was viscous and gloppy, and there were *things* suspended within it, things of varying shapes and sizes, some thin and delicate, some long and knobby, each one bleached stark white.

Bones.

"Lanie, behind you!"

I registered Ryan's cry too late. One strong arm from behind snaked around my throat; another knocked the gun in my right hand to the ground. I flailed against my assailant, still clutching the other gun, and Dr. Brixham ducked down, no doubt fearing a bullet.

And then the man's arm tightened around my windpipe, and dark spots swarmed my vision. I felt someone pluck the gun from my grasp, and then a sharp pinch in my upper arm.

The room swam before my eyes, expanding then contracting. My body was going limp, and I was being lowered to the ground. I watched on helplessly as Dr. Brixham and the other man—Harry? Ian?—conferred together in front of me. I strained to hear what they were saying, but the whole world was shifting and fading…

"Lnyeh! *Lnyeh!* LNYEH!" The insistent voice came to me from somewhere far off, like the words were being bellowed at me from across the Grand Canyon. I frowned and kept my eyes closed, hoping whoever it was would shut up and go away. It felt so good to sleep…

But I was in the land of the conscious now, and I could tell there was no going back. Nubby carpet scratched at my cheek; I was still lying on the ground. How long had I been out? It couldn't have been for long; the fire alarm was still going off…

"LNYEH!" The voice tried once more, and this time I recognized the word, though garbled, as my name. I cracked one eye a millimeter open. Melissa was bent over in front of me, shouting; tears glistened on her cheeks. Scott and Claw Hands stood behind her, the tanks a looming backdrop. Scott's eyes were wide, his hands clenched into fists; the demoness's face was just as shadowed and unreadable as ever.

Melissa was saying something else unintelligible to me, fear etched into her face. I tried to push up off the ground, but my body was rock-heavy, weighted to the earth…

"Bill, are you there?" Dr. Brixham's voice came from somewhere behind me. There was no response; the doctor must be on the phone. "Good. And what about—? Perfect. Have him start a small chemical fire in the lab on the east side, away from that door. And then you work on getting those bodies squared away before the firemen barge in."

"Beauchamp and Friesen are on it?" said a different man's voice.

"Yes." Dr. Brixham heaved a sigh. "God, what a shit show. How much did you give her?"

"Not even half a dose," said the other man, "since I didn't know her medical history. She'll start coming around soon, I'm sure."

"All right, then you stay here. I'll work on fending off the firemen and the rest, but get the two of them hidden away in Ward B, just in case." Dr. Brixham paused, sighed again. "Two men down… The director's going to have my head."

"We have the girl, though," said the other man. "That has to count for something."

Dr. Brixham snorted. "We'll see." His voice was growing fainter; he must be moving towards the exit. "When I was on the phone with him last month he called SPECTR 'history's most expensive séance,' if that gives you any indication."

I heard a door close, then felt a man's hand grip my shoulder. I opened my eyes and found myself looking at a key card dangling from a lanyard. It had a picture of a middle-aged man with a red beard and flinty eyes. The text underneath read *Rob McClintock.* My eyes flicked upward to Rob

McClintock himself.

"You're not Harry…" My tongue was heavy, less like a body part and more like a hunk of meat floating in my mouth.

"Not much gets by you, huh?" Rob said, hauling me to my feet. As I stood, I saw that he'd thrust one of the guns into his waistband. Dr. Brixham must have taken the other one.

My knees buckled, and Rob had to hold me upright. My whole body felt loose, my legs like jello.

"Leave her alone!" came Ryan's shout from the wall opposite the tanks. I saw now that he was in a small barred room—effectively a jail cell. Two other cells lay beside his own, both empty. He was looking towards me helplessly, his eyes glassy.

Scott, Melissa, Ryan—I was surrounded by people who wanted to help me, and yet I'd never been more alone. Claw Hands and SPECTR had won.

"Young lovers," Rob said with a grimace. "History always repeats itself, doesn't it?" I heard a low hiss from behind me—was that Claw Hands?

Rob's fingers dug into my shoulders as he began to move me forward across the room towards an unlabeled door at the back. I went cold as I tried to guess at the unknown horrors awaiting me in Ward B. "In any case," he continued, "you're right—I'm not Harry. It's an alert system. The boss says 'Harry,' I know it's a hostage situation. He says 'Ian,' I know he's incoming and wants me to do something about it."

"Is 'Frank' code for 'you're a *fucking* monster?'" I slurred, just as I gathered all my strength together and wrenched out of the grip he had around my shoulders. The room spun around me like the world's worst fun house, and I hit the floor as he watched on.

"Yeah, you're going to want to take it easy," Rob said, walking over to where I'd landed. "You're up and at 'em, but a haldol and ativan cocktail is nothing to sneeze at. So come with me, and we'll get you off your feet and take a look at that cheek. What did that to you? A dog?" I tried to crawl away, but he tugged me to my feet as easily as if I were a rag doll and began frog-marching me forward once more. Melissa hovered beside us, her expression frantic. She said something to me, and though I couldn't make out the words, it was clear from her body language what she meant.

I'm sorry! I don't know what to do!

"It's okay," I said to her, not caring if Rob overheard the one-way conversation. "You did your best, and I did too."

"So it's true," Rob murmured. We were just a few steps away from the door to Ward B now. "You really can see them." His hold tightened around me, like he'd realized he was clutching some expensive piece of equipment. "Here we go," he murmured, pausing before the door. "Let me just..." He fumbled for the key card with his right hand, still keeping me in close, just as I too grabbed for his key card—or rather, the lanyard attached to it.

I got there first, seizing hold of the lanyard and launching myself to the right. He loosed a choking cry as the lanyard whipped around his neck, cutting across his Adam's apple and yanking him with me to the ground.

And then we were tangled together on the floor, him gasping for air and trying to restrain me, and me reaching for the gun. The room was a gut-churning blur. My fingers brushed cool metal, but he jerked to the left, and with him went the gun. I found it again, grabbed at the grip, but I couldn't get it free from his waistband…

But it felt like the gun was angled in toward his leg.

Bang! Bang! Bang!

He howled and released me, just as white-hot pain shot through my right knee—pain that could only be from a bullet, pain that rocketed me out of my body for the third time that day. I sank back down a second later. Shadows were already squirming eagerly at the edges of my sight.

"Lnyeh!" I heard Melissa shout, then a moment later in crystal clarity, "Lanie!"

"You shot me," Rob blubbered, looking down at his inner thigh. Blood was swiftly staining his pant leg. "You—"

He looked back up at me, and his face drained of what little color it had left. The gun had finally slipped free of his waistband when he'd released me, and I had it aimed right at him.

"*Get out,*" I hissed, trying to still my trembling arms. The gun felt far heavier than it should. "I've already"—my mouth couldn't form the words—"twice today."

And I kept the gun trained on him as he got up as best he could, like a fawn struggling to its feet for the first time, and hobbled away toward the exit.

Chapter 33

I SET THE gun down as soon as he was out of sight, then tried to stand, but the drugs pumping through my veins and the roaring pain in my knee sent me crashing back down to the floor.

Two pairs of blue feet entered my peripheral vision. "Get to Ryan," Melissa begged, Scott seconding her cry. "Hurry, Lanie. You have to get to Ryan." I began to drag myself at a turtle's crawl toward his cell, whimpering each time my right knee bumped the ground. I heard a throaty whine that could only be from Claw Hands.

"You can do it," Melissa breathed. She'd gotten down on the ground beside me, her breath frosting my ear. "Just a little further."

I cried out as I closed the last short stretch, my knee screaming in protest. Ryan was reaching towards me through the bars, gripping my arms, dragging me upwards. I clung to the bars, my energy flagging as I tried not to topple over. The demoness made another low noise, a mewling sort of whimper.

The lock required yet another card; there was also a key-pad for entering a code manually. I gritted my teeth and dug in my pocket for the key card.

But the panel lit up red and gave a short, honking beep when I swiped the card. I heard Melissa's sharp intake of breath; she hadn't expected this. I tried again…

The panel flashed red. "Leave, Lanie," Ryan pleaded. "They'll come back and kill you. You have to—"

"Stop it," I whispered as I flipped the card around, swiped it once more with shaking fingers.

Red. *Beep.*

I couldn't leave him. From simply a live-or-die stand-point, the chances were effectively zero that I could make it out of here alone. I'd barely been able to crawl to Ryan's tank. I was free now, but they'd catch me soon enough.

Yet even that didn't really matter. Leaving Ryan would mean I wouldn't be able to live with myself for whatever small sliver of life I had left. I'd dragged him into all this, and now I had to save him; it was as simple as that…

My ghosts clustered in; I could see their blue in the cor-ners of my vision, could feel the chill of them beside me. My skin was springing goosebumps.

"Scott, I don't know this one," Melissa murmured. "Do—?"

"Try one-six-eight-four-eight?" Scott said. His voice was tight; he didn't sound confident.

The manual code didn't work. I bent my head against the

unyielding metal bars, and Ryan touched his lips to my forehead. The demoness whined once more.

"It's all right," Ryan murmured, covering my hands with his. "Go."

"I w-won't leave you. I c-came to s-save y—"

"Three… ssseven…"

I raised my head. "What?" That sibilant voice… I'd only heard her speak once before—*Leave ussss… ALONE!*—but her voice was unforgettable.

Both Melissa and Scott were gaping at the demoness, just as shocked as I was. Her shoulders were bowed, her face too dark to read. She spoke again. "One-sssixx… eight… three-sssseven… *Sssave him…*"

"Th-thank you," I stammered, and a beat passed between the two of us before she turned and walked away, seeming to shrivel with every step.

The latch clicked and released when I punched in the code. Ryan was through the door in an instant, hoisting me into his arms. "The tanks," I whispered to him, and he nodded. As we crossed the room, Pamela retreated to a far corner, hunching into a ball and rocking back and forth. A wail split the room, high and keening.

The tanks towered over us, bathing us in an eerie blue light, and they radiated a poisonous heat; this side of the room had to be ten degrees warmer than the other. I did my best not to stare at the pale bones floating within the thick gel, tearing my gaze away instead to look at the ghosts.

"You're sure you want to do this?" I asked.

Melissa turned her head towards Scott, her eyes shining like liquid crystal. "I'm ready. Have been ready, for years."

He gave her a long, solemn nod, then faced me. "Yes, I'm ready," he said. His posture was ramrod straight, arms at his sides like a soldier at attention. And perhaps that was fitting. Just like a soldier, he was facing down his death—knew, in fact, that its arrival was imminent. "Thank you."

But before things went any further, he went first to Pamela, still huddled in the corner. Bending down before her, he spoke to her in a low tone, and she lifted her head. My breath caught as I watched them; I felt like a voyeur. Her attention was only for him, as if they were the only two beings for miles.

And then the demoness's head drooped back down to her chest, and Scott got to his feet.

"Yes," he said simply.

They instructed us on how to do it—one switch here, one switch fifteen feet over there, both to be flipped simultaneously. It wouldn't happen immediately, they said. There would a countdown, and then the tanks would slowly start to cool.

Ryan lowered me gently from his arms, and I clutched the supporting machinery, balancing on my good leg.

"On three?" he asked me when he reached the other switch.

I waited for the final nod from my ghosts, then grasped the switch with shaking hands. Dull metal, perfectly ordinary, yet just one movement would bring SPECTR to an end.

"One," he called. "Two…"

Three.

I flipped the switch, and the steady humming of the equipment shifted as new processes initiated. The fire alarm cut out at last, replaced by a robotic woman's too-calm voice. The alarm lights on the ceiling kept flashing.

"Warning—cooling process initiated. Abort time is nineteen minutes and fifty-four seconds. Warning…" The message began to loop.

Ryan walked back to me. "We'd better get going. They'll probably be back soo—"

He was interrupted by a terrible grinding from the bowels of the machinery. There was a clunk, then a light whirring sound, like something within was spinning around uselessly. I saw at least ten lights on a nearby display panel flip from green to red.

"Doesn't seem right…" said Ryan, shifting side to side, and I took his hand. We all stared at the machinery, willing it to work. Even Pamela had started to her feet, hanging back a bit from the rest of us.

And then a new alarm began to sound, its wail far shriller than the previous fire alarm. The alarm lights shifted into overdrive, like the room was gearing up for a pyrotechnics show.

"Warning," said the robotic woman. "CC tanks are overheating. Evacuate immediately. Warning—CC tanks are overheating…"

We ran, then—or Ryan ran, with me gathered up in his

arms. How he, not exactly the bodybuilder type, could carry me and run that fast was mind-boggling at first, but soon I stopped questioning it. Sometimes you can find just the right amount of strength when everything seems lost.

Scott had said a shaky goodbye to me as Ryan headed for the exit. I looked back just before we fled the room and saw him facing Pamela, speaking more quiet words to her. Whatever sad, strange relationship they kept was coming to a close; they were going to spend their last moments together.

Though I was cradled into Ryan's chest, I didn't shut my eyes. Melissa was keeping pace beside us, guiding us through the maze of corridors.

"Turn right here!" she yelled, and I relayed this to Ryan. "Now left at the end of the hall!"

We came to the corridor with Dr. Brixham's office. The two bodies were gone, but a half-mopped up puddle of blood remained; someone had clearly been cleaning up the evidence before being interrupted by the tank alarm.

And then the blood smears were behind us, and we were back in the hallway with the file cabinet room. "Turn there," I told Ryan, and my heart leaped when he rounded the corner and I saw the door that lead to the outside.

"Tell him not to stop when you get out," Melissa said, bending in close to me. "There won't be much time now."

I told him, even as I kept my gaze fixed on Melissa. "I'll miss you," I said. "I wish I'd known you better. And I hope..." I struggled for words as I fought an onslaught of tears. "I hope that whatever's next is better."

Next—what did that even mean? Some shining utopian paradise, with no war or death or destruction? A place beyond comprehension, far removed from human concepts like "spirit" and "soul?" Or just a final fade to black?

Melissa nodded at me, blinking fast. "I know it will be better."

Ryan shoved the door open, and I yelped as the three of us emerged into the sunlight, my still-sensitive eyes instantly tearing up. Though they were nowhere to be seen, I could hear what sounded like every single one of Enville's fire trucks and police cars, their alarms twining together into an awful symphony. They must be around the side of the building, in the parking lot.

Ryan drew in a shaking breath and adjusted his grip on me. "Which way?"

"That way," I said, pointing in the direction of the sirens. It was a risk—surely there would be masses of scientists there, as well as Dr. Brixham—but there would also be firefighters, police officers, people who could hopefully prevent us from getting taken a second time. And we also didn't really have another choice; there was zero possibility of me getting back over the chain-link fence.

I looked to Melissa again. She smiled at me, and I smiled back at her. "I'm so proud of you," she said, then glanced away as we came into view of the parking lot. Like I'd suspected, it was milling with cops, firefighters, and a small army of scientists in white lab coats—most of the latter in the process of fleeing away on foot toward the private access road. A few stragglers gawked at the chaos around them.

"MOVE BACK, EVERYONE!" one firefighter was shouting into a megaphone. A chill coursed through me when I recognized the scientist by his side as Dr. Brixham.

I saw a different firefighter point at us, and the doctor turned.

"Leave that to me," Ryan whispered in my ear. "Don't worry."

"You'll be all right," echoed Melissa, then she let out a gasp, her eyes widening. "Oh! I-I'm hot all of a sudden."

"Faster!" I urged Ryan as my heartbeat climbed to a gallop.

"Lanie," Melissa said, her speech quick, "thank you for everything, and I love y—"

But before she could finish, her blue brightened, grew luminescent. Threads of gold and white shot through her like lightning.

"—you." The sound didn't reach my ears, but I saw her mouth the word just before she took on a sun-like radiance. And then she was gone, a million shimmering particles exploding outward from where she'd just been, like a bursting supernova.

I closed my eyes, and a second later felt the boom, then the accompanying blast of heat as the world exploded.

Chapter 34

THE AIR SMELLED sour and burnt; that was the first thing I noticed as I huddled into Ryan, my eyes still screwed shut. The stench was all too familiar for having only smelled it once seven years ago — that same day that I'd put on my science goggles and trooped outside.

Ryan was holding me tighter than ever, though he'd stopped short. I could hear his heartbeat pounding in his chest, and I focused in on the rhythm, trying to block out the screams and the sirens and the *everything* that awaited me the second I opened my eyes.

Whatever came next, I could take comfort in the fact that he was here with me… That I had freed him… That we both, perhaps, had a shot at living another day.

I opened my eyes.

Ryan had me angled in such a way that the first thing I saw was the building we'd just fled. What moments before had been just another part of Avanic's glittering campus was now a burning ruin. A good third of the structure had blown off and smashed into the adjacent buildings, and flames were eating away at what remained, sending great, dark billows of smoke into the sky.

I'd seen Melissa pass on, but some trepidation had flickered through my mind about Scott and Pamela. Now I wondered no more. Project SPECTR was finished, once and for all.

I turned my head and looked forward, toward the parking lot.

We had quite the audience—more than twenty firefighters, just as many cops, and a good handful of brave (or just rubbernecking and stupid) scientists. Every single one of them was staring at the two of us, and I drew in a deep breath, trying to figure out what to say, but acrid smoke tickled the back of my throat and set me coughing.

"She needs help!" Ryan shouted at one group of cops, breaking the spell. "Please!"

They jogged over to us, dodging the smoking pieces of debris that studded the ground. I heard one of them calling on his radio for an ambulance, though I had no doubt that all the ambulances for fifty miles were already on their way. My heart sank when I saw Dr. Brixham hesitate, then trail after the cops.

"Not him," I called, pointing at the doctor.

Five pairs of eyeballs swiveled over to Dr. Brixham. "We'll handle this, sir," said the policeman nearest the doctor, putting up his hands. "If you'll just—"

But Brixham interrupted him. "So sorry, Officer…?"

"Dugan."

"Officer Dugan," he repeated tremulously. "If I can just

have *one* moment with the girl alone. She—"

"No!" Ryan and I said in unison.

The doctor pressed his bony hands together; I could see him trying to think about how to get at me. His life's work blown to smithereens just seconds ago, and here I was, within tantalizing reach. "But—"

"The young lady seems to be quite clear on this, sir," said Officer Dugan. "Now if you'll please make your way to a safer area…"

The doctor's nose scrunched, like he'd just smelled something disgusting, but he backed away after a few more seconds.

"What's that guy's name?" Officer Dugan asked, leaning in towards me.

"Dr. Brixham. That's B-R-I-X-H-A-M," I spelled. No way was I letting the doctor squirm his way out of what was coming to him.

"Thanks," Officer Dugan replied, then looked to the cop on his right. "Can you just keep an eye on him while he's still hanging around? See who he's talking to, stuff like that? Somehow I have a feeling we'll be having another conversation with him shortly."

I was starting to like Officer Dugan.

Ryan grunted and shifted on his feet; miraculously, he was still holding me, though sweat was pouring down his face by this point. "Err, sorry—can we get her to an ambulance? She's been shot in the knee and injected with two drugs—haldol and ativan…"

I watched their expressions change, could see the second they realized this story ran much deeper than a chemical explosion and an inexplicable grudge between a scientist and a high school girl. Everything around me became a flurry of activity—someone wrapping my knee as the officers took down my information, then being loaded onto a stretcher and wheeled into an ambulance.

As we sped off to the hospital, Officer Dugan himself followed behind with lights flashing. He'd promised to call my parents and Ryan's on the way over to tell them we were safe.

I hoped *they* were safe. Where had my parents been these past few hours? At our house, not two miles from ground zero? Maybe on their way to St. Brigid's? I had no doubt that Felicity had called them after I'd gone missing, and Josefa had likely touched base with them as well about the fake natural gas leak.

The very second we got to the hospital I was being readied for surgery, a swarm of people in scrubs calling for a surgeon, fluids, an anesthesiologist. I didn't look down at my knee when the nurses cut off my jeans with scissors, but I saw their faces tighten. Gunshot wounds couldn't be too commonplace at Enville Memorial Hospital.

"All right," one young nurse said to me, taking my hand in her own. "You're going to be fine, but we're going to have to put you under. Ready?" She shot a glance at the anesthesiologist, who had been figuring out how to proceed given my recent drugging. Those two medications, the EMT had told me on the ride over, were normally reserved for panicking psych patients. They were *not*, she had sniffed, commonly used on clearly lucid sixteen-year-olds.

"Good to go," replied the anesthesiologist.

But *I* wasn't good to go. "Where are my p-parents?" I asked the nurse, starting to cry.

She shook her head at me. "I'm sorry, hon—I don't know where they are, but we have to proceed… Oh!"

Someone had just knocked on the door. Another older nurse cracked it open, listened for a moment, then grinned. "Your mom and dad will be here soon! But they understand we need to get this underway."

"And Ryan?" I pressed them as the younger nurse grabbed for the tissue box. "He's o-okay?"

She bit her lip. "We're really not supposed to discuss other patients…"

"*Please*," I begged, and she glanced at the older nurse, who flapped her hand, giving the go-ahead.

"He's all right. He's being treated for dehydration, and they're keeping him around for observation, just for a few hours."

I felt a weight on my chest disappear. "Then let's do this."

The anesthesiologist placed a mask over my nose and asked me to count backward.

"Ten… nine… eight…"

And then I was back, lying in an unfamiliar hospital bed, watching my parents chatting quietly. I didn't remember waking up; I was just suddenly *there*. I felt a dull ache in my leg and my cheek, but that was all; I had to be on some heavy-duty painkillers.

The window opposite the bed was dark. "What time is it?" I croaked.

They were by my side in an instant. "Hey, kiddo," said my dad, beaming, as my mom sniffled and squeezed my hand tight.

"It's almost seven," she said tearily. "You were in surgery for four hours."

"My knee—it's going to be all right?"

She nodded. "The surgery was successful, so the doctor says with time it should heal well. I'll just call the nurse to check on you." She padded out of the room, leaving me alone with my dad.

"Lanie," he said softly, "I want you to know that your mom and I aren't mad at you or disappointed or..." He shook his head. "Or anything like that. We're confused, sure, but really we're just happy you're alive and here and—" He broke off and quickly looked away.

I felt my own lips starting to wobble. "Dad, these past few months I... I've kept a lot of secrets." I dug my fingers into the hospital blanket. "And I want to tell you about it, but I'm s-scared you won't believe me."

He sniffed loudly and laid a gentle hand on my shoulder, like I was made of glass. "I promise you—" He choked up, then started again. "Lanie, I promise that we will believe you. So when you're ready..."

"I'm ready now," I said, my voice growing a bit firmer. Reality could change in a moment, and death could be right on the doorstep, waiting for you to open the door—maybe even with a paperweight held aloft. No one else could tell this story but me, and it had to happen now.

Because even though Melissa, Scott, and Pamela were gone, they were still counting on me, in a way. They all had surviving relatives, friends, classmates—the people left behind when they'd vanished into the night. People who had only been able to wonder what had happened, guessing at the monsters lurking in the shadows.

"Okay," my dad said. I could read the surprise on his face. "Just so you know, there are a lot of people who want to talk to you. The police, one of our senators, about a hundred reporters... We've had to turn our phones off; they found the numbers somehow." He cleared his throat. "So I think the most pressing order of business is you talking to the police—but again, this is *only* when you're ready. And *only* with your mom and I and our lawyer present."

"Dad, I'm ready."

He took a moment to respond. "All right," he said at last. Something was lurking in his eyes—fear. He wanted to know how his daughter had come to be in a hospital bed with a bullet wound, but he was scared, too.

"It'll be fine, Dad," I said.

"All right," he repeated, jaw clenching. "Our lawyer's meeting your mom and I here in a few minutes, and there's actually a police officer just outside who can take your statement. Officer Dennan, or something..."

"Dugan," I corrected.

"Right."

So fifteen minutes later, after a nurse had given me a few oversized pills to swallow, I found myself surrounded by four adults.

Officer Dugan was in the chair opposite me, and he pulled out a recorder, a pad of paper, and a pencil. "Now," he said, clicking on the recorder and looking up at me. He wasn't smiling, but his eyes were kind. "If you can just start at the beginning and tell me what happened."

I talked and talked and talked, recounting my first encounter with Melissa back in October, how I'd figured out the various catalysts that let me see the ghosts and the demoness, how Ryan and I had mapped their territory, only to discover that Avanic lay at the center. The only piece I skipped over was August Rufner's involvement, saying instead that I'd read about the Connecticut serial killer hypothesis sometime last summer, then connected the dots on my own. Rufner had suffered decades of guilt; that was punishment enough.

True to his word, my dad listened steadily as I spoke, asking only the occasional question, and my mom did the same. The lawyer and Officer Dugan, however, were all raised eyebrows and barely suppressed looks that said *this girl must be on an awful lot of medication right now.*

And then I reached the events of the past twenty-four hours, where the ghost hunter shenanigans took a more serious turn. Stealing away from school in an Uber—that was the sort of thing that was generally agreed upon by society to be bad, but not really illegal. Yet everything after that, I realized as my parents paled and Officer Dugan's note-taking grew furious, was more dubious in the eyes of the law. I'd stolen onto Avanic's campus to rescue Ryan. (Trespassing.) I'd killed two men in self-defense. (Homicide.) I'd shot somebody in the leg with a gun, tampered with private property, and blown up a building. (Reckless handling of a firearm, vandalism, and… terrorism?)

Though Officer Dugan and the lawyer were keeping their cool, I knew they wanted to dismiss the whole story as bullshit—then maybe ask the nurse for a straitjacket. But they couldn't argue with the very real bullet that had been pulled from my knee during the four-hour surgery.

My throat was parched by the time I reached the end. Dugan leaned back in his chair. "And you're the *only* one who was able to see these… spirits?"

"Yes."

"You've been smoking pot off and on, you've been in the midst of finals, all while messing around with… what sort of dreaming again?"

"Lucid dreaming," I answered. "This is *not* my imagination or being tired or—"

"All right, all right," he said, throwing up his hands. He turned to my parents. "Any history of mental illness in this family?"

The lawyer cut me a sharp look. "No need to answer that.

The purpose of this meeting is simply to interview Miss Adams about her experience—that's it."

Dugan hunched forward, his eyes squinted. "Then we're done here tonight. I suggest you get some rest. And stay in town—no going back to your fancy boarding school, at least for the present. We'll need you around for further questioning." And then a court date, no doubt—probably multiple ones. And possible juvie? What the hell was going to happen to me?

"That's no problem," my mom said to Dugan, her eyes narrowing too. "We'll be wanting to keep Lanie here in Enville anyway. It's best for us to be together as a family right now."

Dugan and the lawyer excused themselves, leaving the three of us alone. I looked at both my parents, *really* looked, trying to see exactly how crazy they thought I was. Were their calm expressions just masks, or did they—?

"I believe you," my mom said, interrupting my spiraling thoughts. She glanced sidelong at my dad and took his hand in hers. "Pat?"

"Of course I do," he said. "Just like I said I would."

My mom gave a high, breathy laugh. Her eyes were wide, a tad too much white showing. "I did wonder why you had a baseball bat with you that day Ryan threw up on the rug!"

"And now," my dad said, "I can tell Grandma Ruth that it wasn't just her singing the seventh-inning stretch that day that made you sick."

"Right," I said, trying to conjure some enthusiasm into

my voice even as my heart sank. For just like I'd been able to hear the truth in Rufner's voice over the phone, I could hear my parents lying to me now. Is that what they'd discussed out in the hallway, just before Dugan and the lawyer had come in? *Whatever she says, take it in stride. She needs that most right now. And if she needs psychiatric help, we can discuss that later.*

Well, what could I have expected? Ghosts, demons, astral projection… The whole mess was laughable. Their lying was out of love for me, I knew. Did that make it better or worse?

Hard to say. When they left a little while later, I lay drained and still in my bed. Out in the hall, I could hear someone, probably one of the nurses, humming a tone-deaf rendition of "Santa Baby." Christmas was one week away, and the only present I found myself wanting was for someone to believe me.

Chapter 35

WHEN MY PARENTS got to the hospital the next day, they had three important things to tell me. The first was that they'd heard from Ryan's parents that Dugan had gone straight from the hospital yesterday to interview Ryan— and that his account corroborated nearly everything I'd said. The second was that a good number of Avanic employees were cooperating with law enforcement in exchange for immunity deals. The third was that the story had broken on the front page of all US newspapers, as well as a good number of international ones.

I could see my parents trying to parse all this in their minds. Two kids, both clearly wrapped up in something enormous, both spouting nonsense about ghosts and spirits—yet our stories matched. Then again, only one of us claimed to have actually *seen* the ghosts—unfortunately, not the sketchy stoner, but their own daughter.

I scrolled through the articles on the new phone my parents had given me that morning; they'd found the one I'd abandoned in the basement, the screen smashed beyond repair. Most of the articles were near carbon copies of each other. If Ryan's English teacher had had a say in anything, she would have written up the whole lot for plagiarism.

Illegal experimentation on US minors by CIA front company... the articles cried. *MKUltra sister program Project SPECTR continued operations into the present day... Avanic head Dr. Sydney Brixham arrested...*

No mention of Melissa, Scott, or the other SPECTR victims, I noticed with a sinking feeling, skimming for information that I already knew wasn't there.

I started when the phone began to ring. *New York number.* With some trepidation, I answered the call.

"Hello?"

"Hello, I'm calling for Miss Melanie Adams?" It was a woman; she didn't sound familiar.

"Uhh... yes? That's me."

Her voice went up about three octaves. "Hiii, Miss Adams, how are you? I hope this isn't a bad time. My name is Macy Silvers, and I'm calling from the *National Enquirer.* I would *love* to interview you for an exclusive piece about Project SPEC—"

I hung up the phone.

"Who was that?" my dad asked distractedly. He was working on setting up a new laptop (*not* a Mac, per Ryan's instructions) that I could use to play *Hour of Fate* with Ryan while I was still in the hospital. My doctor was saying it might still be a week until I was discharged—and even after that I was facing months of recovery and physical therapy.

"Reporter," I said, eyeing my phone like it was a bomb about to go off—and a moment later, it did.

Florida number. And then, after I'd sent that to voicemail, a call from California not one minute later.

"How'd they find my number?" I asked, putting my phone on silent before shooting Ryan a text.

> Journalists are calling my phone. I think Hour of Fate is almost set up.

"They're crafty, these reporters," my dad replied. "Ah, okay. All set, and… only three and a half hours of updates to download, then you should be good to go!"

A few days later the story in the papers shifted from discussing the existence of SPECTR itself to the accompanying fallout. Again the stories were all near-identical, all using the same basic phrasing and verbiage. Despite SPECTR being a national scandal, not one journalist seemed curious enough to broach the question of *what* the project's experimentation had entailed.

Key records from Project SPECTR missing… Avanic security camera footage damaged… CIA director facing Congressional hearing next week…

A hearing—but not a trial. The CIA director had known about SPECTR's dirty details; I remembered Dr. Brixham saying how the director had called the program a séance. Didn't he deserve prison time—as well as everyone else who'd known about the project?

The days in the hospital stretched on, and anger within me grew from a spark to a constant heat, always threatening to boil over. Playing *Hour of Fate* with Ryan (I was on my way to becoming a decently skilled cleric) became my escape, a lid I used to tamp down the rage.

On Christmas Eve, my mom received a call from someone at the White House. The president was extending an offer to Ryan's family and ours to go to D.C. for a formal apology, once I got the okay from my doctor to travel. Hopefully this meant that whatever crimes I'd committed to save Ryan would be forgiven. I was pretty sure they didn't let kids who were about to be thrown in prison meet the president.

"Working the damage control, but can't bother coming here himself?" my dad asked, scratching his head as he tried to figure out a sudoku. He'd been working through a whole book of the things as we waited down the days until I could leave the hospital. "Make the kid with the gunshot wound do the traveling? We'll see who gets my vote come next election!"

"Mmm," I replied, scrolling through all the phone numbers in my missed call log. It had to be over three hundred at this point. Then my phone buzzed with a text, and I perked up.

"Ryan?" my mom asked.

"Yeah." I glanced at her, asking a silent question.

"We should really get going," she said brightly, checking

the time on her phone. "I have a few last-minute gifts to wrap, and I'd rather make the pie dough tonight, instead of tomorrow morning…"

"So soon?" my dad asked.

"Presents won't wrap themselves!" she sang and shooed my dad out.

A few minutes later Ryan poked his head through the door. "You know," he said, coming in and setting his backpack down, "I saw your mom in the parking lot, and she actually smiled at me. I didn't think there could be any redemption after the vomiting-on-the-carpet incident, but maybe she's coming around to me!"

"Stop fishing for compliments," I said, gingerly scooting to the far edge of my bed. "You carried her injured daughter out of a building that was about to explode. That would change any mom's mind."

"You're sure?" he asked, waiting for my nod before clambering up and laying gently beside me. Everyone around me nowadays was treating me like some porcelain doll. "How's the leg? And the… everything?"

"Way better, actually. The bruises look bad, but I can't feel them much anymore." My body had bloomed yellow and purple in the first few days—the result of falling in the woods, then out of the tree, then my final, desperate fight with Rob McClintock. "My cheek's doing all right, too." A consulting plastic surgeon had assured me there would be little scarring, and that any scars that did occur could probably be zapped away with some laser treatments. Or, he'd said with a broad grin, I could keep the scars as a reminder of what a bad-ass I was.

I could smell the soap and sandalwood scent of whatever body wash Ryan used, could feel the solid warmth of his body against mine. I leaned my head on his shoulder and felt my internal anger ease.

Maybe it was stupid, this bit I wanted to say next… But when he left again, I knew that anger would return.

"So," I said, dropping my voice, "I've been thinking."

"Yes…?"

"Thinking that maybe we should talk to a reporter."

He interlaced his fingers tight with mine and drew in a breath. "Why's that?"

"The papers aren't talking about Melissa or what Avanic did to Pamela or CC gel or anything at all. It's almost like they're being told what to write. Like they're being given talking points. And now there's this whole thing with the missing records and the security footage, and who knows who's going to get prosecuted, and… I just think everyone should know."

Ryan nodded. "You're right," he said. "They should. But let's just say this conspiracy theory of yours is correct—the government isn't allowing the papers to publish full details or something. I mean, that makes sense, because these are massive human rights violations. But if that *is* the case, then wouldn't it be useless to talk to a journalist? Seems counter-intuitive."

"But… but maybe we could reach out to someone from a

smaller organization. You know, this woman from the *National Enquirer* gave me a call. We could—"

He scoffed. "Yeah, no thanks. I refuse to be interviewed by the same tabloid that brought the world Bat Boy."

"I think that was a different tabloid…"

"Still! Tabloids are gross! Not happening!"

"Okay, okay." I uncurled my fingers from his own, little flickers of irritation igniting within me. "Did you want to play *Hour of Fate*?"

I picked up my computer from the side table and opened Facebook as I waited for his own laptop to boot up. All my social media pages had exploded in the wake of the Avanic story; I had thousands of friend requests to sort through, as well as a slew of DMs from journalists, people from school I'd never talked to even once, conspiracy theorists…

A question scratched at the back of my mind. Two seconds later I was staring at the front page of Uncle Ed's Forum. I scrolled down to the CIA Programs sub-forum, and my jaw dropped.

"Oh my God, we're Internet famous."

Ryan laughed as he typed in his password. A moment later the ethereal *Hour of Fate* theme song filled the hospital room. "Well, yeah. Duh. You ready to play?"

"No, I mean, look at all this." I'd read the news articles, of course, but somehow seeing everyone at Uncle Ed's discussing the Avanic case felt *different*—like the most popular kids at school were dissecting the intimacies of my life. I clicked into the thread, and a strange thrill shot through me when I saw that not only had it been posted by *Uncle Ed himself*, but that it boasted almost two thousand replies — and the last one had been posted only seconds ago.

GreysFdUrMom, 12-24-19, 02:48 PM: I'm starting to think it's something to do with aliens. There's quite a lot of spotter activity in that area of the country. Thoughts?

AJ74, 12-24-19, 02:51 PM: Man, leave off with the aliens, it's definitely not that… But I doubt we'll ever really know. Government has this shit locked down, it's pretty obvious reading the papers. They're already burying the records! Like, we all know by now that MKUltra wasn't just about messing around with LSD. We'll get some watered-down version of the SPECTR stuff, just like MKUltra, but I guarantee you it won't be half of the reality.

"You see?" I said to Ryan, pointing at the last comment. "This is exactly what I said!" The skin on the nape of my neck was prickling.

He leaned in, his eyebrows knitting together into a frown as he read. "Yeah, I didn't doubt you, but what do you want to do about it?"

And it clicked into place for me then. These people might be certifiably weird, but they were *my* sort of weird, and *they would believe me.*

I waved my hand at his computer and mine. "Who needs

journalists? Let's just do it ourselves."

I could see him thinking it over. "We could film some-thing… Or better yet, livestream it. Answer questions as they come in."

I nodded at him, almost giddy. "Post on here, then tell them where to watch the stream. Tell them to tell their friends, to share it around everywhere. Once it's online, no-body can do anything about it."

He shook his head wonderingly. "My parents are go-ing to be *pissed*. They'd rather they never heard the word 'ghost' again."

"Mine too, but… fuck it. We just sort of *have* to do it, right?"

"Yeah," he said, "we do."

My pulse was racing. "So can we do it right now? Is the livestream easy to set up?" For there was no sense in wait-ing. Every day I woke up, checked the papers, and knew the chances of the world coming to know the truth about SPECTR had shrunk even smaller overnight.

And wherever Melissa and the others were now, wasn't there some possibility that they were still watching, that they knew their secrets remained buried?

Ryan's gaze stuttered over to me. He swallowed. "Sure. Let's do it right now."

When you post on a forum of conspiracy theorists that you're the very person at the center of their latest fixation and are here to tell them all about it, it takes some convincing before they decide you're the real deal. The second we made the post, we were deluged with accusations of being trolls and fakes. So we posted pictures of our student IDs with the hope that would be enough, then said we would stream in a few minutes and put up a link.

Just before we were scheduled to go live there was a soft knock on the door. It opened a moment later, and my Grandma Ruth poked her head in.

"Hi, Lanie, just thought I'd pop on by and say hell—oh!" She saw Ryan snuggled on the bed next to me, and her eyes sparkled. "Well, I didn't know you had a *gentleman caller*. I'll get going… Should have given you a ring before I came over. You kids need anything from the food court or anything?"

I squirmed. "No thanks, Grandma. Umm, you're sure you don't want to stay?" *Please don't, please don't.*

"No, no, you kids have fun."

"Okay, thanks. Love you." As I said this, my eyes glanced over at the screen and I blanched. There were two thousand eight hundred fifty-eight people waiting for us to start streaming—and the number climbed even higher the next second.

She paused in the doorway, seeing me pale. "You two watching a scary movie or something?"

"Yeah," I lied. "Not very Christmas-ey."

"Well, I know that's your style." She gave me a wink just before she turned to leave. "Have a good time, hon."

Ryan let out a breath. "Not too subtle, your grandma."

I traced a heart on the back of his hand, then looked over at him, warm waves coursing through me as my eyes strayed from the spray of freckles across his cheeks down to the faint stubble on his upper lip, then up to his kind, hazel eyes. I took in the boy beside me, so smart, so handsome, so caring, and so, so alive.

"She just has good taste," I said, then leaned in for his kiss.

A few blissful minutes later we parted lips, him tending to straightening his shirt and me to my mussed hair. That done, I looked back to the waiting livestream audience to check the numbers.

Almost four thousand—more people than attended Enville High. I sucked in a sharp breath.

"You can do it," Ryan said, placing a hand on my (good) knee. "*We* can. It's just us two in the room, remember. And we can cut it short if it goes weird."

"Right," I said, then didn't let myself think any more about it as I hit the button to start the stream.

And then we were live, the chat filling with messages in an instant—emojis, accusations, dumb jokes, a call from Uncle Ed to "be nice, people, but stay skeptical!" But there were also questions, *real* questions, from people who believed and wanted to know more. So I began with the first Avanic explosion, then the fever and the rest, Ryan interjecting when necessary.

The number of viewers swelled as we told the story. Fifty-five hundred, then six thousand, then nearly eight thousand by the forty-five minute mark.

It was around then that I looked up and realized someone was standing in the doorway—my Grandma Ruth again. She raised her eyebrows and pointed into the room, and I gave her a little nod. She tiptoed inside and took a seat.

I didn't know exactly what my parents had told her, nor how long she'd been eavesdropping outside, listening to us weave the story. But as she sat there quietly, my worries slipped away. Maybe, just maybe…

The chat was flying now, too fast to read anything properly, yet for a second I thought I saw the name D_plexippus, and I called out to him, telling him I would never have figured any of it out without him. The chat filled with thumbs ups and smiley faces, and my spirits soared.

And then, once our voices had gone gravelly and the story had come to a close, we ended the stream. A humming energy seemed to suffuse the little hospital room. It was over, it was done, and Ryan's hand was back in mine.

I looked up.

"Grandma, I—"

She flapped a hand at me. "Don't say a *thing*, Lanie. I just think you kids are so brave, and…" Her eyes glimmered with—sadness? Pride? Then she smiled. "You know, I never could resist a good ghost story."

Chapter 36

I HANDED TEN dollars over to the plump CVS cashier, trying hard not to stare at the red and green reindeer antlers affixed to her headband. There were little bells sewn to the end of each antler, so she jingled with every movement.

"I know, I know," she said, waggling her head. *Jingle, jingle, jingle.* "I'm pushing it now that we're three days past the holiday, but I just like dressing up. Anyway, happy reading! Wait, hang on…" She looked down at the four tabloids I'd just paid for, then at my crutches, then up at me and Ryan, who was standing right beside me.

"Are you…?" she asked, bug-eyed.

"Yup!" I said cheerily as Ryan grabbed the tabloids. She was still watching us, jaw slack, as we left the store.

The livestream had spread like wildfire across the Internet, and traditional media was now playing catch-up. The more mainstream papers seemed to have settled on the narrative that Ryan and I had a tenuous grip on reality, our minds addled by the still-unspecified experiments. What's more, the White House had called to postpone the invitation to visit, ostensibly due to a situation the president was dealing with in the Middle East—but I knew it was really because of the livestream.

The checkout aisle tabloids, on the other hand, were all in with the ghost stuff. *Teens TELL ALL about Avanic's GHOST SPIES!* they screamed. *Sinister Director's Graduate Research Focused on the Paranormal! SPECTR Survivors' Story Resolves FIVE Cold Cases!* Beneath that last headline were old yearbook pictures of each of the SPECTR victims—as well as a smaller headline at the bottom of the page teasing an article about a reptilian commune deep in New Mexico's Chihuahuan Desert. Clearly some intrepid journalist was having fun perusing my favorite place on the Internet.

Some good had come from the questionable coverage. Just before Ryan had picked me up that morning, I'd logged onto Facebook to confront my shocking amount of DMs, and noticed an odd, concise message sticking out from the rest, sent from a just-created dummy account.

A-
Thank you, and all the best.
-A.R.

D_plexippus had deleted his video and forum post, on my private request to him after the livestream. Rufner, tortured by his unspeakable secret, was in the clear.

Back in Ryan's car (borrowed from his brother, since my doctor had forbidden me to drive for a few more weeks) we divvied up the tabloids. "They're using my yearbook photo from freshman year," I moaned as I opened up the first article.

"That's nothing compared to this one of me," he said with a scowl, holding up a picture of him in an *Hour of Fate* T-shirt. He was giving the camera a dopey smile and a thumbs up, and his eyes were half-closed, blinking at the camera flash. "I thought I'd scrubbed that one off the Internet… Oh wow, look at this." He pointed at an artist's crude charcoal rendering of my demoness on the opposite page. "Is that at all close…?"

I shook my head. "Not even a little bit. I guess you were right. These tabloids really are garbage."

He nodded and tossed them into the back of the car to join the trash from the drive-through burgers we'd scarfed earlier. "So, you still up for the movie?"

"Of course," I said, giving him a kiss on the cheek. "Drive on."

We'd considered the horror send-up about Santa's elves, which had scraped a winning twenty percent on Rotten Tomatoes—but, after a little deliberation, we'd settled on a romantic comedy instead.

That night I dreamed of greasy burgers and reptilians basking in the scorching desert sun and cackling half-elf half-human CVS cashiers. It was a consequence of all the effort I'd put into inducing lucidity that now I was always partially conscious when I dreamed, even though I didn't wish to be.

This wasn't uncommon, I'd learned from the people on Beyond the Veil—and with time, they said, my brain should relax and allow me deep, unconscious slumber once more.

But that hadn't happened yet, so every night I was faced with a choice. *Should I check if she's there?* And every night, I put it off, telling myself it wasn't the right time, that maybe it would *never* be the right time, that checking would only delay my "healing"—whatever that meant.

Still, I couldn't deny my curiosity. Plus it *felt* like the right thing to do, like there was something in my chest pulling me towards her clearing—a tightly knotted string that I would only be able to untie if I went there myself.

So that night I batted away the half-elves and ordered the lizard people back to the depths from which they'd sprung, until I was floating in red-black nothingness—*my realm*, as Melissa had called it.

Enville, I thought as clearly as I could, and a murky cluster of shadows to my right shifted. I sped in that direction, the darkness slowly resolving into a ghostly simulacra of my town. I soared above like a hawk riding the winds, over Ferngrove Lane, my house, the woods. There was Avanic, the building Ryan and I had fled from still lying in ruins. And there was the little clearing within the woods—not a glint of blue to be seen.

I drifted down to the ground, touching down softly on the leaf-strewn forest floor. Spinning in a slow circle, I searched the shadow-trees for a girl who wasn't there. They surrounded me like a dark, solemn tribunal—watching, judging. Everything was hushed, and the air hung still, the whole world holding its breath.

"Melissa?" I whispered.

No answer.

So that was that. Yet as the seconds ticked on, the knot in my chest kept tightening.

But now there came a fluttering from behind me as a breeze set the leaves around my feet dancing. The tree branches creaked, and the wind circled me, warm and gentle, smelling of summer, of things green and growing… And were those the faintest strains of a young woman's laughter, tangled in the wind's sighing?

The knot in my chest was loosening, the string going slack…

Another distant peal of laughter, joyous and carefree.

I closed my eyes and released myself from the dream.

AUTHOR'S NOTE

Ghosts, demons, astral projection... The whole mess was laughable.

It's a pretty good summation from Lanie, isn't it? You can't really fault her parents for not believing her. I mean, would *you* believe her? I sure wouldn't.

Specter is a work of fiction through and through, an amalgam born of my love for horror, the weird, and conspiracy theories. (And serial killers! For whatever reason I can never really get away from those pesky serial killers in my books...)

But even though the events of *Specter* are thoroughly rooted in the fantastic, there are nuggets of truth in the book. People really can achieve lucidity in their dreams, for example, and there are many online guides about how to go about doing so. Whether the dreamer can achieve Lanie's level of lucidity is up for debate, however. Out-of-body experiences, too, are a real dissociative phenomenon, though their cause is definitely rooted in the scientific rather than the paranormal.

Similarly, I used actual historical events as inspiration for

Project SPECTR. Terrible crimes have been perpetrated on unwilling test subjects in the name of scientific research, from Josef Mengele's Nazi-era human experimentation to the Tuskegee Syphilis Study to Project MKUltra. That CIA program, mentioned only briefly in the book, was primarily concerned with mind control and the development of truth drugs for use against the Soviet Union. MKUltra had a large scope and thousands of participants, many of them unconsenting; the program most infamously dosed unwitting test subjects with LSD and other psychedelic substances. It is unlikely that MKUltra's full impact will ever be known, due to the unbridled experimentation without proper scientific procedure, consent, or follow-up, as well as the CIA's deliberate destruction of records.

All this is to say that while *Specter* is a work of fiction, the world we live in is a strange one. So as Uncle Ed would no doubt say, be skeptical and be curious. Truth is often stranger than fiction.

ACKNOWLEDGMENTS

I don't know how many times I've heard some iteration of how lonely the book writing process can be. I must be the luckiest writer on the planet, since I've found just the opposite. This book has been a team effort, from the planning to the drafting to the editing, and I am so grateful to my family, friends, and professional contacts for their incredible support.

To my NaNo CT North crew, who form my Connecticut writers anchor. (As well as the world's only Secret Youthberry Club!) Marina Black, Dawn, Chelsea, Auny, Brooke, Kat, Karoun, and everybody else—I remain in awe of your speed and your diligence. I'll stay comfy in last place for word wars, watching you all zoom ahead.

To Sheyla Cordero, the best damn Spanish tutor on iTalki. Thanks for clearing up all the confusion about evacuating.

To Mary, for her invaluable consulting services.

To Ally Grosvenor, beta reader extraordinaire and official illustrator of KJG Enterprises. You are an amazing artist, the most thoughtful of readers, and the bestest of friends. Check out Ally's gorgeous chapter illustrations for *The Gold in the Dark* on katiejgallagher.com.

To my mom, dad, sister, and everyone else in my family. I'm so grateful to you for being my lifelong cheerleaders through all the crazy phases. Costuming, zines, Chinese, singing, dance… You guys have seen it all, while hardly batting an eye. I love you all so much.

And to John—my husband, my alpha reader, and my partner-in-crime. *Specter* would not exist were it not for your epic pep talks and pull-no-punches editorial skills. How many times have we sat over coffee and a Jalisco turkey sandwich debating one word? I love you, and here's to more books to come.

Thank you so much for reading *Specter*! If you enjoyed this book and have a spare moment, I'd love it if you would write a review on Goodreads or wherever you bought the book. Reviews are key to helping new readers discover my books. Also, if you want to be notified about new books, sign up for my newsletter at katiejgallagher.com, follow me on Instagram @katiejanegallagher, or follow me on Amazon!

And again, thank you so much for spending time with my book! That means the entire world to me.

All the best,
Katie

KATIE JANE GALLAGHER is the author of the serialized YA fantasy *The Gold in the Dark*. She was born and raised in Illinois, and the magical Naperville Public Library was her home away from home until she ventured to the East Coast for college. Katie graduated magna cum laude from Connecticut College with a BA in Chinese language and literature. She currently lives in Connecticut with her stupendous, half-human half-neanderthal husband and their dopey boxer dog.

You can sign up for Katie's newsletter and get a free *Specter* short story here:
KATIEJGALLAGHER.COM/FREE

Or follow her on Instagram
@KATIEJANEGALLAGHER

AUTHOR PHOTO: HUDZEN PHOTOGRAPHY